WHO WAS BEHIN
THAT SPELLED L
AMERICA?

Could it be Cuba's "Maximum Leader," in re-
venge for his recent debearding at the hands
of Remo and Chiun?

Could it be the Emperor of the Anchors, Don
Cooder, in his ultimate act of peeved
petulance?

Could it be the KNNN news king, Jed Burner,
Captain Audacious himself, with his newest
wife, the aging exercise queen, Layne Fondue,
out to give cable a stranglehold on the
nation?

And what would anyone want with Cheeta
Ching and her unborn baby, a package that
was like a time bomb waiting to go off?

*These were good questions, and Remo and
Chiun wanted answers in the worst way—no matter how many smoke screens they had to plunge
through, how many covers they had to rip
away, or how many suspects they had to tear
apart. . . .*

The Destroyer

#93

TERMINAL TRANSMISSION

Created by
WARREN MURPHY & RICHARD SAPIR

A SIGNET BOOK

SIGNET
Published by the Penguin Group
Penguin Books USA Inc., 375 Hudson Street,
New York, New York 10014, U.S.A.
Penguin Books Ltd, 27 Wrights Lane,
London W8 5TZ, England
Penguin Books Australia Ltd, Ringwood,
Victoria, Australia
Penguin Books Canada Ltd, 10 Alcorn Avenue,
Toronto, Ontario, Canada M4V 3B2
Penguin Books (N.Z.) Ltd, 182–190 Wairau Road,
Auckland 10, New Zealand

Penguin Books Ltd, Registered Offices:
Harmondsworth, Middlesex, England

First published by Signet, an imprint of New American Library,
a division of Penguin Books USA Inc.

First Printing, July, 1993
10 9 8 7 6 5 4 3 2 1

PUBLISHER'S NOTE
This is a work of fiction. Names, characters, places, and incidents either
are the product of the author's imagination or are used fictitiously, and any
resemblance to actual persons, living or dead, events, or locales is entirely
coincidental.

For Don Hutchison, and the Book of Amos 5:26. (We can't explain it, either!)

Not to mention the Glorious House of Sinanju, P. O. Box 2505, Quincy, MA 02269.

1

The greatest domestic crisis since the Civil War struck the United States of America at exactly 6:28 P.M. Daylight Savings Time on the last Thursday in April.

Approximately thirty million citizens scattered throughout the nation and in Mexico and the lower reaches of Canada saw the crisis unfold on their television sets. And every one of them, no matter what broadcast station or network they were tuned to, UHF or VHF, saw the exact same thing.

A dead black rectangle where a moment before busy phosphor pixels had been generating kaleidoscopic images of entertainment, information, and commercials.

The blackness was relieved by thin white letters in the upper right-hand corner. The letters spelled out two words.

The words: NO SIGNAL.

TV speakers everywhere, in private homes, in hospitals, in offices, in neighborhood bars, reproduced the same staticky carrier wave hissing of dead air.

Then a voice began speaking in a monotone:

"There is nothing wrong with your television set . . ."

Don Cooder was late.

The news director was in a panic. The floor manager was running from restroom to restroom in the Broadcast Corporation of North America headquarters building on Manhattan's West Forty-third Street, peering under stalls for a pair of trademark ostrich-hide wrangler boots.

"Try the ledge," the harried domestic producer cried. "He sometimes hides out on the ledge when he's unhappy."

Everybody who wasn't frantically racing around the Bridge—as the BCN newsroom was called—preparing the 6:30 news feed to the affiliates, raced to the nearest window. Don Cooder was late. Nobody knew what it was about, but everybody knew what it could mean. Their eyes were stark and frantic.

Troubled voices called back reports.

"He's not on the third floor ledge."

"He's not on the fourth floor ledge."

"He's not on *any* of the ledges!"

"Maybe he fell off," said a lowly desk assistant.

In the great TV-screen-blue newsroom set a hush fell. Faces, so strained a moment ago, lit with entirely different lights. Ambition leapt to some. Relief to others. And all eyes went to the Chair, more coveted than many modern thrones, which now sat spotlit but empty. Power flowed from that elegant seat, situated in the exact geometric center of the Bridge, which had been designed to make the anchor desk seem to be the center of the universe, but in practice made many viewers change channels thinking that they had tuned in to an old *Star Trek* rerun.

"Maybe he fell off . . ." the producer muttered.

"Maybe he jumped!" said the director.

"CBN star anchor Don Cooder succumbs to ratings pressure!" the chief news writer cried. "Makes dramatic leap into oblivion!"

A dozen lips whispered the rumor. Faces froze, some in shock, others to conceal their pleasure. The makeup woman broke down weeping for her job.

The domestic producer, his face paling, took charge. He began issuing husky orders.

"Camera crew to the sidewalk. If Cooder's a messy spot on the pavement, we'll want to lead with that." He shouted after the running figures, "If he's dying, try to get his last words."

"What about the headlines for the affiliates?" asked the director, gazing at the digital clock which read 06:28:57.

"Somebody get Cheeta Ching! I'd be damned if we go black again because of that Aggie prima donna."

An intern leaped from the room.

In her office in the outermost concentric ring that orbits the Bridge, CBN weekend anchor Cheeta Ching, nine months, one week, and three days pregnant, and as bloated as a floater freshly fished out of the East River, looked up from her script for the evening broadcast of *Eyeball to Eyeball with Cheeta Ching* as her door unceremoniously crashed in. The can of hair varnish she had been emptying into her raven tresses dropped from her long fingers.

"Miss Ching!" an intern panted. "You're on."

"What are you talking about? I'm not on for two hours yet."

The intern fought for his breath. "Cooder fell down the rabbit hole again," he gasped.

"His job is mine!" screeched Cheeta Ching, self-styled "superanchorwoman of the nineties," as she bolted from her desk and trampled the unfortunate staffer before he could get out of the way.

The run from Cheeta Ching's office to the Chair was a straight unwavering line. After hours, Cheeta had timed the run with a stopwatch. Her best time had been 47:03 seconds.

That was before the home pregnancy test had come up blue, of course.

Still, Cheeta gave it her best. She had known for years—ever since Don Cooder had let the *BCN Evening News with Don Cooder* remain black for an unprecedented six minutes because a *World Wide Wrestling* match had spilled over its allotted span and into his time slot, that it could happen again. And she was ready.

Because Cheeta Ching knew that if she landed in the coveted anchor chair at the right moment, Cooder's job would be hers.

Flinging off her Georgio Armani taupe wool faille maternity skirt, she ran through the halls in her Victoria's Secret chenille slip.

The thought of the high seven-figure salary, the perks, and the intoxicating power that lay at the end of the run drove her to pound down the carpeted hall like a water buffalo in heat. Staff pressed themselves against the walls before her. A cameraman, seeing her careen toward him, hit the rug and covered his head with a script. A technician opening a door flung himself back. Too late. Cheeta hit the closing door like a linebacker; it flew back and broke the technician's nose and glasses where he stood.

The Chair was within sight now. Cheeta could see it clearly through the semicircle of indoor glass windows that overlooked the Bridge from the inner concentric ring of offices.

The director, spotting her, waved her on frantically with a script that flapped like a wounded dove.

"Mine! It's mine!" Cheeta shrieked.

The last door crashed open under the blind force of her padded shoulder. Cheeta was panting now. Only a stretch of a few cable-strewn yards stood between her and the highest-paid job in television news.

Staffers shouted encouragement.

"Come on, Cheeta!"

"You can do it, girl!"

Then a bosun's whistle shrilled and the floor manager shouted, "Admiral on the Bridge! All hands! Admiral on the Bridge!"

That's me! Cheeta thought wildly. *I'm the admiral on the Bridge now.*

And from out of nowhere, a pinstriped blue shape blindsided her. Heart pounding, Cheeta understood immediately what it meant. Her bloodred fingernails extended like talons as she made a last, desperate lunge for the Chair.

And an ostrich-hide boot stomped on her instep while a hard hip like a whale's jawbone knocked her down. An immaculate shoe sole flattened her nose.

And over the squeal of the Chair's springs adjusting to 185 pounds of human ego, a deep, masculine voice growled, "There's only one admiral on this bridge. And don't you forget it."

Cheeta Ching tried to struggle to her feet. But all around her sycophantic shoes had appeared, preventing her from rising.

"Don, where have you been?" the relieved producer asked.

"None of your business."

"Don, so great that you're here," said the chief news writer.

"Don Cooder is great, no matter where he is."

"Don, here's your script for the affiliates update," said the director.

"Don Cooder doesn't need a script to read headlines. Just tell me what they are and I'll wing it."

"Senator Ned Clancy issues denial on love-nest rumor," the director recited in an urgent voice. "Dr. Doom inaugurates toll-free death line. Scientists dub strange new AIDS-like disease HELP."

"Here's your lavaliere, Don."

"Will somebody please let me up?" Cheeta snapped.

"Quiet, Cheeta," the producer said coldly. "Just lay there until the commercial break."

The feet went away and the floor manager was calling out, "Quiet, please. Don Cooder headlines for affiliates! Five seconds! Four! *Quiet!*"

Then the voice of Don Cooder, pitched into a low resonant tone, began his clipped recital.

"Senator Ned Clancy issues denial on love-nest rumor. Dr. Doom inaugurates toll-free death line. Scientists dub strange new AIDS-like disease HELP. All that and more coming up soon, so stay with us."

Cheeta started to rise.

The stampeding feet returned.

"That was great, Don. You nailed it in one take."

"Fabulous ad-libbing, Don."

"Will somebody help me up," Cheeta said through clenched teeth. "I have my own show to prep."

She was ignored.

"Here's the script, Don."

"We're losing the bumper, Don."

"One minute to air, everybody!" the floor manager announced.

"Don, we'll lead with Dr. Doom and follow up with the love nest story," the director was saying.

"I think we should lead with the love-nest story, don't you?" Cooder shot back.

"Absolutely, Don," the director returned without skipping a beat. "But it's not written as a lead."

"I'll wing it."

"Fifteen seconds to air!" the floor manager called.

The feet went away again and Cheeta Ching tried again. Her expanded center of gravity was not helpful. She was on her back, and it felt like a cannonball had been placed on her stomach so that a trained elephant could sit on it.

Grimacing, Cheeta rolled over—and collapsed panting.

Out of the corner of her eye she spotted the red ON AIR sign flaring up.

"This is the *BCN Evening News with Don Cooder*," the stentorian voice of Don Cooder announced. "Tonight, beleaguered democratic senator Ned J. Clancy, married barely a year, is contending with rumors of marital infidelity. With us now is Washington reporter Trip Lutz."

Cheeta was on her hands and knees now, behind the anchor desk and out of camera range. And she felt as if she were being weighed down by an abdominal tumor the size of Rhode Island. She tried to crawl, but the floor manager caught her eye. He was on his knees waving a Magic Markered sign that said: STAY THERE FOR THE FIRST SECTION. PLEASE!

Cheeta flipped him the bird. She started crawling.

And an ostrich-hide cowboy boot came around to plant itself on the small of her back. Cheeta Ching went down hard. "Oof!"

And the hated voice of Don Cooder returned, saying, "Thank you, Trip. In other news . . ."

"Ugh," Cheeta said.

"The retired pathologist and self-styled 'thanatologist' known as Dr. Doom has discovered a fresh wrinkle in the toll-free number game: Dial and die."

"Uhh," Cheeta groaned.

"AT&T reports their lines are jammed for the second consecutive day in the wake of the controversial new service for the terminally ill."

"I think my water broke," Cheeta grunted.

"This just in," Cooder said. "Reliable sources tell BCN News that weekend anchor Cheeta Ching is at this moment giving birth at a location not far from here. Speaking on behalf of her colleagues here at the Broadcast Corporation of North America, we wish her Godspeed and a joyful labor."

And the boot heel pushed down harder.

Cheeta Ching's flat, reddening face slammed to the rug and turned sideways. Then she saw it. The line monitor, which showed the picture that millions of faithful BCN viewers were simultaneously watching in the privacy of their own homes.

The line monitor was as black as a virgin Etch-a-Sketch.

If there was one cardinal, inflexible rule in on-set broadcast journalism etiquette it was: Quiet on a live set.

But if there was a prime directive it was: Never, ever go to black.

The prime directive was far, far more important than on-set etiquette.

And so Cheeta Ching took a deep breath and, steeling herself, let out a shriek calculated to scale a salmon.

In the ringing aftermath, Don Cooder barked, "This just in. Cheeta Ching has given birth to a healthy . . ." Cooder cocked an ear for the answer.

"We're in black!" Cheeta shrieked.

All eyes swung to the line monitor.

It was nestled in the cluster of monitors that displayed incoming satellite feeds, previews of about-to-be-aired reports, and waiting commercials. The other monitors were busily cutting between segments. But the line monitor, the crucial monitoring terminal, was like a glassy black eye.

A black eye that would be seen by sponsors and network brass alike. A black eye that would cause viewers all over the country to fidget, grumble, and grope for their remotes.

A black eye that would be tomorrow's headlines if it wasn't corrected in time.

"Don't just stand there!" Cooder shouted. "Put up color bars!"

In the control room, the technical director worked the switcher frantically. "Color bars up!" he shouted.

"No, they're not! Hit it again."

The technical director, his eyes widening as the seconds—each one worth over a thousand dollars in commercial airtime—ticked away, shouted, "How's that?"

The producer blinked at the line monitor. "N.G."

"We're going to get creamed in the ratings," Cooder said in a voice twisted with raw emotion.

"No, we're not," the floor manager said matter-of-factly.

"Huh?"

"The other networks. They're black too."

The monitors marked ANC, MBC, and Vox all showed black.

Relief washed over the newsroom as the truth sank in.

"Must be sunspots or something," a stage hand muttered.

"Right, sunspots."

"I never heard of sunspots blacking out TV like this," the technical director said doubtfully.

Telephones began ringing all over the set. In the circle of offices around the Bridge. All over the building.

The word came in. It wasn't a local phenomenon. Broadcast television had gone to black all up and down the East Coast.

"What a story," someone said.

"Let's get on this, troops," Don Cooder said, tearing off his IFB earpiece and storming about the Bridge like an admiral in red suspenders. "Work the phones. How big is this story?"

As it turned out, very big.

"There's no TV in Illinois," a woman at the satellite desk reported.

"St. Louis is black, Don," a reporter added.

"Montana is without reception," chimed in another correspondent.

"How can anyone tell?" said Cooder, who was from Texas.

"LA is down too. And San Francisco."

"It's nationwide!" Cooder crowed. "And it's our new lead story. We'll lead with 'Sunspots Suppress Television Across Nation.' "

"But we don't know it's actually sunspots," the director pointed out.

"It's good enough for the lead. We can always update. Get our science editor on it."

"Feldmeyer? He's on vacation, remember?"

"Then get the backup."

"There isn't one. We lost our backup in the last round of budget cuts."

Don Cooder squared his magnificently photogenic shoulders. It was not for nothing that *TV Guide* had dubbed him the "Anchor of Steel."

"What do we have for video on this thing?"

The news director blinked. He pointed to the line monitor.

"Just this. A dead screen."

"We can't broadcast a dead screen," Cooder complained.

"We *are* broadcasting a dead screen. *That's* the story."

Don Cooder blinked. His perpetual glower darkened. His eyes, which *People* magazine had described as "cathode-ray blue," reverted to the Texas sunsquint of his field reporter days.

"We can't go on the air with this," he mumbled. "A dead screen is terrible television. Folks will turn us off."

"Don, get a grip. We can't go on the air. Period."

"No one can break this story until the air clears?" Don Cooder demanded.

"Right, Don."

"When the air clears, the competition will be over this like piss on a flat rock, right?"

"I guess so," said the director, who never understood his star anchor's homespun aphorisms.

"I'm not waiting for the air to break. I'm breaking this story here, now and first. And all of you are my witnesses."

"What are you going to do, Don?"

Without answering, leaving the carefully prepared script on his desk and the teleprompters standing frozen in time, Don Cooder, the highest paid news anchor in human history, strode from the Bridge to the nearest outside office. He threw up a window sash, stuck out his head and broad shoulders, and in a voice loud enough to startle the pigeons roosting on nearby Times Square buildings, proclaimed, "This is a *BCN Evening News* Special Report. Don Cooder reporting. All over the continental United States, broadcast television was blacked out at the start of the first national news feeds. The mysterious force responsible for this tragedy has yet to be identified, but for now, in this slice of time, for the first time in the over forty-year history of television, America is staring into a blackness more terrible than the Great Blackout of 1965. And the blackness is staring back. Who will blink first? That is the question of the hour."

The producer tapped him on the shoulder. "Forget it, Don."

"Shut up! I'm broadcasting. The old-fashioned way."

"KNNN is on the air."

Don Cooder straightened so fast he bumped his intensely black hair against the window sash. He

wheeled, leaving sticky strands of hair adhering to the
wood. "What!"

"It's true. They're been broadcasting uninterrupted
all along."

"Damn! Did they scoop me?"

"Afraid so."

"Damn."

Cooder strode into the control room, where a monitor showed a calm anchor speaking in a flat voice
under the world-famous Kable Newsworthy News Network logo—a nautical anchor.

"Those bastards! They can't bigfoot me like this!"

"Now you know how it feels," came a groaning
voice from the floor—Cheeta Ching, draped over her
big own stomach and breathing through her mouth the
Lamaze way.

"You deserve to be bigfooted," Cooder growled.
"If only your public could see you now. You look like
a beached whale suffering from acute jaundice."

"Somebody help Miss Ching," the floor manager
called from the huddle around the monitor cluster.
They were all tuned to KNNN. The volume was up.

Don Cooder pushed into the huddle, fuming.

"What are they saying?" he demanded.

"Bare bones stuff. All broadcasting is black. Only
the cable lines are getting through. No one's figured
out why yet."

"Damn. There goes all of prime time. We'll never
recapture those viewers." His intensely blue eyes went
to the line monitor where the mocking white letters,
NO SIGNAL, showed mutely.

He was reaching for the volume control when the
line monitor blazed into life. The burst of light was
so unexpected that Cooder blinked. When his sight
cleared, a sight more blood-chilling than the Attica
riots and the 1968 Democratic National Convention
put together was framed on the screen.

The sight of two stage hands helping a wobbly
Cheeta Ching into the anchor chair. His Chair.

Don Cooder's head snapped around. The number

one camera tally light was a red eye pointed directly at Cheeta Ching.

"We're live! We're back on!" he shouted, pitching across the news set.

A cable snagged a boot heel before he got three feet. His face slammed into the carpet. For a moment, Don Cooder lay stunned.

And floating to his ears came the hateful voice of his chief rival, her tones syrupy and triumphant, saying, "This is the *BCN Evening News with Don Cooder*. Cheeta Ching reporting. Don is off tonight."

And as millions of Americans settled back into their seats, those who had patiently stayed with BCN heard above the treacly voice of Cheeta Ching a raging bellow of complaint.

"Let me up! Let me up! I'm going to strangle that Korean air-hog if it's the last thing I do!"

2

His name was Remo and all he wanted was to die.

That was all. A simple thing. No big deal. People died every day. Remo knew that better than most. He had personally helped hundreds, if not thousands, of deserving people into the boneyard. And now it was his turn.

So why did they have to make it so hard for him?

He had been dialing the toll-free number all morning. The line was busy. Remo would hang up, wait a few moments and then stab the redial button. But all he got was a busy signal beeping in his ear.

"Dammit," Remo said, hanging up.

"What is wrong?" asked a squeaky voice.

"I still can't get through."

"You are not doing it properly," said the squeaky voice.

"Yeah? Well, you try it for once."

From the east-facing windows of the great square room which had windows on all sides, a tiny Buddhalike figure squatted on a reed mat. It was swathed in crimson silks that were trimmed in shimmery golds. The bald top of its head gleamed like a polished amber egg, framed by twin clouds of hair that concealed the tips of delicate ears.

"It is not my burden," said the figure.

"We're coequal partners. It's half your burden."

"Only if you fail or die, which should be the same thing, otherwise the house will be shamed forever."

Remo blinked. "The house would rather I die than fail?"

"No. The house prefers success. But will accept your death with proper lamentations and vows of vengeance."

"What about living to fight another day?"

"This is my task in the event of your failure," the immobile figure sniffed.

Remo pointed at the phone. "How can I fail if I can't get through?"

"How can I meditate on the approaching day of joy with you banging two pieces of plastic together and pacing the floor?"

"It stops the minute I get through."

The tiny figure suddenly arose. It turned. The lavender, scarlet, and gold silks of its kimono rustled and settled as the frail-looking figure of Chiun, Reigning Master of Sinanju, padded on black sandals over to the telephone set on the only article of furniture in the great bare room, a low taboret.

He was a tiny wisp of a man. His round head sat on a thin wattled neck like an orange on a pole. The face might have been molded of papyrus and kneaded around matched agate eyes.

The Master of Sinanju floated to the taboret and lifted the receiver with a hand whose skin was shiny with age. He did not bring the instrument to either delicate ear, but instead held it at arm's length, as if it were a distasteful thing. With the other, he stabbed the one button and then the 800 area code.

Remo started to say, "The rest of it is—"

"I know the rest," snapped Chiun.

And as Remo watched, the Master of Sinanju began tapping out the correct exchange.

"How do you know the number?" Remo asked.

"I am not deaf. I have been listening to the annoying chirps all morning."

Remo looked startled, "You can tell the number by the chirps?"

"As can any child," sniffed Chiun, tapping the first

three numbers of the last group of digits. He paused, his long-nailed fingers hovering over the keypad.

"Ah-hah," said Remo. "Stuck on the last number."

"I am not!"

"Then what are you waiting for?"

"The proper moment."

Remo watched. The Master of Sinanju stood frozen, the receiver in one hand, the other like an eagle's claw prepared to pounce on the tiny square eggs of the keypad.

Remo folded his lean arms. Chiun was up to something. He wasn't sure what.

"You're going to lose the call," Remo warned.

Then the finger descended. The long colorless nail touched the five key and Remo's face quirked up. Five was the correct digit. Chiun had not been stuck after all.

Then, with a disdainful toss, the Master of Sinanju put the receiver in Remo's hand and padded back to his floor mat and his meditation.

Remo brought the receiver to his ear. The phone was ringing.

"How did you do that?" he called over to Chiun, who had returned to his mat.

"It is the correct method."

"For what?"

"For calling radio talk programs."

"You been doing that?"

"Thrush Limburger is very entertaining for a fat white with a loud voice."

"When did you start listening to *him*?"

"Since he speaks the truth about this lunatic land I serve."

Then the ringing stopped and a crisp nursey-sounding voice was speaking.

"This is the office of Dr. Mordaunt Gregorian," the nursey voice was saying. "If you are calling from a touch-tone phone, please press the correct option. If you are not calling from a touch-tone phone, please stay on the line and if possible someone will assist you. But do not count on it. We have many patients to process."

"Wonderful," Remo growled. "I got his answering machine."

"If you are a reporter calling to interview Dr. Gregorian, press one."

Remo gave the one key a miss.

"If you are a lawyer calling to sue Dr. Gregorian, press two."

"I'll bet that's a busy line," Remo muttered.

"If you are calling because you wish to die, press three."

Remo pressed three.

There was a long pause, then some musical chirping that made Remo think of tin crows, and a crusty male voice said sharply, "This is Dr. Gregorian. State your business."

"I want to die," Remo said.

There was a hesitation on the line. Then, "State your disease."

"Leprosy."

Another hesitation. "State your prognosis."

"I'm falling apart."

The line hummed. Remo figured the man was writing everything down. At least he had gotten through to him.

Then, "State your preferred manner of crossing the River Styx. Barbituate pill. Lethal injection. Or suffocation."

"I'll take the pill. Where do I show up?"

The line hummed. Then, "State your sex."

"Male. What do I sound like—Madonna?"

The crusty voice didn't answer. There was a pause and Remo heard a relay click. Then, once more sharp, the voice said, "Your application has been rejected. Do not call again. Have a nice day."

The line went dead.

Remo slammed the phone down so hard the keypad 0-for-operator button bounced off the ceiling.

"I was talking to a freaking machine!" he complained.

"You could not tell?"

"I thought it was the real Gregorian."

"I do not believe there is any such person," said Chiun.

"If I can just lay hands on the guy, there won't be. He makes me sick to my stomach."

"A strange thing for an assassin to say."

"Hey, I'm a professional. The guy is a ghoul."

"A ghoul to some is a boon to others," Chiun said.

A frown touched Remo's face. It was a strong face, dominated by deep-set dark eyes and pronounced cheekbones. The frown brought out the innate cruelty of his tension-compressed mouth.

"He's out there snuffing people for money," Remo snapped.

"And what is it we do, you and I? If not snuffing?"

"That's different. We're professionals."

"Sit."

Still frowning, Remo toed a tatami mat into place before his mentor. Crossing his ankles, he scissored his legs downward until he had assumed the traditional lotus position, feet crossed, wrists on knees. Remo's wrists dwarfed his lower legs. They looked thick enough to conceal baby I-beam girders.

The rest of him was lean enough for a diet commercial. There wasn't an ounce of extra fat on his exposed arms. His muscles were understated, but well-defined. He was dressed casually in black chinos and a fresh white T-shirt.

"Life is cruel," intoned Chiun. "Many are born. Almost as many die before their prime. All die in their own time. One day I will die, as will you."

"Nobody could kill you, Little Father," Remo said simply.

Chiun lifted a finger in stern correction. "I did not say kill, I said die. Even the magnificence that is embodied in my awesome form must one day wither and expire like that of any lesser creature."

Inwardly, Remo winced. This frail wisp of a Korean had come into his life more than twenty years ago, transforming him into the superbly trained human machine he was now. Chiun had not been young then. Now, even though he admitted to only eighty winters, Remo knew the old Korean had surpassed his one hundred year mark some time ago. He showed it in tiny ways. A faint fading of the bright hazel eyes. A thickening of the wrinkles that sweetened his parchment features. The color of his sparse beard and eyebrows in some lights seemed more of a smoky gray that the crisp white of days gone by. Remo shoved those thoughts into the furthest, darkest corner of his mind. He did not like to dwell on the future.

"In my heart, you will never die," Remo said simply.

Chiun nodded once. "Well spoken, but untrue." He raised a thin finger once more. "I do not know how many years lie unspent in this shell, especially without the powdered bones of a dragon to prolong my span."

Here we go again, Remo thought. Since their last assignment, Chiun had been bemoaning his "sad fate." A Brontosaurus had been found living in the heart of equatorial Africa. The Master of Sinanju, under the impression that the creature was some unknown species of Africa dragon, had talked the head of the organization for which they both worked into letting them rescue the dinosaur from a terrorist group. Chiun had had an ulterior motive. He coveted a dinosaur bone because it was a traditional Oriental belief that the bones of a dragon, ground to powder and mixed in a potion, insured longevity. No amount of argument about the differences between dinosaurs and dragons could sway him. It was only when their superior had ordered them to see to it that the Brontosaurus was safety transported to America for study did Chiun finally, reluctantly, noisily give up on the idea of prolonging his life at the expense the last surviving Brontosaurus.

Remo decided he didn't want to argue the point once again and simply let out a short sigh. Chiun seemed to get the hint—a major miracle.

"But it is of no moment," he said dismissively. "I understand these things. Dragons are important. Old men who may have lived out their usefulness are not."

"It's not like that at—"

"Hush. I was speaking of death." Remo subsided. "I will tell you a story now," Chiun added.

Remo shrugged. "Why not? Maybe it will help me think."

"You would need a new brain for that."

"Har de har har," said Remo, folding his lean arms.

Chiun rearranged his skirts before speaking. "Many are the stories I have told you of my glorious village," he began, his voice deepening, "the pearl of the East, Sinanju, from which sprang the awesome line which you—a mere white—have been privileged to belong. How the village had the misfortune to perch on the coldest, grayest, most barren waters of the West Korea Bay. How the soil gave up no seedlings. How, in even the good times, the people suffered want and privation."

"That part I know by heart," Remo grumbled.

"Good. For one day, as the next in line, it will be your happy task to pass on the story of my ancestors to your pupil."

"Yeah, and I'll tell them the truth."

"Truth! What truth?" The Master of Sinanju spanked his hands together. "Quickly. Speak!"

"I'll tell him how the villagers were so lax they ate the seeds instead of planting them," Remo said. "How they never went fishing because the waters were too cold and they couldn't be bothered to build boats. So the village leader was forced to hire himself and the strongest men of the village out as hired killers and mercenaries to support the lazy ones. Until the days of Hung, who died in his sleep before he could teach Wang, who left the village to meditate and fell asleep in a field, then woke up understanding the secrets of the universe. I still don't know how *that* worked, but anyway, Wang had discovered the sun source and he went back to the remaining mercenaries and cut them down because they weren't needed anymore. After that, Wang and his descendants had a lock on the title of Master of Sinanju."

Remo paused to see how he was doing.

The visage of the Master of Sinanju was frozen, its webby wrinkles deep with shock. The parchment yellow of his tiny features were slowly turning red, like Donald Duck in a particularly strenuous cartoon. His tiny mouth was a tight button. And as Remo watched, his cheeks began to bulge like Dizzy Gillespie blowing on his trumpet.

When his breath exploded out of his mouth, the words of the Master of Sinanju came like a violent typhoon.

"That is not how the legend goes, pale piece of pig's ear!" Chiun hissed. "You have everything wrong and nothing right!"

"You forget I've been to Sinanju," Remo countered. "If you and I didn't send them CARE packages every year, they'd probably all move to Pyongyang and go on welfare."

"An outrage! My people are country folk. They would not dwell in cities, as I am forced to."

"Then again, North Korea doesn't *have* welfare," said Remo. "And what does this have to do with Dr. Gregorian?"

"You have not only gotten it all wrong, you have left out the most important part," Chiun complained.

Remo scrunched up his face in thought.

"Oh, yeah. Every other martial art, from Karate to Kung Fu, was stolen from us. And nobody got it right either. Which is why if Bruce Lee were triplets and still alive, either one of us could take him with our big toe tied behind our back."

"No! No! The babies! You forgot the babies."

"Right. The babies," said Remo, wondering why if Chiun were telling him a story, how come he was doing all the work? "The first Master left the village because the food situation got so bad they had to drown the babies in the bay."

Chiun lifted an admonishing finger.

"First the females," Remo added, "because they weren't good for much except for making more babies, which might not be needed anyway, and then the males—but only if it was absolutely necessary."

"And this is called?" Chiun prompted.

" 'Sending the babies home to the sea,' " said Remo. "Another word for crap."

"Crap?"

"That's right, crap. They were drowning innocent infants. Calling it something fancy and talking about how they'd all be reborn in a better time doesn't change what it was."

Chiun cocked his head like a curious chipmunk. "Which is?"

"Murder, plain and simple."

"No, it was necessity. Just as this Dr. Gregorian is performing a necessary service. Snuffing."

"Crap."

"And what would you do if those days were to return and you were Master, Remo?"

"Me?" A cloud of confusion passed over Remo's face. What would he do? Of course, it was unlikely. Each year the United States sent a submarine crammed with gold to the village of Sinanju in payment for Chiun training Remo in the art of Sinanju. Hardly any of it was spent, either. The human race would probably die out before the gold ran out at the rate it was being spent. But that wasn't the point. Remo was being tested. His brow furrowed deeply.

"I wouldn't drown any babies, that's for sure."

"You would send them away?"

"Probably."

"To wander alone and unloved, to be eaten by wild animals—those who did not starve?"

"I'd've put them up for adoption then," Remo said firmly.

"And what of the piteous wailing of their mothers, who would not eat in the grief of not knowing the fate of their children, and without whom there could be no future generations?"

"Okay, I wouldn't put them up for adoption. I'd . . ."

"Yes?"

Remo hesitated. He was on the spot. "I just wouldn't," he said flatly. "I'd find a way. Something would come to me. I wouldn't give up until—"

"—until all had expired in the agony of their empty bellies," Chiun snapped. "You may be a Master of Sinanju, thanks to my indulgence, but you will never possess the grace and wisdom of a true Master. You have a white mind. It sees poetry and reduces it to garbage. Oh, I have tried to drill those traits out of you, Remo, but I can see the error in my ways." He shook his aged head ruefully. "It is very sad, but I have no choice."

"To do what?" Remo asked suspiciously.

"To stay alive long enough to see that the boy who will soon issue from Cheeta Ching's mighty womb is properly trained in the art of Sinanju."

"I'm glad you brought that up," Remo said. "I've been wanting to clear the air."

"This is easily done. Simply leave the room and the air will clear itself. Heh heh heh." Closing his eyes, the Master of Sinanju rocked in time with his own cackling. "Heh heh heh."

"Why are you on my case all of a sudden?" Remo asked, barely masking the hurt in his voice.

"Since you have become testy with unwarranted jealousy," Chiun returned.

"Jealous? Me? Of what?"

"Of the boy who is about to be born."

"One," Remo said. "You don't know it's a boy. Cheeta's not saying."

"A grandfather knows these things."

"Two, it'll be a cold day when I'm jealous . . . Wait a minute—did you say *grandfather*?"

"Merely an expression," said Chiun, looking away. "Think nothing of it."

Remo hesitated. For nine months now, ever since Cheeta Ching had announced her pregnancy after a brief interlude with the Master of Sinanju, Remo had believed the child was Chiun's. Chiun had not discouraged this belief. After all, Chiun had been infatuated with the Korean anchorwoman for over a decade now. And Cheeta had been trying to become pregnant by her husband—with a noticeable lack of success—for years. It all added up, although no one was speaking on the record.

"Let me get this straight," Remo pressed. "Are you saying you're *not* the father?"

"I am not saying that," Chiun said evasively.

"Then you're not *denying* that you're the father?"

"Cheeta would not be with child were it not for my grace and wisdom."

"Then you *are* the father!"

Chiun lifted his bearded chin proudly. "I admit nothing. Cheeta is a married woman. I will not shame her with rumors. Nor will I be lured into making rash statements by jealous persons."

Remo's dark eyes narrowed. The Master of Sinanju made a show of arranging his riotous kimono skirts.

"I am *not* jealous," Remo repeated.

"No? Then why are you running hither and yon, snuffing Emperor Smith's enemies as if there were no tomorrow? You are hardly ever home anymore."

Remo made a violent, sweeping gesture that took in the entire room. "You call this pile of stone home?"

"You will be fortunate indeed if your next emperor bestows upon you a castle," Chiun said aridly.

"This isn't a castle," Remo said hotly. "It's a freaking church turned into condos and foisted off on you by Smith. I can't believe you fell for his lame sales pitch. He tells you it's a castle with a great meditation room. This is the steeple, for crying out loud!"

"It is true," Chiun said in an injured tone, "that this castle is not as large as I would have liked, but this is a new country and sadly deprived of royalty. Its castles are lamentably few. I was forced to settle."

"I got news for you, you settled for a freaking church-turned-condo."

"Also," Chiun added, "there was the urgent need

to prepare a suitable dwelling for the boy who is to be born."

"If Cheeta and her brat move in, I'm moving out."

"I would not trust you to change the diapers of a son of pure Korean blood," Chiun sniffed disdainfully, "you who would not grant a starving child the boon of sending him home to the sea, but instead let him be eaten by wild wolves."

Remo threw up his hands in surrender. "What does this have to do with that ghoul, Gregorian?"

Chiun's evasive gaze suddenly locked with Remo's. "Just as the young depend upon those who have more wisdom than they to end their lives in times of difficulty," he said, "so too do the old."

"You saying that euthanasia is okay?"

"No. Not okay. Merely preferable."

"To what?"

"To granny dumping, for example, a cruel practice in this barbarian land you love so much."

"I would never dump you."

"That is not the question," Chiun shot back. "If I lay broken in body and mind, pleading for a gracious snuffing, you would deny me the clean blow that would send my essence winging into the peace of the Void?"

"That's easy. Yeah. I would not kill you. No way."

Chiun's face fell. "Then I have failed you, and you are not worthy to change a single precious diaper."

"Good," Remo said, folding his arms. "I'm glad that's settled, because I don't change diapers."

"And if you were wise, you would leave this man Gregorian alone. He has done nothing to you."

"Hey, he's probably our next assignment."

"Which you have been hectoring Emperor Smith into granting you. If only to still your beseeching tongue."

"Smith dislikes him as much as I do. He's exactly what the organization was set up to deal with. The guy found a technicality in the law that lets him get away with killing every halt and lame basket case who can't—"

"Commit suicide for themselves?"

"That's not what I mean. And he only kills women. You ever notice that? Never men. I just got refused because I'm a man. You heard it."

The Master of Sinanju sniffed delicately. "Perhaps when my time comes and the pain is unendurable, I will call upon this Dr. Boon to ease me into the Void with dignity and grace."

"Doom. They call him Dr. Doom," Remo snapped.

"He has been misnamed by cretins. He is truly Dr. Boon."

"Forget it," said Remo, rising from his mat. "I'm going for a walk. I need some fresh air."

"Since you are unwilling to bestow upon me the gift of a graceful snuffing out in my time of future need, perhaps you will find it in your cold white heart to turn on the television set for one of my venerable years. It is nearly time for Cheeta Ching."

"This is a weekday. Cheeta's only on weekends," said Remo, snatching up the TV clicker and pointing it at the TV.

"You are forgetting her special program, which is not on until later. But Cheeta will soon give birth. I am certain this joyous event will be the first thing that Don Cooder speaks of. I would watch him—but only for tidings of Cheeta."

"Suit yourself," said Remo, turning on the TV. It was twenty-eight minutes past six. "And, speaking of that barracuda, isn't she way overdue? Like into her ten or eleventh month?"

"The perfect child is not produced in a mere nine months," Chiun said, his tone dismissive. "The Great Wang was in gestation for fifty weeks. Cheeta is only doing her duty properly."

"If you ask me," Remo said as the set warmed up, "she's waiting until sweeps month starts."

"Sweeps?"

"Next week May sweeps begin. And—" Remo stopped. He looked at the screen. It was black as a bat's daydream of nirvana. In the upper righthand corner the words NO SIGNAL showed thin and pale.

On his mat the Master of Sinanju started.

"Remo! What is wrong!"

"I dunno," said Remo, dropping to his knees. He tried changing the channel manually. On every channel, he found the same unrelieved blackness and the same NO SIGNAL legend. "Damn, it's on all channels."

Chiun was beside himself now. "Remo, I cannot miss Cheeta."

Remo adjusted the contrast knob. The NO SIGNAL came and went. "Something must be wrong with the set," he said.

"Quickly, bring the other device from the lower floor."

"Tell you what—since it's ninety seconds to Don Cooder, how about we just go downstairs and watch it in the privacy of the kitchen?"

"Is there nothing you would do for me, who have exalted you to greatness?" Chiun said huffily.

"Turn on the TV for you? Yes. Cook dinner? Some days. Rush downstairs and drag a twenty-two-inch Trinitron up a flight of steps? Maybe on your next birthday."

"Ingrate!" sniffed Chiun, throwing off all semblance of age and feebleness. He became a silky flash that disappeared down the stairs like a specter of lavender, crimson, and gold.

Out of curiosity, Remo followed him down.

The Master of Sinanju had turned on the downstairs TV, which was set on an island in the middle of a spacious kitchen.

"Remo! Remo! Come see, come see!"

Remo stepped in and saw the same thing the upstairs TV had showed—a block of broadcast tar.

The TV was speaking.

"Do not adjust the picture."

"Remo, what does this mean?" Chiun demanded.

"Could be an early warning bulletin or something," Remo muttered.

"The problem is not in your set. . . ."

"Definitely not a reception problem. They're saying so."

"Is this is the end of the world?" Chiun squeaked. His voice betrayed rare fear. "Have the ignorant whites succeeded in ending their so-called civilization? Oh, now I will never hold Cheeta's beautiful boy in my arms."

"Don't panic yet. Listen."

We are controlling transmission. . . . We will control the horizontal. . . . We will control the vertical. . . . We can change the focus to a soft blur . . ."

The TV screen remained black, the NO SIGNAL message unwavering.

"Or sharpen it to crystal clarity. . . ."

"Wait a minute," Remo said suddenly. "I recognize this. It's the opening to an old TV show, *The Outer Limits*."

"I see only blackness," Chiun said, frowning.

"We're getting the audio signal. But no video."

"I do not know this audiovideo mumbo jumbo," Chiun spat.

Remo tried changing the channel. Every station was the same. Even the New Hampshire and Rhode Island stations which they normally couldn't get or which came in full of snow. There was no difference in picture quality.

Chiun's eye went to a wall clock whose second hand moved in time to the cartoon cat's eyes and wagging tail. "It has already started!"

"Relax. This is a reception problem. If we can't pick it up, I'll bet no one can."

As Remo ran up and down the channels, the sonorous voice had fallen silent. Static hissed steadily.

"Well?" Chiun said impatiently.

"Hold it. What do you think I am?"

"A white. Therefore one who understands machines."

"Well, I don't understand this machine. Every channel is the same." Then the voice began speaking again.

"Do not attempt to adjust the picture."

"Something's wrong," Remo said slowly.

"Yes! I cannot watch television."

"No, this *Outer Limits* thing is back on, but I'm on a different channel now."

"The trouble is not in your—"

Remo switched channels.

"—set. We control the—

"—horizontal. We con—

"—rol the vertical."

"This is weird," Remo muttered. "Whatever's doing this, it's on every channel."

"I can see this!" Chiun wailed, beseeching the ceiling with upraised arms. "I wish to see Cheeta instead."

"Uh-oh," Remo muttered.

Chiun dropped his arms. "What?"

Remo hesitated. A few months ago, there had been a grave Cuban-American crisis. The Havana government, in retaliation for what it wrongly believed was a latter-day Bay of Pigs invasion, had stepped up its government broadcast power and overwhelmed all TV in south Florida. As it happened, the counterattack had interrupted a Cheeta Ching newscast—thereby incurring the bitter enmity of the Master of Sinanju. The matter had been resolved without Chiun having fulfilled his vow to decapitate the Cuban leader. If it were happening again, Remo knew there would be no stopping Chiun this time.

"Maybe I should call Smith about this," Remo said quickly.

"Yes! Yes! Call Smith. Smith will know. Ask if he has had word of Cheeta. Ask if he will tape all news of Cheeta, that I might miss none of it."

"All right, all right. Let me dial in peace."

There was a wall phone and Remo picked up the receiver, one eye on the Master of Sinanju, who stood before the blank-faced TV set as if looking upon an injured pet. His eyes were stricken.

Remo was about to press down on the one button—the foolproof code by which he could reach his superior—when abruptly the screech-owl sound of Cheeta Ching's voice filled the kitchen.

"This is the *BCN Evening News with Don Cooder*. Cheeta Ching reporting. Don is off tonight."

"Cheeta!" Chiun crowed. "It is Cheeta! My ancestors have heard me. My prayers have been answered."

"If they have," Remo growled, "they must have a heck of a lot of pull with the FCC."

"Hush."

Remo left the phone and came to Chiun's side.

"Tonight," Cheeta Ching was saying, "*BCN Evening News* was blacked out nationwide just as a search for missing anchor Don Cooder was called off."

"You lying witch!" a voice cried from offstage. "You said your water broke!"

"Wasn't that Cooder's voice?" Remo said.

"Hush!"

"As yet," Cheeta continued unperturbed, "no clear understanding of the electronic disturbance has been ascertained. There are reports, unconfirmed at this time, that the broadcast blackout was not confined to BCN."

"It wasn't my fault!" Don Cooder's disembodied voice cried.

"That *was* Cooder," said Remo. "Where is he?"

"Remo!"

"In our efforts to stay on top of the headlines, BCN has video of the unprecedented phenomenon."

The screen went black except for the NO SIGNAL message, and the sonorous voice repeated its monotone mantra: *There is nothing wrong with your television set. . . ."*

"Remo," Chiun squeaked. "The TV is broken again!"

"No, this is a tape."

"But why are they showing this?"

"It's the headline for the night. What else are they going to show? Don Cooder standing around with nothing to do?"

"They could show Cheeta's beauteous face, dwelling on her perfect nose, her lips so—"

"Vampire-like."

"Philistine!"

The wall phone rang suddenly and Remo said, "Karnac predicts that's Smitty."

"Tell him I am out."

"Sure thing," said Remo, picking up the receiver. "Sinanju diaper service," he recited. "You soil 'em and we'll boil 'em."

A voice that sounded the way bitter lemons smell said, "Remo. Smith here."

Remo stepped out into the hall, the receiver cord uncoiling behind him. He eased the door closed. "Tell me this isn't Cuba all over again," he whispered.

"Remo, I do not know what it is. But for nearly seven minutes broadcast television was knocked off the air from Yellowknife to Acapulco."

"Could the Cubans do that?"

"Theoretically, with a powerful enough transmitter, they could. But that is not what appears to have happened. Except for cable owners and satellite dish receivers, on-air television signals did not reach their affiliates, and somehow the affiliate signals were blocked before they could be received by home sets."

"Is that what the 'no signal' message meant?"

"Yes. I want you and Chiun to stand by."

"I wasn't having any luck getting hold of Dr. Doom, anyway."

"I must remind you that he is not yet an assignment—and certainly not a problem of this magnitude."

"Problem? There was no TV for a few minutes. Big hairy deal. The worst thing that could have happened was for everybody to go to the john at once and mess up the plumbing."

Smith's humorless voice was clipped. "Remo, stand by. I must gather more information. Just stand by."

The line clicked. Remo returned to the kitchen to hang up and look in on Chiun.

Cheeta Ching was going on and on in her screechy voice. As Remo listened, he realized she was simply repeating the essential story: Broadcast TV had been blacked out. No one knew why. It was a three-sentence story, but like a stuck phonograph record, she couldn't get off it.

From time to time, a hand would appear in the background, waving or shaking a fist. It apparently came from a figure who was presumably flat on the floor, and from the occasional glimpse of a human form being prevented from rising into camera range by kneeling stage hands.

"Looks like Cooder finally wigged out on camera," Remo remarked. "They must have pulled Cheeta in as a substitute anchor."

"Hush."

Twenty minutes later, after Cheeta had had on-air conversations with virtually every BCN correspondent, all saying the same thing—which is to say, nothing—Cheeta Ching fixed the viewers with her dull, sharklike eyes and smiled without sincerity.

"In other news, I'm happy to report that my pregnancy continues on schedule with all signs pointing to an imminent delivery. Stay with BCN News for further updates and bulletins on this momentous developing story. This is Cheeta Ching reporting."

"Which momentous story?" Remo asked. "The blackout or the baby?"

"Oh, Remo do not be ridiculous. Of course it is the baby."

"That's what I was afraid of," said Remo, rolling his eyes ceilingward.

3

Dr. Harold W. Smith rarely watched television.

Even when it was new, he seldom spent more than a passing hour a month watching television. He much preferred radio. With radio, it was possible to do something constructive and listen at the same time. To a lifelong workaholic like Harold Smith, the demands television put on a person's full attention meant only one thing: TV would not last. It was a fad, a vehicle for novelty programs like wrestling matches and roller derbys, soon to pass.

So back in the so-called Golden Age of Television— the early 1950s, when he would come home from his long days at the then-new Central Intelligence Agency, Harold Smith would ignore the tiny round-screened television despite the serious dent it had made in his government salary, and he would turn on the radio instead. Why bother watching a broadcaster reading the news off a script when radio commentators performed the same service and stimulated the imagination at the same time?

Yet millions did. Further proof that TV would not last.

But it was not long before the television shows expanded to thirty minutes and began including footage of events. And as music tastes changed and rock and roll seemed to more and more crowd out the tasteful standards Harold Smith enjoyed, he listened less and less to his old console Atwater Kent—a graduation gift from his uncle Ormond.

Reluctantly he retired it into the attic.

Grudgingly Harold Smith fell into the habit of watching TV news. *The Huntley-Brinkley Report* had been his favorite—although Howard K. Smith—no relation—had also been good. He was able to stomach Harry Reasoner, despite his unseemly frivolity.

Today, the current crop of anchors left much to be desired, so Smith had swallowed hard and invested in home cable, paying out of his own pocket the installation charge and the monthly access fee despite the fact that he was well within his rights to charge the fee to either of his operating budgets.

Smith had two. The lesser of them was the operating budget for Folcroft Sanitarium, a sleepy but efficient private hospital on the shores of Long Island Sound in Rye, New York. Harold Smith was Folcroft's director, and had been since his retirement from the CIA back in the halcyon days of Huntley and Brinkley.

The other operating budget was Smith's to do with as he wished. It wasn't literally true, but in practice there was no one above Smith to tell him that no, he could not siphon off $53.50 each month to equip his Rye, New York home and Folcroft office with cable. Even if he had been subject to auditing, the paltry $53.50 would have been hardly a blip on a CPA's radar screen.

For Smith's total annual operating budget, the budget in which Folcroft was a minor expenditure, exceeded many millions of dollars in taxpayer's money.

Harold W. Smith was the head of CURE, sanctioned by the President of the United States—but answerable to no lawmaker, no congressional oversight committee, no one. It had been set up in the early 1960s to operate outside the constraints of lawful government. Its mission: to keep order in an increasingly chaotic society, resorting to extraconstitutional activities when deemed necessary by Harold Smith.

In those difficult early days it had often been necessary. Smith had run the organization from his Folcroft office until the day a successor to the martyred president who had set up CURE in the first place had given Smith authorization to take the next necessary step: create an enforcement arm.

A candidate had been chosen. An ordinary man, soon to be made extraordinary. First Smith had the subject executed. The subject had been a Newark cop, seemingly no different than others who pounded the urban streets of a declining America.

Smith had arranged for his badge to disappear, only to reappear in an alley beside the bludgeoned body of a pusher. The death penalty had been in effect in those days, and the subject had been quickly rail-roaded into a death cell.

It had all been arranged in advance. The execution had been a fraud. The "body," in a pill-induced coma, was spirited to Folcroft, where a plastic surgeon went to work on the subject's face, while Harold Smith, in his Spartan office, went about the grim task of cov-ering his tracks. All records of the declared-dead New-ark cop were purged from Social Security, IRS, and Marine Corps records. The man had been an orphan, unmarried, and thanks to Smith, disgraced. So it was a simple matter to virtually wipe all but the fading memory of one Remo Williams from the official record.

Smith had felt no remorse. A greater good would be served. And it was, once Smith had presented Remo Williams with the cold choice—volunteer or die for real. Remo had been placed in the hands of the last Master of Sinanju, a forgotten line of assassins on the verge of fading from the human stage, for training in the ultimate martial art, called Sinanju, which had taken its name from a desolate village in the bleakness of Communist North Korea.

In time, Smith had his enforcement arm—a human killing machine, professional, unstoppable, invincible, which he had code-named "Destroyer."

For twenty years, Harold Smith had fielded innu-merable crises as head of CURE, the supersecret gov-ernment agency that officially did not even exist, drawing vast sums from a secret operating budget, sanctioning covert operations that involved mayhem, murder, and extortion, utterly unaccountable to anyone, yet in all that time he had personally accounted for every penny to the highest authority Harold Smith personally knew—his own conscience.

The president who had invested Harold Smith with his enormous power and responsibility had never lived to see how Smith had exceeded the trust placed in him. But if he had, he would have experienced absolutely no misgivings.

And so, on a Tuesday evening in April, Harold Smith sat in a comfortable overstuffed chair in the privacy of his home enjoying a night alone, with his wife away at his sister-in-law's, and saw the greatest crisis in his career of public service begin as a KNNN update.

"This just in to Kable Newsworthy News Network News," the cool-voiced anchor had said. "As they were preparing their evening news programs, the three major broadcast networks experienced a unusual simultaneous service interruption. The disruption appears to be nationwide. More on this story as it becomes available."

Smith took his remote from his coat pocket and pointed it at the cable box. The channels marched before his eyes. It took him only one cycle before he realized two incontrovertible facts.

First, that all satellite reception and cable-only stations were broadcasting unimpeded.

Second, all other stations were blacked out, UHF and VHF.

He listened to the sonorous voice advising viewers that the trouble was not in their sets and, not being a watcher of episodic television, failed to recognize it as an old program theme opening.

That was not important. For Harold Smith recognized something more important—that he was witnessing the tip of an iceberg more terrible than any that had threatened the democracy he had sworn to safeguard.

Smith turned on a tabletop radio, and the sonorous voice broadcasting on all TV stations issued from the radio speaker in perfect time with the TV. There was no tape delay.

Turning off the radio and lowering the TV volume, he picked up a well-worn briefcase that was never far away. Smith placed it in his lap, defused the explosive charges in the locking latches, and exposed a portable computer and telephone handset.

This was his link with the secret computers at Folcroft, the nerve center though which he monitored the affairs—public, secret and subversive—of a computer-linked nation. He lifted the handset, dialed a number from memory, and was relieved to find his enforcement arm reachable.

Only after he had put Remo Williams on standby did Harold Smith call the President of the United States, the only person outside CURE to know about the organization.

Smith had not spoken to the new president, who had taken office months before, trusting to the outgoing chief executive to have broken the news of the existence of CURE. He imagined the revelation of the secret organization that kept American democracy stabilized for nearly thirty years had come as a distinct shock to the new man. Normally, Smith left it to each successive president to make contact with him.

But this was a crisis. He just hoped he could convince the latest occupant in the White House of its gravity.

The President's raspy Southern voice was curious. "Smith?"

"Of course," said Smith. The phone was tied by computer link into the dedicated line that had rung a red dialless telephone in the Lincoln Bedroom of the White House. No president since CURE's inception ever failed to answer it. Harold Smith did not make casual calls. "Mr. President, I am calling to warn of a grave danger to this country."

The President's tone lifted an octave. "What is it?"

"Are you aware of the nationwide television blackout?"

"Yes. But the White House is wired up for cable. We weren't affected."

"Sir, a powerful force has showed itself. For what reason, I do not know, but it has the capability to knock broadcast television off the air nationwide."

"They're saying it's sunspots," said the President.

"Who are saying this?"

"The networks."

"Sunspots would not do what this power has accomplished," Smith returned. "Somehow, by some science I cannot fathom, this power has managed to intercept all TV video signals, at the same time broadcasting an audio signal of its choosing."

"Could this be the Cubans up to their old tricks?"

"Doubtful. This appears to be a quantum leap beyond Havana's technical capability. Let me explain the situation as I see it. For years we have feared Cuban interference with our broadcast reception. We know that they possess a transmitter that could be boosted to over 100,000 watts—powerful enough to overwhelm U.S. TV transmissions nationwide. In short, they would override ordinary signals across all frequency bands with an overriding multifrequency signal of their own."

"I follow, Smith."

"This is not the phenomenon we are witnessing here."

"No?"

"No, Mr. President. This power is somehow preventing the outgoing signals from every local broadcast station from getting onto the air. At the same time, it is able to put out an audio signal of its own."

"Science isn't exactly my field, Smith."

"My limited grasp of television theory tells me that this is an amazing and very threatening breakthrough. The power behind this has tonight tested his equipment. Now that he know it works, he will show his hand."

"How?"

"He will jam every TV station in his broadcast radius. Soon. Within the week at the very latest. And if there are demands, he will broadcast them."

"That's a heck of a lot of deduction from a seven-minute blackout."

"Mr. President, I have placed my people on alert. I suggest you do the same. Particularly, be prepared to triangulate the audio signal so that we may trace this interference to its source or sources."

"You think there is more than one source?"

"While it is possible to drown out all TV signals through one centrally positioned broadcast tower, we can't discount an array of jamming stations. Each of them must be tracked down and terminated."

"I'll start the machinery, Smith. Please stay in touch."

"Of course, Mr. President," said Harold Smith, hanging up.

It has gone as well as could be expected, Smith reflected. The succession had gone as it always did, noisy but bloodless. Still Smith was going to miss the old President. He was probably the last one of Harold Smith's generation.

Sadly he closed his briefcase, shucked off his slippers, and drew on his well-polished wing tip shoes. He had not so much as loosened his tie upon coming home, but he tightened the knot as he stood up.

Smith was a tall graying man of retirement age, the flesh tight on his prominent bones. His face was pinched, a pair of rimless glasses perching precariously on his patrician nose. A congenital heart defect gave his skin an unhealthy grayish pallor that matched the hue of his three-piece suit. His eyes, faded from years of dull bureaucratic work, were a similar gray. Even his fingernails looked gray. His Dartmouth tie was hunter green.

For the work that lay before him, Smith would need the speed and power of his Folcroft mainframes. He picked up his worn briefcase.

Smith went out into the night, a cold feeling in the pit of his stomach. He had tried to impress upon the President the seriousness of the event, but he doubted the President had fully grasped the potential for harm tonight's seven-minute blackout foreshadowed. The man had not turned down the music that had been playing in the background during their conversation. It had sounded like Elvis Presley.

As he drove his battered station wagon to Folcroft Sanitarium, Harold Smith hoped the President would not have to deal with it.

For just the tip of the iceberg filled Smith with dread.

4

Remo Williams was on boom-box patrol.

Ever since he and Chiun had moved into the converted-church condominium—occupying all sixteen units—in the city of Quincy, Massachusetts, Remo had been stuck with boom box patrol. It was one of his least favorite duties.

There was a high school next to the Gothic-Swiss-Tudor fieldstone building Chiun considered his castle, and at night teenagers sometimes hung out, playing loud music. Mostly rap. Remo hated rap. He despised heavy metal. Disco gave him headaches. Rock was okay—as long as it was pre-Beatles rock. Why was it, he wondered, that each successive evolution moved further away from melody and toward pure beat? He figured popular music was on its way to extinction. Not that it mattered much. If the local kids were playing Mozart at an estimated 130 decibels, Remo would still have to put a stop to it.

Loud music was offensive to the Master of Sinanju's easily offended ears. Especially with *Eyeball to Eyeball with Cheeta Ching* about to come on.

So Remo had slipped out the front door and was moving toward the disembodied squawk of a rapper extolling the virtues of shooting uncompliant girlfriends in the face with his Glock.

"This is a no-noise zone," Remo called out by way of greeting.

"And this is a free country," a voice shot back.

The voice sounded black but the face was white as bleached flour.

"This is a no-noise zone before it's a free country," Remo countered.

"That's not what they taught us in school, man."

As Remo approached, he saw that the loiterers were a mixture of white and Asian kids, wearing sweatshirts and turned-around Red Sox caps. Somewhere he had read that the biggest, deepest secret in the music industry was the fact that rap music was strictly a suburban teenager phenomenon. Remo wasn't sure what urban kids listened to. Bluegrass, for all he knew.

The sight of the Asian faces alarmed him more than the music bothered him. Chiun had a thing against Asians. True, he was no fan of white people, considering them inferior to Koreans, especially North Koreans, especially North Koreans from his village, and particularly inferior to Chiun's immediate family, but especially inferior to the Master of Chiun himself.

But white Europeans had never invaded Korea, nor their kings cheated previous Masters of Sinanju. Much.

When Chiun had discovered that he had moved into an area with a healthy Asian population, he had all but gone ballistic. It had been all Remo could do to talk him out of embarking on an Sarajevo-style ethnic cleansing campaign.

Reluctantly, Remo had agreed to go door to door and ask his Asian neighbors to kindly, if it was not too much trouble, move to another city. He was almost relieved to discover that almost none of them spoke a word of English. That let him off the hook. But Remo began to feel awkward himself. He personally preferred neighbors who spoke English.

Approaching the mixed white and Asian teenagers listening to black music, his mixed feelings returned. He represented a five-thousand-year-old Korean tradition—the first white man to become a Master of Sinanju—spoke fair Korean himself, and was more comfortable shopping at the local Asian market than the nearby supermarket. He could eat the stuff from the Asian market and survive the experience. The supermarket stuff was 99 percent lethal to his Sinanju-refined digestive system.

Remo had been raised by nuns at St. Theresa's orphanage in Newark. For a long time, he had felt torn between the country of his birth and the honor and responsibility that had been placed on his shoulders. Somewhere along the line, he had become more Sinanju than Newark.

"Tell you what," Remo said in the spirit of compromise, "you can stay if you behave, but the box shuts down."

A quick hand reached for the volume control knob. Remo started a smile that became a grimace when his eardrums were abruptly assaulted by a screeching voice emanating from the dual speakers.

Remo swept in, grabbed up the box and thumbed the off switch.

"Show you a trick," he said.

And like a basketball player, Remo heaved the box into the night sky with both hands. He made it look casual. Five thousand years of Sinanju Masters stood behind the gesture. Five thousand years of unlocking the secrets of the human mind and body. Five thousand years of applying principles Western learning had not even approached.

All eyes shot upward. The box receded into a silvery gleaming dot. And kept going.

This impressed the trio.

"Whoa!"

"Way cool!"

"I wouldn't stand there if I were you," Remo remarked.

"Why not?" one teenager asked, not dropping his gaze from the seemingly stationary gleam above.

"It's going to come down."

"Yeah, I know. And I'm going to catch it. It cost me $47.50."

"It'll cost you both arms of you're lucky enough to catch it," Remo said.

"Says you."

"Says Newton's third law. What goes up, must come down."

"Newton's third law says for every action there's an equal and opposite reaction."

Remo shrugged. "So sue me. High school was a million years ago."

The trio kept their eyes on the night sky. Various expressions played over their young beardless faces. One twitched. Another, the truth dawning on him, took three giant steps backward, his eyes going very wide.

"It's sure taking a long time to fall," one muttered.

"Take the hint," said Remo.

Then the third teenager shouted, "I see it! I see it! It's coming back."

"I got it! I got it!" said the first teenager.

They bumped heads, jockeying for position.

Remo was tempted to let nature take its cruel course, but at the last minute relented.

He swept in, caught a shirt collar in each hand and pulled the two bumping would-be boom-box rescuers out of the way as the box screamed back to earth and shattered into a thousand bits of plastic and electronics, incidentally cracking the asphalt noticeably.

The trio were slapping at their arms and faces. Their fingers came away bright with tiny drops of blood.

"Ouch! Ouch! What hit me?"

"Shrapnel," said Remo. "Now go spread the word. Anyone caught making noise after dark ends up picking plastic out of his face—if I'm in a good mood."

The trio looked to the shattered box, to Remo, back to the box, and fled.

As he walked back to Castle Sinanju—as Chiun called it—Remo muttered, "Beats evicting the entire neighborhood."

From the squat Gothic steeple, windows aglow on all four sides, issued a sudden shriek of anguish. Chiun.

"Now what?" said Remo, whipping through the front door.

Remo burst into the meditation room and stopped in his tracks.

The Master of Sinanju was hopping about the room, his hands clutching at the puffs of cloudy hair that floated over each ear.

"Don't tell me it's another blackout!" Remo said.

"Worse! Worse!" Chiun leveled an agitated finger at the screen.

Remo looked. There was the stony face of Don Cooder, looking steely-eyed into the camera. He was speaking.

"In our efforts to bring you up to date on the crisis along Network Row, we are preempting *Eyeball to Eyeball with Cheeta Ching* for a special live *24 Hours*. Tonight: '24 Hours on Blackout Street.' "

"What about Cheeta!" Chiun cried.

"Cheeta Ching will be seen at this time next week," Cooder said. "Unless, of course the big moment arrives, in which case BCN will cut in live for special labor coverage."

"They're planning to broadcast the *birth*?" Remo grunted.

Chiun said, "Of course. It will be a day of celebration."

"Bulldookey," said Remo. "Look, I'm sorry Cooder's horned in on Cheeta's face time, but these things happen."

"Why do these calamities keep happening to Cheeta? It is not fair!"

"Hey, you got your dose of Cheeta for the night. Lighten up."

"My evening is ruined."

"Why don't we just watch this? Who knows, Cheeta may start having contractions and you'll get to see it all in its gory glory."

As Remo settled onto one of the mats facing the screen, the Master of Sinanju ceased his pacing.

"Why are you interested in this?" he asked suspiciously.

"Smitty thinks that blackout may be something for us. Might as well get current."

"It is not the work of that bearded ruffian, Castro, is it?"

"Smith doesn't think so. We threw a pretty good scare into him last time. He still hasn't shown his face in public."

"No doubt his beard has not yet regrown itself," Chiun sniffed.

"Rat's nests aren't built in a day," said Remo cheerfully.

They watched in silence. A graphic filled the screen. It showed a green circle indicating the area of broadcast interference. It was a big circle. All of the U.S. as well as most of Canada and Mexico were in what Don Cooder referred to as "the null zone."

"While the source of this disruption has not yet been identified," he was saying, "sunspots cannot been ruled out. For more on this important story and how it may affect you, here by telephone is vacationing BCN science editor Frank Feldmeyer."

As a Quantel graphic still of Feldmeyer showed on the screen, the correspondent's comments ran as a voice-over. He was a square-faced man whose features were made smaller by oversized horn-rimmed glasses.

"Don, this phenomenon, if it is a natural one, is utterly baffling. Somehow, all video output was intercepted and substitute audio broadcast in its place. Sunspots might account for one, but not the other."

"Frank, are you saying this could be man-made?"

"Don, there doesn't appear to be any other explanation. Beyond that, it's too early to tell."

"It's too early to tell," Cooder intoned.

"Didn't Feldmeyer just say that?" Remo asked Chiun.

Chiun said nothing. His hazel eyes were narrow in thought.

Cooder was back on the air now. His ruggedly handsome black-Irish face was fixed. There were bags under his eyes large enough to double as coin pouches.

" 'It's too early to tell,' " he repeated. "Portentous words. What can they mean? Is this just a glitch of the electronic age, or—something *more*? Something that will darken all of our lives? For another perspective, here is White House correspondent Sheela Duff."

The picture cut to the White House correspondent standing, appropriately enough, on the White House lawn. She was speaking into a handheld microphone that looked like a candy box with a giant BCN logo.

"Don, here at the White House there is no sign of a crisis atmosphere."

"That's because there's no freaking crisis," Remo grumbled.

"But reliable sources assure us that the President is aware of the situation and cognizant of its meaning."

Cooder asked, "Sheela, as you know, Havana tried to jam U.S. airwaves not long ago. Is this an unscheduled rerun of that old crisis?"

"No, Don. As the graphic you just showed indicates, Cuba is not the epicenter of the so-called null zone. In fact, reliable reports are that Cuban TV and radio were knocked off the air at the same time. In fact, Havana is angrily pointing the finger of blame at Washington. As are, I might add, the Canadian government and the Mexicans."

Cooder came back on. "Let's look at that graphic again, shall we?"

The graphic came on. Remo leaned into the screen.

"Looks like he's right," he said. "Can't be Cuba. Otherwise the blackout would reach clear down to Peru. The transmitter must be in the U.S."

"I understand none of this voodoo," Chiun said darkly.

Don Cooder was saying, "If I read this graphic correctly, and I want to be sure I understand this . . . Frank Feldmeyer, are you still with us?"

"Yes, I am Don."

"I know you can't see the graphic, but it shows a circle encompassing most of North America. What should we be looking for?"

"The center."

"For those of us not well grounded in science, that's the middle, correct?"

"Exactly, Don."

"Actually it looks to me like Canada is the center," Remo muttered.

"The epicenter appears to lie in the heartland of the United States itself," announced Don Cooder.

"Any idiot can see it's Canada," Remo complained.

Don Cooder went on, obviously making it up as he went along. "For those just tuning in, at this hour, the known facts are these: U.S. TV blacked out for seven minutes. Cause: Unknown. Motive: Unknown. Suspicion: Somewhere in the U.S. heartland a pirate transmitter waiting patiently. For—what? No one knows."

Don Cooder paused, fixing the camera with his unblinking eyes. "For the story of those most affected by this, here's our national correspondent, Hale Storm."

The image changed to show the prettily handsome face of BCN national correspondent Hale Storm, looking as dashing as if he had stepped out of a soap opera—which he had. BCN had hired him from one of their own soaps in an effort to broaden their female audience base.

"What was the first thing to go through your mind when the blackout hit?" Storm asked an off-camera figure.

The face of Don Cooder, looking pensive, appeared. He was informal in a fawn-brown cardigan sweater.

"I was at the anchor desk—we call it the Chair around here—and had just read the lead-in headlines when the producer noticed the line monitor had gone black. At first, he thought it was an internal glitch, but I knew that couldn't be. Here at BCN we have the finest technical staff in television. I immediately pitched in and, sensing something more serious amiss, discovered that the other networks were black too."

"Very astute, Don."

Don Cooder offered his trademark forced smile and said, "Don Cooder has been in this news game a long time, man and boy. He can smell a story."

Chiun nudged Remo. "Why does he refer to himself in the third person?"

"Maybe he's schizo," Remo offered. "What I want to know is why are they interviewing each other. Shouldn't they be talking to the man in the street?"

"Why should they waste their time speaking with peasants?" Chiun wanted to know.

"Maybe because the story affected maybe sixty million people, and only a few dozen TV employees, that's why. These news guys all think they *are* the news."

"They are obviously very important," said Chiun.

"What makes you say that?"

"They all look very much like the President of Vice, who is an important person as well."

"Come to think of it, the Vice President does kinda look like he should be reading the news, not making it. And he's just like the network anchors. They're practically all airheads. They get paid a ton of money to just sit there and read."

Out of the corner of his eyes, Remo noticed Chiun's wispy beard tremble. And he knew he had made a mistake.

"They are paid how much to simply sit and read?"

"Uh, I forget," Remo said evasively.

"I will settle for a rough estimate."

"Oh, I heard Cooder gets oh, four or five."

"Thousands?"

"Millions."

"Millions! To simply *read*!"

"Cheeta isn't exactly paid in seashells, either, you know."

"That is different. She does not read mere news, but recites poetry in her lilting voice. She is a fountain of culture in a barbarian land. No amount of money can be too much for her."

"And she's just the weekend anchor."

Chiun's eyes narrowed. "Why are they called anchors?"

"Good question. Ask Smith next time we see him. He knows all kinds of useless stuff."

The taped interview with Don Cooder ended and the live Don Cooder returned to do a live interview with the national anchor who had just interviewed him. Then, Don Cooder interviewed the producer, the news director, and up on to the president of the news division, who vowed that this would never happen again, but if it did, BCN would be there to cover it. Round the clock, if need be.

How BCN could cover a disruption that would prevent them from broadcasting was not explained, and no one thought to point out the lapse in logic. Everyone spoke in crisp, authoritative sentences, wore expensive suits, and boasted perfect helmets of hair that could decorate storefront manikins. Some possibly had.

At the end of the broadcast, the camera closed in to frame Don Cooder's face and he said, "*BCN Evening News* pledges to keep you up to date on this developing story. Until next time," he added, giving the peace sign, "Rock on."

Immediately, a local anchor came on with a teaser for the eleven o'clock news.

"TV blacked out nationwide. The story at 11."

"Why do they do that?" Remo complained.

"Do what?"

"We just watched a half hour of national coverage and the local station immediately jumps in trying to get us to watch it all over again at eleven."

"I do not understand these American customs," Chiun sniffed. "I only know that I will have to wait until the weekend before beholding the sight of Cheeta the Beauteous."

"You'll make it."

The Master of Sinanju arose like a pale column of smoke. He had changed to evening white. "I will retire now," he said.

"Kinda early, isn't it?"

"Awake, I will only feel sadness. Perhaps in sleep I will dream of Cheeta the Fair."

"Does that mean I gotta resume boom box patrol?"

The Master of Sinanju paused at the door. He turned, his face stern.

"If I am dreaming of Cheeta, and rude voices awaken me, there will be heads adorning the gates by dawn."

"Trust me," said Remo. "You'll sleep peacefully if I have to sleep outside."

"I would not mind," said Chiun, padding off to his bedroom.

And hearing those chilly words, Remo's spirits fell.

5

The office of Harold W. Smith was a Spartan cube that looked as if it had been furnished in 1963 from a municipal auction of sixty-year-old surplus school equipment.

The desk was a scarred slab of oak; the leather executive chair in which Smith sat was cracked with age and the corrosive action of human perspiration. Smith had sweated out countless crises in the chair.

There was a faded green divan that might once have sat outside a school principal's office for discipline-problem students. The file cabinets were a mixture of dark green metal and oak. Intelligence analysts could have pored over the contents of those cabinets for a hundred years and would have been forced to conclude that Folcroft was no more than a stodgy private hospital.

Behind him, Long Island Sound was a crinkling expanse of moonlit India ink visible through a picture window of one-way glass so prying eyes could not read Harold Smith's lips or peer over his shoulder at the computer terminal that occupied one corner of Smith's pathologically neat desk.

The illumination was fluorescent—as an aid to Smith's nagging eyestrain. One filament shook nervously. When the day came that it finally burnt out, Smith would replace it, not before.

As he worked the keyboard, Harold Smith was not even aware of the annoying problem.

From this terminal, Smith could reach out with invisible fingers and touch virtually every computer net accessible by phone line. Right now, he was monitoring the internal computer systems of the three major networks and Vox TV.

On his screen appeared, in rotation, news stories being written in distant terminals by network newswriters, internal office memos, and electronic mail.

All four networks were busy. According to their computer activities, there was a great deal of gossip and speculation going on, but no hard facts. Doggedly Smith logged off one network and switched to another. It sometimes seemed to him that it had been easier in the early days of CURE, before computers revolutionized American business. In fact, it had been more difficult. It was just that the proliferation of computers meant that much more raw data was accessible to Smith—and hiring a staff to keep track of it all was out of the question.

As Smith secretly prowled the Multinational Broadcast Corporation database, unknown fingers were typing a fragment of electronic mail.

"This weird fax just came in," the fingers wrote. "And the brass all went into a huddle."

Smith dropped out of the MBC net and accessed the AT&T software that processed telephone calls. He brought up the MBC headquarters active billing file and backtracked the most recent incoming calls. There was no way to differentiate between voice and fax transmission calls, except that the latter were usually brief. In the last five minutes, Smith found, MBC had received six incoming calls. Only one was long-distance. It was from Atlanta, Georgia.

Smith dropped out of the file and brought up the American Networking Conglomerate billing file. ANC, too, had received a long-distance call from Atlanta. The number was the same. Ferociously, Smith accessed the BCN file.

There had been no call from Atlanta. Then, as Smith watched, one appeared.

Like a demented concert pianist, Harold Smith dropped out of AT&T and called up the BCN database. Most faxphones, he knew, were tied into computer software so that on-screen text could be faxed by the simple press of a hot key, without bothering to generate a hard copy. Smith raced from screen to screen, breathing like a jogger in motion, looking to see if an incoming fax was appearing anywhere in the system.

Then he found it. Line by line, it began manifesting itself on his own terminal.

"My God," he croaked. "It is worse that I imagined."

Without taking his eyes off the screen, Smith reached for one of the many telephones on his desk. From memory, he called the Atlanta number that was the source of the fax. The other telephone rang six times. Then there was the click of a backup line cutting in, followed by more ringing.

As the fax completed itself in ghostly green letters, a telephone voice was speaking in Harold Smith's ear.

Smith groaned, a low inarticulate sound. The voice had told him exactly where the fax had originated.

If it meant what he thought, a new and terrifying kind of conflict was about to be played out. And the battlefield would be an electronic one.

6

Cheeta Ching was afraid to leave her office.

Normally, Cheeta Ching wasn't afraid of man, beast, or machine. Behind her back, she was known as the Korean Shark. Even her coworkers feared her. But if there was one colleague even she feared, it was senior BCN anchor Don Cooder.

Theirs had been a long-running feud, dating back to the days before she had jumped rival MBC for BCN. Cheeta had never wanted to leave MBC. Certainly not for a lateral slide from MBC weekend anchor to BCN weekend anchor. She would never have done it. Never in a million years. Except for Don Cooder.

With Cooder in the Chair, BCN was dead last in the ratings, heading for the ratings cellar with a millstone around its corporate neck. Nobody expected him to last. And as the pressure had mounted, the hothead from Texas had become increasingly unstable.

There was the famous seven-minute walk-off. The shouting matches with presidential candidates. Being kidnapped by irate taxi drivers. It was only a matter of time, the industry knew, before Don Cooder cracked like an overboiled egg.

Cheeta Ching knew that she was making a potentially disastrous career move. She also understood that if Cooder went off the deep end, whoever was his heir-apparent was certain to land her lucky ass in the Chair. And Cheeta Ching wanted to be the proud owner of that lucky ass.

Industry critics all but wrote her professional obituary when she accepted the BCN weekend anchor slot. In interviews, she shrugged off all predictions of doom. After all, she was Cheeta Ching. *The* Cheeta Ching. The only female Korean anchor on earth. Or at least outside Korea. Nothing had ever stood in her way.

Except, she had discovered to her everlasting chagrin, Don Cooder.

The man was like a starfish attached to an oyster with that damned Chair. He couldn't he pried up, knocked off, or smashed loose.

Not that Cheeta Ching hadn't tried. During one of their smoldering feuds, she had hired a group of thugs to jump him outside his Manhattan apartment crying, "What's the frequency, Kenneth?"

It should have sent him over the edge. It didn't. The man was a barnacle, inert and immovable.

After that, Cheeta shifted tactics, announcing the start of her heroic struggle to become pregnant. As Cheeta saw it, the publicity value would be incalculable. She was over forty, female, and a symbol to career-minded women across the nation. To have a child would have made her the ultimate emblem of having it all. And why not? It had worked for Candice Bergen.

Except that Cheeta Ching couldn't conceive to save her life.

It was embarrassing. *Entertainment Weekly* called her the "Little Anchor Who Couldn't." Don Cooder had ramrodded onto the air a special report, "Why Superwoman Can't Ovulate."

It was especially embarrassing because her husband was a gynecologist-turned-talk-show-host. They did it in every position except free-fall—but only because Rory's fingers couldn't be pried loose from the open aircraft door. He was petrified of heights.

Next, they resorted to every fertility drug known to man. Her biological clock ticking, every tabloid holding her up to ridicule, Cheeta Ching grew desperate as a starved barracuda.

Then, like a miracle, a man had appeared in her life. A Korean. Of course. Only a fellow Korean, a member of the most perfect race ever to grace a sorry world, could have helped barren Cheeta Ching to total, womanly fulfillment.

His name had been Chiun, but out of respect for his years, Cheeta always called him "Grandfather." She had never spoken of him to her husband. There was no need to crush his spirit. Rory had been certain that the oysters and Spanish fly omelette breakfasts he had endured for more than two years had done it.

For nine months now, Cheeta Ching had basked in the glow of positive press. *BCN Weekend Report* ratings were soaring, even as Cooder's were sinking. She had been cover-featured by *People* three times—once each trimester. *Vanity Fair* had a standing cover-shoot offer, preferably showing mother and child nude. Breast-feeding. In the rarified world of the celebrity anchor, Cheeta Ching was Queen of the Mountain—and determined to grind her stiletto heels into the eyes of the competition. It was only a whisper in the halls, but already they were talking about making a major change when Cooder's contract came up for renewal.

The Chair was as good as Cheeta Ching's.

All she had to do was live long enough to plant her lucky behind in it.

It was almost eleven o'clock now. Cheeta had been locked in her office since she had signed off the 6:30 feed and rushed from the newsroom.

"It's for your own good," said the producer, as he escorted her to her office. Security guards ringed her with drawn guns. Down the corridor, Don Cooder was incoherent with rage, screaming, and frothing at the mouth.

The remaining security force was sitting on him.

"I'm admiral now, right?" Cheeta had asked breathlessly.

"We'll talk about it later. Okay?" the producer returned.

"What about the seven o'clock feed?"

"It's a slow news day. We'll just replay the 6:30."

"Who's going to do the West Coast update?"

"Don't worry about that," the producer promised, shoving her into the office and closing the door. "Better lock it to be safe."

As the producer hurried away to deal with his temperamental anchor, Cheeta banged in the door and asked, "What about my *Eyeball to Eyeball* edition?"

"We'll let you know when the coast is clear."

Cheeta spent the next hour with one ear pressed to her locked office door, listening to the horrible sounds coming from the newsroom as the staff attempted to placate Don Cooder.

"We'll give you a raise, Don."

"Don Cooder's very soul has been wounded. It will take more than mere money to bind up his mortal wounds," he announced.

"We'll increase your operating budget. Add that backup science correspondent you wanted."

"You insult Don Cooder with a bribe of another color."

"How about you do a special special tonight?"

"A *special* special?"

"Yeah. On the blackout. You can do it in the *Eyeball to Eyeball* slot."

Cheeta tried to choke it down, but the shriek of anguish came out of her too-red mouth as raw sound.

"You bastard!"

"I'll do it," said Don Cooder in a suddenly placated tone.

At eight o'clock, Don Cooder had gone on the air, his hair sprayed into submission, his wild eyes almost calm.

As she watched on her office TV, Cheeta Ching's greatest hope slowly dwindled to nothingness. Namely that the brass would see the seven-minute blackout as a repetition of the famous seven-minute Don Cooder walkout and can the prima donna once and for all.

"My time will come," she hissed at the screen, while

eating cold *jungol* soup. Once, the baby kicked.
Cheeta slapped her belly and he settled right down.

When it was over, Cooder was knocking at the
door, saying in an imitation Robert DeNiro voice,
"Come out, come out, wherever you are."

Cheeta sat very still in her desk and said nothing
until the clumsy sound of his boots creaked away.

Less than an hour later, he was back doing a Jack
Nicholson.

"Heeerre's Donny."

Cheeta refused to respond. Fortunately, no ax came
splintering through the panel. Cooder went away
again. From time to time, furtive footsteps returned
to her office door. Cheeta ignored them, mentally
vowing to outwait him, just as she would outlast her
arch-rival in the long haul.

Hours had passed without any further sign of Cooder.
Cheeta called around the studio. No one had seen him.
But no one had seen him leave the building either.

With any luck, Cheeta hoped, he had gone to the
john to have his long-overdue nervous breakdown. If
only someone would tell her for sure. The cold spicy
soup was repeating on her. Either that or she was
having the weirdest contractions.

Cheeta was steeling her nerve for a tentative hall-
way reconnoiter when her office fax tweedled and
began emitting annoying noises.

She turned in her seat and watched the sheet slide
from the slot. She ripped it free and read it.

It was short:

BROADCAST CORPORATION OF NORTH AMERICA:
UNLESS TWENTY MILLION DOLLARS IS DEPOSITED IN
SWISS BANK ACCOUNT NUMBER 33455-4581953 BY NOON
TOMORROW, THE NEXT BLACKOUT WILL BE SEVEN
HOURS, NOT SEVEN MINUTES. THINK OF WHAT THAT
WILL DO TO YOUR RATINGS.

                                          CAPTAIN AUDION

"Audion?" Frowning. Cheeta went to her word

processor. Her chief asset as a news reporter had been her aggressive take-no-prisoners style and her flat-but-photogenic features.

As weekend anchor, it had been her attention-getting voice and her mane of raven black hair.

Writing had nothing to do with any of it. She was paid over two million dollars a year to be a corporate logo that talked. The truth was, Cheeta Ching could barely spell. So she input the word "Audion" and waited for her electronic on-line dictionary to help her out with the unfamiliar term.

The database responded instantly.

AUDACIOUS: Brash, outrageous or unconventional.

"That's not what I asked for," Cheeta complained. Then she noticed she had misspelled the word and the database had given her the nearest equivalent. She retyped the word again, this time using both typing fingers.

AUDION: A triode or vacuum tube used in early television development.

"Hmmmm," said Cheeta, swiveling back to her fax-phone. As a journalist, she had received her share of anonymous death threats—most, she was convinced, came from Don Cooder. As a precaution, Cheeta had an AT&T Caller ID device attached to her phone that gave a digital readout of the last number that had called. She pressed the memory button.

A ten-digit number marched along the readout screen and froze. Picking up the phone, she dialed it. The phone rang six times, and there came the click of a second line cutting in.

A crisp woman's voice at the other end said, "Burner Broadcasting."

Cheeta hung up an instant ahead of her own gasp.

"Thank you, thank you, thank you," she told her

nest of inanimate electronics. "You have just given me the greatest story of my career."

"Story?" A low voice called through the door. "What story?"

Cheeta froze. Forcing a lilt into her barn owl voice, she called, "Fooled you, Don. Just testing to see if you're still there."

"I'm not Don Cooder," said the unmistakable voice of Don Cooder.

"And I'm sleeping on the office couch tonight," returned Cheeta Ching, getting up to turn off the lights.

After waiting a full minute, she got down on her hands and knees and peered under the door.

An unblinking bloodshot blue orb was staring back at her.

"Comfy?" she asked the eye.

The eye refused to answer. Neither did it blink. It was pretending it wasn't there. Or something.

Noticing some dust along the carpet edge, Cheeta puffed at it hard.

"Arggh," said the eye, going away. Ostrich-skin boots hopped and danced out in the well-lit corridor.

"Something in your eye?" Cheeta taunted.

"You'll never read news in this town again," Cooder warned, stomping off.

"Pleasant dreams," she returned, struggling to her feet. She threw herself on the divan and moved her bloated body so the springs creaked noticeably. The stomping stopped. But in the quiet that followed, Cheeta could hear labored breathing. Cooder had obviously tried the old trick of walking in place to give the impression he had gone away.

After a while, heavy footsteps did pound away, sounding disappointed.

Cheeta went to her window, which overlooked the studio's Forty-third Street entrance. A dark figure in a Borsalino hat and holding a hand up to one eye flung itself into a waiting taxi, which roared away like a fat yellow jacket.

Cheeta eased the door open a crack. Seeing the

coast was clear, she slipped out the back door and hailed a taxi with a two-fingered whistle.

"La Guardia," she told the driver.

"Ain't you Cheeta Ching, the anchor lady?"

"No, I'm Cheeta Ching the superanchor," Cheeta spat back. "And after tonight, no one will doubt it."

"Fine. Just don't have your brat in my back seat, okay?"

"You should be so lucky," Cheeta snapped back. "My baby is going to be bigger than Murphy Brown's." She reached into her purse, fished around, and her tightly knit eyebrows separated in dull surprise.

Noticing her expression in his rearview mirror, the cabby asked, "Forget your wallet?"

"Worse. My pills."

"Should I turn around?"

"No," Cheeta said firmly. "The story always comes first. Besides, I'm only going to be away a few hours."

7

The biggest flap ever to hit television had turned into the story of the decade with the transmission of a handful of extortionary faxes to the four broadcast networks—and no one knew what to do with it.

At MBC, Senior Anchor Tim Macaw ran his hand through his boyish salt-and-pepper hair as he read the fax over and over with innocent-looking, uncomprehending eyes. In an age where maturity of face and voice lifted ratings, he was rarity—a youthful anchor. Critics dismissed him as Tom Sawyer with a sixty-dollar haircut and dressed up in a Pierre Cardin suit. But he appealed to blue-haired elderly women, and while it was not much of a demographic niche, he sold of lot of Efferdent and Tylenol.

"Captain Audion? Is this on the level?" he asked his producer.

"No one knows."

"But it *could* be for real?"

"There's no telling."

"Should we break in with a bulletin?"

"If we do, it could be the worst gaff since KNNN almost aired that hoax report that the last president had died."

Tim Macaw frowned, his youthful features gathering like a Kleenex dropped into water.

"I'm not taking responsibility for this," he said petulantly.

"Good. I'll kick it upstairs. It sounds like something for legal anyway."

"Yeah, this is legal's turf."

And two of the most powerful men in broadcasting went their separate ways, relived that they had avoided a potentially career-wrecking bear trap.

At ANC, Dieter Banning had just drawn on his trademark trenchcoat and was about to leave for the night when *Nightmirror* correspondent Ned Doppler rushed in, clutching a shiny but smudged fax.

"Dieter—this just came off the newsroom fax."

Dieter Banning was widely considered to be the smoothest, most cosmopolitan anchor in modern television. His round Canadian consonants were invariably delivered in impeccable style. He projected the image of a man of the world—cool, unflappable, and one of the few anchors on TV whose hair looked like his own.

"What kind of bullshit is this?" he yelled, cigar ashes falling on the fax signed "Captain Audion."

Ned Doppler snatched the fax away, his protruding ears red.

"Don't burn it, your moron!" he snapped. "It may be news! I'm giving you the option of going live with it."

Banning wrinkled his pointed nose at the fax. "Is it for real?" he muttered, feeling for something lodged in his left nostril with a thumb.

Doppler shrugged. Banning frowned. The two men stood, toe to toe, sizing one another up like gladiators in some electronic arena.

Both were thinking the same thought.

If I go on the air with this, it could be a career maker. If I don't, it could break me. On the other hand, if it's a hoax I'll never live it down.

"Has it been checked out?" Banning pressed, wiping his thumb clean on the inside of his lapel.

Doppler fixed Dieter Banning with his frank, expressive eyes, like twin marbles sunk into Silly Putty. In spite of his protuberant ears and overfreckled cheeks, and despite his resemblance to a boozy Howdy Doody, Ned Doppler was considered by many to be the most trusted man in TV news since Walter Cronkite.

"How do you check out an anonymous fax?" he retorted.

"You know," said Dieter Banning, flicking cigar ash onto a carpet that looked as if it had been pulled from a burning tenement, "I'm just going to pretend I never saw this. How's that?"

"It's your career," Doppler growled.

Banning smiled broadly. "Only if you have the balls to use it on *Nightmare*."

"It's *Nightmirror* and you know it."

"I was thinking of your next night's sleep," grinned Dieter Banning, striding from the room.

Ned Doppler stood watching him go. "Putz," he said softly. It was ten past eleven. He was on live in twenty minutes and he didn't have his lead written.

He fished into his pocket for his lucky quarter. It would not be the first time he was prepared to risk his career on the outcome of a coin toss . . .

Eventually, a producer at the fledgling Vox newsroom bit the bullet. He called his counterpart at BCN.

"Yeah, we got one," said the BCN producer. "Did you?"

"Yeah. Think it's legit?"

"Sonny, if you don't know by now, you ain't never gonna know." And the BCN producer slammed down the receiver and raced to his office TV. He turned on Vox, hoping they would break the story. That way, BCN could use it, falling back on the Vox report for credibility. If it went sour, Vox would take the heat. If not, it was a story BCN would dominate. Vox ran their newsroom as if it were a sitcom, complete with studio audience, orchestrated applause, and canned laughter for the human interest stories. They weren't even in BCN's class.

But Vox didn't break in with a bulletin.

Unhappily, the BCN producer pulled his handkerchief out of his pocket and draped it across the mouthpiece of his office phone. He called his counterpart at MBC.

"This is your counterpart at another network," he said through the muffling handkerchief.

"BCN, right?"

"You can't prove that."

"Sure I can. I just got off the phone with both ANC and Vox. They got faxes signed Captain Audion, too."

"Damn. Are you cutting in with it?"

"Why don't you tune in and find out," said the MBC producer, hanging up.

For the BCN news producer, it was pressure beyond belief. All of his competition had the story now. It was just a matter of minutes—perhaps seconds—before someone broke in.

As the seconds crawled past and salty sweat oozed out of his forehead, he decided that the network that was dead last in the ratings could afford to give the one-armed bandit of destiny a hard pull.

"Is Cooder still in the building?" he snapped into his intercom.

"No, sir."

"Then get me Ching. I know she's still here. She's been circling the Chair like a shark, hoping to go into labor live."

"Miss Ching left fifteen minutes ago."

"Is there *anybody* still in the building who can read news?"

"I'd be happy to give it a shot," said the secretary in a hopeful voice.

"Forget it."

The BCN producer settled heavily into his executive chair. He turned on ANC. It was almost time for *Nightmirror*. That goofball Doppler was sure to run with the story. He had looked silly for years and it never seemed to hurt his career.

But *Nightmirror* made no mention of the fax. Neither did MBC or Vox.

Potentially it was the story of the decade. All four networks were on ground zero—and no one knew what to do with it.

8

Harold Smith had his tiny portable black-and-white set perched on his Folcroft desk. The reception was snowy and one of the rabbit ears was bent. He was watching *Nightmirror*. Had he been a viewer of TV during the medium's infancy he could be forgiven for mistaking the blurry talking head on the screen for Howdy Doody or a *Mad* magazine cover.

The sonorous voice of Ned Doppler came through the static like an audio beacon.

"And so it remains, seven minutes of television time lost to mankind. That's 420 seconds to you and an estimated 40 million dollars in lost advertising revenue to the networks. Will it matter? Stay tuned. I'll be back in a minute."

Harold Smith switched off the set, knowing that Doppler always came back only to say, "That's tonight's report. I'm Ned Doppler." Sometimes he did a program update. But never came back with any statement of substance. The tag was simply a device to trick viewers into watching the final block of *Nightmirror* commercials—usually for a national retail chain that had a hundred-year reputation and was recently found to have engaged in a pattern of racketeering and fraud in their automotive repair and appliance divisions. Smith had personally exposed them after being overcharged seven dollars on a muffler patch job.

Smith gave the other networks a final scan and

switched off the set. It was midnight. None of the networks had floated so much as a hint of the extortionary fax transmissions. Perhaps they had dismissed them as crank faxes. Possibly none of them understood they were not the only recipient. At any rate, the networks were unlikely to break programming with bulletins now, with much of the country asleep or preparing for bed. It was the flip side of the same cynicism that motivates political leaders to schedule their press conferences an hour before the midday or evening news.

Smith recalled a nonsense adage: If a tree falls where no one can hear it, does it make a sound? Wryly, he wondered was it news if no one reported it?

Harold Smith knew the faxes were real. He knew this because he had an excellent idea who had originated them. Not in the absolute sense. But all the signs pointed in one direction.

Clearing his throat, he reached for the dedicated line to Washington.

"Yes, Dr. Smith?"

The President's answer was slightly hoarse. He had picked up on the fifth ring. Smith did not apologize for waking him. That was not how CURE worked. Although ultimately answerable to the executive branch, the President could not mandate CURE operations. That would invite possible political abuse. The chief executive could only suggest missions. Or he could issue the ultimate directive—to shut down CURE forever.

In this case, Harold Smith was merely keeping his president informed.

"Mr. President," he said, "the four major networks have received extortionary faxes demanding twenty million dollars from each, or all broadcast television will be blacked for a seven-hour interval."

"Is that so bad?" was the President's first question.

"It could be catastrophic. The public would be cut off from their most immediate source of news, not to

mention passive entertainment. And the advertising
revenue loss would exceed . . ." Smith consulted his
computer ". . . 600 million dollars."

"But there's still KNNN. This only affects on-air
broadcasting, right?"

"Mr. President, I have traced the faxes to their
transmission source. They all come from the Kable
Newsworthy News Network headquarters in Atlanta."

"What?"

"I have confirmed this to my satisfaction. KNNN
appears to have launched a campaign to demoralize if
not destroy network television."

"Smith, I find this very hard to believe. Here at the
White House, we could hardly get by without
KNNN."

"Mr. President, any hoaxer with access to a KNNN
telephone could have sent those faxes. But to knock
coast-to-coast television off the air requires enormous
money and extremely sophisticated equipment."

"I know the competition out there is pretty fierce,
but isn't this taking it too far?" the President said
weakly.

"There is reason to believe that KNNN head Jed
Burner is directly culpable," Smith added. "This is no
prank."

"You have proof?"

"I admit it is circumstantial, but it appears telling.
The fax was signed Captain Audion."

"Audion?"

"An old-style vacuum tube critical to early TV
reception."

"So? KNNN is cable."

"You might recall that in his more flamboyant days,
KNNN president Jed Burner was known by the sobri-
quet of Captain Audacious."

"Audacious. Audion. Hmmm. Isn't that kind of
obvious?"

"Only if the fax source is known to the people Captain Audion is attempting to extort. It was a blind fax.
He cannot know I have determined its origin."

"How do *you* know these things, Smith?"

"Sorry. Privileged."

"The last guy told me you were like that. All right," the President said tightly, "what do you suggest?"

"The national economy, never mind public peace of mind, cannot afford a seven-hour blackout. I am putting my people in the field."

The President's swallow was audible. His raspy voice became tinged with reluctance. "If you think this warrants it."

"I do."

"Well, I guess there's nothing more to say, is there?"

"No, Mr. President. I just wanted you to know."

Harold Smith returned the red receiver to its cradle and lifted the blue contact phone handset, reflecting that it was always difficult breaking in a new chief executive. Now more than ever it was fortunate that CURE stood prepared.

There were a great many questions that remained to be answered, but one thing was certain. After tonight, the threat of a television blackout would be nullified.

The Destroyer would see to that.

9

The first problem Remo encountered was getting out of the Atlanta airport.

Remo had been in airports all over the world, ranging from tiny cubicles in distant deserts to urban mazes. But this place was Byzantine. There was more space in the complex than out on the runways. Most of it seemed designed to impress other airport architects.

Remo got lost twice before someone directed him to the automated buses.

He got on the first one that arrived, and it began talking to him in a silly-ass 1950s robot voice.

"Welcome to Atlanta. Welcome to Atlanta. This is Terminal A. The next stop is . . ."

"Shut up," Remo snapped.

". . . Terminal B. If you would like me to stop at Terminal B, press . . ."

"Shut up!"

"Welcome to Atlanta. The next stop . . ."

There was no one else on the bus, so Remo gave the wall a kick.

"iiiisssss . . . *squawwk* . . ."

Immediately, he felt better. But not by much.

Once outside, Remo hailed a cab. The dogwood-scented city air was sultry entering his lungs. It was still too full of hydrocarbons and metallic traces for his taste, but it least it was a change. Remo wasn't so sure he liked living in New England. The climate and foliage reminded him of North Korea.

"Where to, friend?" the cab driver asked in a mellow Southern drawl.

"Peachtree," said Remo.

"Which Peachtree?"

Remo frowned. The call from Harold Smith had told him to go to the KNNN headquarters on Peachtree. That was all. It seemed enough.

"There's more than one?" he asked.

"More than one? There's dozens. Take your pick." The cabby began ticking off items on his thick fingers. "Peachtree Lane, Peachtree Road, Peachtree Street, Peachtree Circle and then you got your Peachtree Avenue—"

Remo brightened. "Avenue! That's it, Avenue."

"Good. Now is that Peachtree Avenue *East*, or Peachtree Avenue *West*?"

Remo's face fell. "Happen to know where the KNNN building is?"

"Which one?"

"The one on Peachtree," Remo said.

"There's *two* on Peachtree. They call them KNNN South and KNNN Not South."

"Not South?"

"You hang a North on a business down in these parts, you might as well torch it the next day."

"Take me to the nearest one," Remo sighed, settling back into the cushions. He was starting to feel glad the Master of Sinanju had decided to stay behind.

After receiving the word to move on KNNN from Harold Smith, Remo had reluctantly awakened Chiun. He would have preferred not to. But he knew that he would catch hell either way.

The first words out of the Master of Sinanju's excited mouth were, "It is happening? Is the baby coming! Tell me!"

"No, that's not it," Remo said hastily.

The Master of Sinanju had stopped in the middle of a frantic lunge for his traveling kimono, which lay neatly folded at the foot of his sleeping mat. "What? Then why do you awaken me?"

"Smitty wants us on this TV blackout thing," Remo had explained. "He thinks Jed Burner is behind it."

Chiun's haughty chin came up. "I do not know that name."

"You're one of the lucky ones. They used to call him the South's Loudmouth. He runs KNNN. That's where I'm headed. Now let's go."

To Remo's surprise, Chiun had tucked his hands into the sleeves of his sleeping kimono.

"I cannot go," he said stiffly. "If harm come to both of us, there will no one to take care of the boy."

"What's wrong with the freaking mother?" Remo had shouted.

"The boy needs a father," Chiun had said in a thin, remote voice.

"Sounds to me like the little bastard's going to have his pick," Remo shot back.

"I should be at Cheeta's side," said Chiun, averting his face.

"Then why aren't you?"

"Remo. It would be unseemly; Cheeta is a married woman. There are those who would gossip."

"Beginning with her husband. He'd have you both on his TV talk show so fast your head would spin."

"I have seen his program. It is filth."

Remo got control of his voice, "It's called *The Gabby Gynecologist*," he explained patiently, "and doctor talk shows are the latest thing."

"I will accept talk. But they show pictures. Gross pictures."

Remo folded his arms. "No argument there. But if anything breaks on Cheeta's condition, you might as well be with me as sleeping."

"How so?"

Remo repressed a smile. The hook was baited. Now to reel in the unwary fish . . .

"Where I'm going," he said, "I'll to be on the ground zero of TV news for the entire world. If Cheeta's water breaks, KNNN will probably have it on the air before Cheeta even knows it's happening."

"In that case," Chiun said, "I will remain here, my ears glued to KNNN."

"The expression is eyes. Eyes are glued to TVs, not ears."

"Glued eyes cannot see and I intend to resume my sleep. But I will leave the television device on, so that if the name of Cheeta Ching is spoken, I will snap awake and race to her side."

Remo frowned. "Last chance. The scuttlebutt is that Cheeta's been keeping her legs crossed until sweeps start, anyway."

Chiun's hazel eyes grew round with shock. The hair over each ear shook imperceptibly. "Is this possible— to hold the baby within the womb until the mother wishes to release it?"

"For normal woman, I don't know. For Cheeta Ching, I wouldn't put anything past her. She's so rat- ings crazed, she'll do anything for more face time—or whatever they'd televise."

"So speaks the green voice of jealousy," Chiun sniffed.

"So speaks a man who's had more than one run-in with that barracuda," Remo snapped.

"My mind is made up."

And it was. Hurt, Remo had left. It was hard to believe. Chiun actually cared more about some brat who hadn't even been born yet than he did about Remo.

All during the flight to Atlanta, Remo's eyes had felt hot and dry and there was a funny tightness in his throat. He couldn't figure it out. . . .

Now, racing through downtown Atlanta, he was angry. And he was going to take his anger out on whatever was behind this.

Up ahead, Remo could see the distinctive KNNN Tower emblazoned with its world-famous corporate symbol—a nautical anchor. The roof was a clump of satellite dishes, like crouching spiders searching the heavens for prey.

"I just hope that this is the right building," Remo growled.

The cab driver hoped so too. His passenger was wearing a really fierce expression. And the way he was gripping the upholstery and shredding the stuffing gave a man a queasy feeling in the pit of his stomach.

10

Jed Burner was the last person on earth anybody would have thought capable of transforming the face of television news.

"TV? Ah don't watch it," he had boasted upon assuming control of a tiny Atlanta UHF station his suddenly deceased father had built from the ground up. "TV's for setters. Ah'm ah doer. Ah've probably watched all of ah hundred hours of TV in mah entire life. Tops."

"So what do you want us to do, Mr. Burner?" asked his nervous station manager on the occasion of new owner Jed Burner first setting foot in the station he had inherited.

"How much this station gross in a yeah?" Burner had asked looking around the master control room and pressing buttons that interested him. Videotape squealed as it went into reverse and a thirty minute episode of *Adventures in Paradise* went onto the air backward. No one noticed.

"Currently we're losing a half million per quarter."

The sandy-haired man with the crinkling sea-blue eyes paused, took his Havana cigar out of his mouth and said, "Find me a sucka."

"Mr. Burner?"

"Ah'm unloadin' this sinkhole. Now get hoppin'."

The staff of WETT-13, "Your Window to the Sunny South," hopped out of the new president's office, their eyes dispirited. They hadn't expected any better. Jediah Burner was a playboy, a sailor of fast boats, a winner of gaudy brass trophy cups and a relentless pursuer of busty blondes. No one expected him to take the helm of anything as stationary as a troubled TV station.

A week and hundreds of cold calls later, they hopped back into his office.

"Who made the best offer?" Burner demanded.

"The ones who hung up laughing," said one.

"The others told us to shove it," added another.

Jed Burner eased his lanky frame into his seat, put his deck-shoe clad feet up on his desk, and tilted his yachting cap back with a cocked thumb. His eyes crinkled humorlessly.

"What we gotta do," he said slowly, "is turn this scow into a sloop. Make it shipshape. Give it some value."

The staff looked to one another. No one quite knew what that meant. Exactly.

The station manager took a helpful stab at it, though.

"We could put a sail on the roof, I suppose."

Jed Burner fixed him with a nautical eye. "Main or jib?"

"Reef?"

Burner's feet came off the desk and a tanned-brown fist slammed the green felt blotter. "Now yoah talkin'! We need us a new motto, if we're gonna catch us a friendly wind."

"The Flagship of the South?"

"Damn fine thinkin', theah. Get on it. Ah got me some practice runs to make. Anybody wants me, tough. Ah'm gonna be writin' mah name all over the Chesapeake. The Americas Cup ain't that far off."

And with that, Jed Burner left. The staff didn't lay eyes on him again for two months. But they heard about him. Twice he was reported missing. Once, his sloop had been boarded by the Cuban Coast Guard, but he had ended up having lunch with Fidel Castro. Each time, he turned up alive, smiling, and posing for

the cameras with a vacuous blonde—sometimes two—
rubbing herself against him.

Every time he resurfaced in the station, he had
ditched the blonde, but never his smile or his cigar.

"We're still in the toilet," he grumbled on one of
those rare occasions, looking at the most recent Arbitron book.

The station manager wore a glum face. "We tried
everything, sir."

Burner scratched his beard. "Maybe we need a bigger sail. . . ."

"The one we got keeps getting blown off the roof.
We've gone through seven already. It's been costing
us dear."

"Dammit. Do Ah gotta do everythin' around heah?
If a sail won't do it, fetch me up an anchor."

And with those fateful words, Jed Burner stalked
from the building in search of a headwind and head—
not necessarily in that order.

The staff looked to one another helplessly.

"Did he mean an anchor anchor or a news anchor?"
asked the program director.

"It don't matter none," the station manager returned glumly. "We can't afford either."

"Let's price both and go with the cheaper option."

If the Savannah Nautical Supply House had been
having their annual November sale a week later,
WETT-13 might have gone the way of the Confeder-
acy. They could have had a nice stainless steel two-
fluker for $367.99. A bargain. But they missed the
sale by thirty-six hours and couldn't afford full price.

On the other hand, Floyd Cumpsty was willing to
anchor the *WETT-13 News* for free.

"I'll even brown-bag my lunch so as not to put any
strain on the station cafeteria," Floyd said with the
youthful sincerity of a man who knew where he
wanted to go in life.

"The station cafeteria," the personnel manager
said, "is that broken down candy vending machine
you passed in the hall. And why do you wanna go
and work for nothing, boy?"

"I hear they make big money reading the news up North. I figure I can learn, get experienced, and seek my fortune up there."

"Sounds reasonable. Except for the living up north part. But first I gotta see if you have the qualifications."

"Yes?"

"Can you read, son?"

"Yes, sir. I'm a high school graduate."

"That hair sitting on your noggin, it the real McCoy?"

"Yes, sir."

The personnel manager stood up and offered a firm hand, "Then let me be the first to welcome you aboard the Flagship of the South. You're our first official anchor."

In those days, there was no news department. In fact, there were no scripts. The WETT anchor assembled his own scripts by cutting up newspaper headlines and changing enough words that no one sued. Then he read them into the camera, frequently mispronouncing words.

No one sued. But a lot of people watched. At first, with their jaws hanging slack in disbelief. Then, with their bellies shaking in laughter. *WETT News* became a favorite in dorm rooms and seedy bars. People caught on to the headline trick and big money was won and lost on which words the anchor would mangle.

Ratings rose. They did not soar. But a quarter point here and an eighth there meant that in six months they had crept up one whole point. Enough to become a blip on the local TV screen and lure in a few thrifty advertisers.

Eight months of steadily rising ratings later, Jed Burner called.

"Hey! How's the boy?"

"Fine, Mr. Burner. And my name is David. David Sinnott."

"Now don't get all fussy with me, boy. Ah'm here

off the coast, just cruisin' along, with Bubbles and
Brenda. Ah heah we got us some upward movement
in them poll things."

"They're called ratings. And we've jumped a point.
It's not a lot, but—"

"It ain't beans and you know it. Don't you kid a
kidder, heah? Now Ah got mah friends in town callin'
me about this thing we got on the air."

"WETT News?"

"Yeah. That. Whose damnfool idea was that?"

David Sinnott winced. "It's bringing in some advertising now," he said hopefully. "Elmer's Linoleum
Emporium, a couple independent filling stations, and
we think the A&W Root Beer people are interested—"

"It bringin' in enough that Ah can sell this talky
white elephant?"

"No, sir."

"My friends are also tellin' me they don't see hide
nor hair of no anchor on mah roof."

"Oh," Dave Sinnott said, only then understanding
that his boss had meant an anchor anchor. "Well, we
priced anchors and they were a little out of our
range."

"Listen to me, boy: You take that new advertisin'
money and you sink some of it—Ah don't care how
much—into a shiny new anchor so mah friends won't
think Ah'm some kinda windy blowhard."

"Yes, sir."

"Only you don't put it on the roof. Since we got all
these nice folks watchin' that fool news show, Ah want
it up on the wall behind that idiot what's doin' the
readin'."

"Yes, sir."

The nautical anchor was in place in time for the five
o'clock news that very day. And it hadn't cost a thin
dime. Dave Sinnott had bartered advertising time for
the thing, which required four strong backs to carry
it into the building.

The news anchor took one look at it and refused to
go on the air.

"Are you kidding?" Floyd said tearfully. "This will ruin my career."

"Boy, your career's done. You just don't know it yet. Now you get your raggedy ass planted in that chair and you read."

Floyd Cumptsy cut his copy of the *Atlanta Constitution* more slowly that day, like a man who had come to the end of his string.

Half way through the broadcast, the anchor fell to the floor with a resounding crash. The other anchor—the one who was reading—kept on reading, his face turning red and his heart sinking along with his future.

Then the calls started coming in.

"Put up that damn anchor."

"Are you just going to let it sit there?"

"It's the best darn part of the show."

Dave Sinnott knew public interest when he saw it. Not bothering to wait for the commercial break, he walked onto camera range and personally hoisted the anchor into place. It immediately fell, breaking his foot in two places.

He hopped off the screen, venting choice curses.

The switchboard was flooded with more calls. Taxis began dropping off excited viewers, offering to put the anchor up themselves. Fistfights broke out over the privilege.

The first three who offered got the job. As the seated anchor droned on and on, slowly sinking into his chair, three Georgia Tech boys got the other anchor up and banged it into place, all but drowning out the weather with their hammering.

The next day, offers to syndicate *WETT News* poured in.

"How many buyers we got?" Jed Burner demanded over the cellular phone hookup when he got the word.

"Thirty," Sinnott said proudly, "and they're still coming in."

"What's the best of the lot?"

"Two thousand."

"Two thousand? Some prime jerk wants to buy mah whole station foah a measly two thousand dollahs?"

"They don't want to buy the station. They want to buy broadcast rights to WETT News."

"Explain it so a lil' ole sailor boy can get the nut of it, will you, son?"

"We have over thirty cable stations vying for the right to rebroadcast WETT News. The best offer is two thousand dollars. Per episode. Seven days a week is fourteen thousand dollars, times fifty-two weeks is—"

Jed Burner interrupted with a question. "What's cable?"

"It's TV that is carried on wires. They gotta hook it up special. They also call it pay TV."

"How come?"

"People pay for it."

"You joshin' me, son. TV's free. It's like oxygen. You buy a set and plug 'er in and you're set for life. Except for the commercials. Think we can get better ratin's if we cut out those dang commercials?"

"Mr. Burner, if we had more commercials we'd be in the black."

"Tell me some more about this cable thing," Jed Burner said slowly.

Station manager Dave Sinnott patiently explained cable. He tried to keep it simple. He knew his boss had the approximate attention span of a gnat.

"Never work in a million years," Jed Burner said at the end of it.

"It's not doing so bad now. These cable outfits are hungry for product. And they'll throw just about anything on the air. That's why our news looks so good to them. It's different."

"All them wires. Ridiculous. But back to this heah rebroadcast rights thing, are these good offers?"

"Depends on what you compare them to."

"Try comparin' them. Just to humor a poor cracker."

"Well, compared to a locally produced show with its budget, these are right handsome offers," Sinnott admitted.

"Ah hear a 'but' in your voice, boy."

"Compared to what network affiliates pay for the big news shows produced up North, it ain't cowflop."

Interest flavored Jed Burner's cornpone voice. "By what kinda margin?"

Sinnott floated some figures and the silence on the line was prolonged. The rush of ocean water past a fiberglass hull was indistinguishable from static in his ear.

He was about to ask if his boss had fallen overboard when Jed Burner's voice came back on the line. Gone was the loud, obnoxious attitude which, combined with his brash personality, had caused the print press to dub him "Captain Audacious."

"You listen here. Forget all that rebroadcast stuff. Ah want you to take that there dinky news show we got and you build it up. Heah? Built it up so that it's bigger and better than the Northern shows. With me so far?"

"Yes." The station manager's voice was a froggy croak.

"Then you offer it around. But you undercut them network scuts. You undercut 'em good. Ah want *WETT News* carried on every station in the cotton-pickin' country."

"Impossible!"

"Ain't nothin' impossible. What's it gonna take?"

"Money. Millions."

"Okay, you got the millions. Ah got a few shekels jinglin' in mah jeans. Mah daddy made himself a fair pile afore he passed on, even if he did kinda let this station thing go to pot. Anythin' else you'll be needin'?"

"Yes," Sinnott said, crossing his fingers, "a bigger anchor."

"Son, you got not one, but two anchors. Moolah's no object. Just make sure it's nailed down real good this time."

"That's not the kind of anchor I meant."

"What other kind is there?"

"The news reader. They call them anchors, too."

"Then we already got two anchors. Am Ah right?"

"We need a bigger one."

"Which should be bigger?"

Sinnott thought fast. "Both. Especially the talking one."

"Guy looks pretty hefty to me."

"Ah meant a bigger name. One more recognizable. One of the network anchors."

"Who's good, but cheap?"

"Don Cooder."

Then Jed Burner blurted out the question that was subsequently reported in *Time, Newsweek, TV Guide,* the *New York Times*—the question that would haunt him in the months and years to come.

"Who the hell is Don Coodah?"

At first, it was seen as a colossal joke. The brash entrepreneur who ran a station no one wanted, trying to launch a national newscast based on a spoof of the news.

It would never have gotten off the ground had the station manager not understood that he had hit the bottom of his television career. It was make *WETT News* work or manage a Burger Triumph. If Dave Sinnott could find one that would take him on.

It was 1980, and the booming cable TV industry, barely a decade old, was facing its first challenge: Satellite TV.

Dishes were already beginning to appear in backyards and hotel lawns and bar roofs in anticipation of the next boom in broadcasting.

Meanwhile, broadcast TV, reeling from the challenge of cable, fought back on every front. The first casualty was their own anchor system. Virtually overnight, the old guard of anchors, seasoned professionals, many of whom learned their craft on radio, were unceremoniously canned.

And a crop of young manicured and tonsured celebrity anchors were brought in to replace them. Thus, the cult of the anchor was born.

Overnight, the cream of television broadcast journalism was on the street.

WETT News had its pick. So Dave Sinnott hired two of the best of the dispossessed anchors.

They weren't flashy. They weren't backed up by computer graphics or identifying Chyrons, But they could read copy off a teleprompter and switch to script without skipping a syllable.

Virtually overnight, *WETT News* was respectable.

"We have to change our name," Dave Sinnott, now doubling as uncredited news director, said one day. "Folks are still laughing."

"Is that bad?" Jed Burner asked via transatlantic telephone.

"Very bad. We have to be serious now. An image change would help."

"Okay—but we gotta keep the word News in there. How about Kable News—KN?"

"Cable is spelled with a C."

"No, Kable *was* spelled with a damn C. And you gotta add somethin' dignified."

"Like what?"

"Do Ah gotta come up with all the brilliant stuff in this operation? A dignified word. Try to get the word 'news' into it some more."

"Twice?"

"Why not? We're the news that *is* news. The newsy news."

"How does Newsworthy News sound?"

"Sounds dang dignified. Everything people say Ah ain't. Haw. Listen, gotta go. Dixie here's gettin' that dewy look about her. Ah want us up and runnin' in a yeah. Got that?"

"A year? You want a national news network in a *year*?"

"Yeah. Normally Ah'd of given you only six months. But I can't on account of Ah'm embarkin' on a round the world cruise, just me and mah forty footer—and Trixie and Dixie and Hortense."

"Hortense?"

"Somebody's gotta do the scullery stuff. Ah told mah attorney to write you all the checks you want. If

Ah come back in a yeah and find Ah'm dead broke and there's nothin' to show for it, Ah'm gonna take that expensive anchor of yours, tie you and him both to the real anchor, and drop you-all in white water. Catch mah drift?"

"If it can be done, you'll have it, Mr. Burner."

And so the race to launch the first national news network had begun, run by a man who had almost unlimited capital and nothing to lose.

When the first commercial Satcom satellite went up, Dave Sinnott purchased a transponder.

Then he had an office building behind WETT headquarters razed to the ground and a satellite dish farm laid out in neat white rows, like ridiculous but very attentive sunflowers.

KNNN quadrupled its anchor staff, broadcasting twenty-four hours a day, just reading news. It was rough, it was hectic—and it carried over its original local audience just from the sheer ineptitude of it all.

"The locals love it," he was informed in a staff meeting. "They're laughing twice as much."

"It's not *supposed* to be funny now!" Sinnott complained.

"And they're asking after the anchor."

"Which one?"

"Well, the one with the flukes mostly, but we're getting fan mail on the readers too."

Dave Sinnott sighed, giving in to the inevitable. "Put it up again," he said weakly. "No, scratch that. Make it part of our logo. Burner'll like that."

After six months, Sinnott received a staticky call that had been patched through from the sloop, *Audacious*.

"This heah's Jed," the familiar boisterous voice announced.

"Where are you?" Sinnott asked.

"Becalmed off the Cape of Good Hope. Just like Vasco Da Gama, except he didn't have a lot of broads yappin' in his ear day and night. Listen, Ah been listenin' to the shortwave broadcasts. Folks is laughin' at me. What you're doin' up there?"

"We're in all fifty states, twenty-four hours a day. By satellite. No wires."

"They're sayin' Ah'm losin' a cool million a week."

"In another six months, we'll be all turned around."

"If you hadn't a said that, Ah was gonna turn mahself around and come wring your neck. You got six months, boy, or you're gonna have barnacles all over your back teeth. You and that anchor."

"There are sixteen of them now, Mr. Burner."

Dave Sinnott redoubled his efforts. He created bureaus in seven states. And all over Canada. That only added to the roughness of the broadcasts as miscued remote reporters were caught picking their noses on camera, and anchors could be heard belching and farting.

Once, an aging anchor stroked out on camera. Ratings roared. Millions turned in to his replacement hoping for a repeat performance.

Then Sinnott hit upon an idea worthy of his boss. The skies were full of satellites beaming network newsfeeds to affiliates for use on their local broadcasts, and these same transponders would relay local news clips for network use. Except the networks refused to release their clips until after their 7 P.M. feeds. In other words, the affiliates were expected to pitch in to help the networks and in return they got stale leftovers.

It was the era of the ninety-minute local newscast. News was booming. Local stations from Dry Rot, Georgia to Bunghole, Oregon were fielding news crews equipped with microwave vans and satellite uplink capability. And even then they were starved for pictures.

So KNNN offered them instant access to their feeds. Free. In return for reciprocal access to theirs.

It was unheard-of. It was absurd. Everyone expected a hitch or trick or catch. There wasn't one.

Once KNNN hooked a few affiliates here and there,

the others came like lemmings. And the networks howled. But there was nothing they could do. Everyone was satellite dependent. And every hour of every day, the transponders relayed raw transmissions up and down, between cities, among states and across oceans, feeding a growing insatiable appetite for the news.

There was no stopping it.

By midyear, KNNN News became the most watched news program in human history—not necessarily because of its content.

While broadcast news grew increasingly slick, polished, and show bizzy, KNNN News offered a relaxed alternative. Down Home news. It became their official slogan.

At the end of the twelfth month, Jed Burner docked, dropped anchor, and was airlifted to KNNN Headquarters on West Peachtree.

He hardly recognized the place. It was a beehive of activity. People were running around, frantic and white-faced.

"What in hell's goin' on?" he roared.

"We've gone black," a harried voice cried.

Jed Burner brightened. "Damn fine. And right on schedule."

"It's the third time this month!"

"Now we're talkin'!"

He burst into the station manager's office.

"Ah heard the good news, boy."

Dave Sinnott stopped shouting into the phone long enough to ask, "What good news?"

"We're in the black!"

"No, we've *gone* black. It's not the same thing."

Jed Burner puffed furious cigar smoke. "Explain it to a li'l ole country boy."

"We've lost our uplink to the satellite transponder."

"You ain't doin' so good," he warned.

"We can't get the TV signal up."

"Yeah . . . ?"

"That means it can't come down to the earth stations for rebroadcast!"

"We're dead, then?"

"No. We lose our picture a lot, actually."

"How about our financial picture?"

"We turned a profit two months ago. Everbody's watching us, from the White House on down to the outhouse."

"They laughin'?"

"Maybe some."

"They stickin' with us?"

"Not for long," Sinnott admitted.

"We're losin' ratin's, then?"

"That's not how it works anymore, Mr. Burner. People don't watch TV like they used to. They don't just sit and watch a show. They skip around, graze a little here and there. Channel surfing, they call it. We're perfect for that. As soon as five thousand people turn us off, there's another six tuning us in."

"What's that mean?"

"It means," said Sinnott, his chest puffing up in justifiable pride, "that on any given week, anyone with a satellite dish or a cable box is watching us. *Everyone.*"

Jed Burner seized his cigar as the thought sunk in. He made faces. The thought appeared to be sinking more slowly than it should.

"Don't you realize that this means?" Sinnott blurted. "You can sell this station for a bundle."

"Sell! Are you loco? Ah ain't sellin' mah pride and joy. And what's more, you're fired for suggestin' such a dastardly thing."

"Fired? I made KNNN what it is today."

Jed Burner poked his station manager in the chest with his cigar. "With mah money. And Ah'll pay you six figures a yeah to go live out your lucky-dog life in obscurity. From now on, KNNN was mah idea, mah vision, mah—"

"But that's not fair!"

"Son, life ain't fair, but it was mah money that done

it. That's all that counts in life. Who's signin' the
damn checks. Now be a smart fella and take mah
generous offer."

Dave Sinnott did. It was either that or continue
working for a lunatic.

Jed Burner called a press conference that very day.
He looked tanned and fit in immaculate white ducks,
and he was holding two very photogenic blondes
rented for the occasion.

"It was mah idea," he said through cigar-clenching
teeth. "From the start."

"What about Dave Sinnott?" he was asked.

"I didn't catch that name, boy."

"He was your station manager."

"Front man. Just in case Ah piled up on a reef
somewhere. All the time Ah was away Ah was guidin'
things by telephone."

"Isn't that an unusual management style for a TV
network?"

"If Ah'm gonna cover the entire globe, Ah had to
see it with mah own eyes, didn't Ah?" Burner
countered.

"Globe?"

"That's right. KNNN is nationwide after only a
yeah. We're puttin' news bureaus all over the dang
world now. We're gonna be global inside of two
yeahs."

The assembled press gasped.

And Jed Burner took his cigar out of his big mouth
and beamed broadly.

"They don't call me Captain Audacious for nothin',
boy."

True to his word, KNNN went global. When wars
broke out, KNNN was there first, booking the best
hotels. If there was a coup, KNNN was first on the
scene. In the global village, KNNN was the town crier
of many faces—fast, rough, sloppy, but instant.

Jed Burner explained it like this in a *Playboy*
interview:

"Not everybody's got the time to brew a good pot of coffee. We're the instant brand. Folks want brewed, they wait for the networks to serve some up. You want it now, you got it—on KNNN."

For one roller-coaster decade, KNNN could do nothing wrong. If their coverage of the Gulf War infuriated some viewers, it didn't matter. There were always more. Presidents swore by KNNN. The Pentagon watched it constantly. If the farting and the belching died down as more anchors were added and coffee and lunch breaks inaugurated, people still tuned in hope of catching KNNN at an awkward moment.

And as KNNN's fortunes climbed, the networks declined. Strapped for operating funds, they closed bureaus all over the globe. KNNN snapped up the leases the next day. Before long, the networks were carrying KNNN footage on a regular basis, trading off economy for the humiliation of advertising their chief rival.

The night broadcast TV went black for seven minutes. Accompanied by his latest trophy wife, his hair now as gray as an old salt's, Jed Burner was on his 129-foot yacht equipped with helipad and Superpuma helicopter.

The deck phone rang. It was his private secretary.

"Mr. Burner," she said tightly, "the networks are blacked out."

"Screw 'em. They're dinosaurs." He clapped and hand over the telephone mouthpiece and hollered in the direction of the bow. "Honey, you're gonna pull a pretty hamstring if you keep bendin' yoahself into petzel-like shapes."

A shrill female voice called back. "I'm practicing for my next video."

"Ain't you done enough of them things? Ah don't want nobody sayin' a wife of mine's gotta work her butt off for a living."

"My last workout video grossed two hundred million."

"For Gosh sake's, woman, don't stand so close to the dang rail! You might tumble over and drown that sweet two hundred million dollah butt of yours."

The telephone continued squawking. "Mr. Burner? Mr. Burner? Are you still there."

"Huh? Oh, yeah. Ah'm heah. What was you sayin' about the TV?"

"They just came back on. It looks like all broadcast stations across the country were knocked off the air. It's never happened before."

"Fucking fantastic!"

"Sir?"

"That means all those frustrated couch 'taters grabbed up their clickers and tuned in to lil ol' us. Are our anchors on top of this?"

"Yes, sir. We were the first to air the story."

"Honey, KNNN is *always* the first to air a story. So don't you go all redundant on me."

"Yes, Mr. Burner."

Hours later, the phone rang again.

"Mr. Burner, Cheeta Ching is here in your office. She's demanding an interview with you. What do we tell her?"

Jed Burner wrinkled his sun-beaten forehead, crinkling his sea blue eyes and asked the last question the man who transformed the way America gets its news would be expected to ask.

"Who the hell is Cheeta Chang?"

11

Cheeta Ching, oblate as a satiated python in her dark red Carolyn Roehm maternity coat, teetered on her stiletto heels in the anteroom of Jed Burner's office.

"I heard that!" she hissed. "He asked who I was!"

The KNNN secretary clapped a brown hand decorated with gold fingernails over the telephone receiver.

"I'm sure Mr. Burner misunderstood you, Miss Ching."

"He did not! And he got my last name wrong. It's Ching, not Chang. Chang is Chinese. Chinese anchors are three-for-a-buck. I happen to be one hundred percent Korean. Who the hell does he think he is?"

Fear was in the secretary's liquid eyes now. "Please don't be upset, Miss Ching. I am sure we can work this out."

"Prove it. Answer this: Whose number is 404 555-1234?"

"Why, that's Mr. Burner's private number. How did you get it?"

"Not important. Tell that mouthy ignoramus I got his fax." Cheeta lifted her voice into a sandblasting screech. "You hear me, Captain Audion?"

"It's Audacious," said the secretary, clapping a firm hand over the phone mouthpiece.

"It's Audacious," echoed the muffled voice of Jed Burner. "And tell that sweet-talkin' woman Ah'm on my way."

"Yes, Mr. Burner." The secretary hung up.

Cheeta blinked. It seemed too easy. "He's coming?" she asked in a taken-aback voice.

"That's what he said."

Cheeta's puzzled frown was a pancake question mark.

"I think," the secretary said, "your voice reminded him of his wife."

Cheeta calmed down. "I've always admired Layne for telling the truth about Vietnam. Is she still getting death threats?"

The secretary indicated a vent near the ceiling. "See that? Behind the grille there's a marksman with a .454 Casull all set to pop you if you make a wrong move."

Cheeta's neck and ears paled. But her face didn't change color visibly. It couldn't. It was too heavily made up.

"And there's other security all about the building," the secretary further explained, "including antiaircraft guns up on the roof. Folks have long memories. Especially down here."

"Personally, I supported her work in Haiphong," Cheeta said in a too-loud voice.

From the vent, the cocking of a rifle came distinctly.

"Better get up on the roof," the secretary said, urging Cheeta to the elevator.

"Why the roof?"

"Cause Mr. Burner has his helipad up there. He's flying in."

Cheeta Ching walked backward on red heels, one eye on the dark ceiling vent. Her center of balance wasn't what it should have been, and when she stumbled back into the elevator, a heel caught and the door closed on the sound of her yelp of pain as she landed on her hormonally inflated backside.

"Going up?" an unfamiliar voice asked.

Cheeta looked up. A man was standing in the elevator. He wore a rumpled raincoat of some sort. It was open and the man's hairy legs showed.

Oh God, a flasher, thought Cheeta—until her gaze, traveling up the man's muscular calves, came to his sinewy thighs. He was not wearing pants. He wasn't even wearing underpants. But he wasn't naked either. He wore some kind of green plaid miniskirt. Her almond eyes shot upward. The man's face, made insect-unrecognizable by wide sunglasses and shaded by a wide-brimmed hat, was looking down at her with a cold remoteness.

"Nice timing," he said.

Then a gloved hand came out of a raincoat pocket and pointed a silenced gun barrel at the largest target in the tiny elevator.

Cheeta Ching's bulging stomach.

Jed Burner was listening to the familiar screechy voice over the rotor whine.

Normally, it was hard to carry on a conversation in the Superpuma. It was as soundproofed as a helicopter could be—which meant that holding a conversation under the whirling rotor mast was akin to hearing confession in a giant Mixmaster.

"She'll be perfect!" Layne Fondue—despised by a generation of US servicemen as "Haiphong Hannah" Fondue—was saying.

"Ah never heard of her," Burner snapped.

"She's the most popular TV anchor in journalism."

"So? Ah don't traffic in star anchors. They cost too damn much."

"I'm not talking about hiring her for KNNN. I want her in my next exercise video, *Layne Fondue's New Mother Workout*."

"We wouldn't need her if you'd just get pregnant like Ah keep tryin' to get you," Burner shouted back.

"I think I must have inhaled some Agent Orange during the war," Layne muttered, primping her pile of streaked hair that made her resemble a hungry Pekinese. "It blocked my tubes or something."

"You ask me, you ain't tryin'. Ah settled down so Ah could have a son and heir, and all Ah get is yappin'. Ah want yappin, Ah'll buy a cockah spaniel. Which come to think of it, you're gettin' a trifle doggy around the edges."

"You sexist pig!"

Burner beamed broadly. "Say it again. Ah don't think the Almighty got the word yet."

Layne Fondue took nothing from nobody. Unless one counted her career, which she had wheedled out of her famous actor-father. She had enjoyed a brief career as an ingenue, rode the celebrity activist circuit in the sixties and seventies while her physical assets succumbed to gravitational erosion, and as her politics went out of fashion, found a comfy niche as the premier exercise guress.

The fact that she had gone to Haiphong, Vietnam and done political commentary for the North Vietnamese, denouncing US soldiers as "baby-eating cannibals," had earned her the unshakable nickname of "Haiphong Hannah."

She was tough, she was hard, and she turned around in her seat and slapped her husband in the mouth.

Jed Burner picked his cigar off the floor, examined the stogie for damage, and blew on the gray ash. It burned red. He put it into his mouth, inhaled long and deep, eyes closed as if thinking.

While his wife watched, slowly relaxing, he sucker-punched her to the floor and kept her there with one foot.

"Let's get somethin' straight, heah," he said calmly. "Ah didn't marry you. Ah acquired you. That makes you mah property. In a manner of speakin'."

"You can't talk to me that way, you smug cracker!"

"Ah'm doin' it. And you gotta take it. Yoah pushin' fifty. You ain't crow bait. But you hang on a man's arm and smile and coo at his friends so he looks good. Ah like that. Folks respect me for my broadmindedness marryin' a pinko and reformin' her, makin' her respectable again. Not that you were all that respectable to start with." He rolled the cigar in his mouth. "Now do you behave or do Ah gotta really get rough?"

"I hate it when you pull that macho crap!"

Jed Burner beamed. "Then why ain't you strugglin' harder?"

*   *   *

The KNNN tower was once described by *Architectural Digest* as the only modern office building with a serious toadstool infestation.

In fact, it looked like just about any major office building in downtown Atlanta. There was too much glass, too much design, and an atrium with enough wasted space to warrant the architect being court-martialed.

Except for the satellite dishes. They added that distinctive toadstool touch. There were three of them, each one aimed at different satellites orbiting somewhere in the heavens. Only one actually pointed at a satellite hanging over the Atlantic. The rest of the KNNN transponders were out over the Pacific. The signal was relayed over ground-based microwave towers to an earth station that connected with the Pacific birds. That was how KNNN fed a news-hungry world.

The satellite dishes made a shadowy cluster around the KNNN helipad, from which KNNN correspondents would be rushed to the Atlanta airport to wing their way to the world's trouble spots.

They also made excellent cover for when the Superpuma touched down.

"Better stay low," Jed Burner told his wife. "We're agoin' in."

Layne Fondue flattened and closed her eyes. She crossed her fingers as well. She was not big on obeying her husband. Except at times like these.

A lot of people thought she had married Jed Burner for his money. That was ridiculous. Layne Fondue was wealthy in her own right.

Or that it was a case of opposites attracting. That was absurd. Both were as mouthy as two human beings could be.

The real reason that the despised Haiphong Hannah—the most hated woman since Tokyo Rose or Axis Sally—had married Jed Burner was that he had almost as many enemies as she did.

The chief attraction was that Jed Burner came to

the altar with a fabulous security system in tow. It was as simple as that. Theirs was a marriage of convenience—and mutual survival.

Layne figured if the worst happened, the bullet was as likely to catch him as her. She calculated her odds of surviving an assassin's bullet doubled whenever they traveled together.

So she stayed flat, with her husband's heavy foot on her left breast as the Superpuma settled onto the anchor-shaped helipad.

"Honey, we're home," Burner said, popping the door and stepping out.

"Coming, dear."

Layne Fondue sat up and followed Jed Burner as he slipped down a flight of steps to his private elevator.

That's when all the shooting began.

12

Melvin "Moose" Mulroy liked his job a lot more before his boss got married.

Not that being head of security for the burgeoning Kable Newsworthy News Network was ever easy. It was just that there were triple the headaches involved in bodyguarding two flaming lunatics as one.

Moose Mulroy's troubles had started when Jed Burner married Haiphong Hannah Fondue. That was the bitch. Oh, it was one thing to pluck an aging spoiled rich kid falling overboard in a mint julip stupor. It hadn't happened so much since Captain Audacious had settled down.

But bodyguarding Haiphong Hannah was another matter. Moose Mulroy was forty-three years old—old enough to remember Layne Fondue when she had been a two-bit actress stepping everyone's lines on the silver screen. Nothing to write home about. No Jayne Mansfield. Certainly no Bridget Bardot—to Moose Mulroy the height of distaff thespian talent.

Moose had indelible memories of Layne Fondue's infamous trip to Haiphong, Vietnam to lend comfort to the enemy. He still had his "Hang Haiphong Hannah" bumper sticker on the back of his aging Thunderbird.

Now a lot of people disliked Jed Burner. He was a mouthy loose cannon. And an open mouth made a mighty tempting target. But folks hardly ever tried kill him. Mostly, he was about the business of getting into trouble on his own hook.

But Haiphong Hannah was a mare of another odor. People were always sending her death threats, obscene faxes, and the occasional Fedex surprise package.

Moose didn't mind the live tarantulas so much. And the deer ticks hadn't been so bad. No one had actually acquired Lyme disease either time.

It was the crazies showing up at reception with the hidden weapons. That was the bitch.

The metal detector caught most of them before they got past the lobby. Except for the anticolorization nut-job with the hang glider. And Moose had personally brought him down with a lug nut and slingshot. That way, it looked like an accident, and no one sued.

The Vietnam vet with the plastique girdle had everyone sweating for three hours the day he showed up, demanding Haiphong Hannah be brought to him. But Moose had talked sense into that one.

At least he hadn't stormed the building shooting. Those were the guys who made Moose Mulroy break out in cold sweats every time the big revolving door went *whisk-whisk-whisk*.

The revolving door was going *whisk-whisk-whisk* now. The sound snapped Moose's attention as rigid as his spine aligning in anticipation of trouble. He fixed his eyes on the man walking in through the atriumlike lobby, towering for twenty stories of glorious, glassy, totally wasted space.

Immediately, Moose became suspicious.

He wasn't a suit. But he wasn't a cameraman either. They usually wore polo shirts and raggedy jeans.

This guy wore chinos and a T-shirt. He looked kinda fruity, except that he walked with a casual, almost aggravating, cock-of-the-walk grace. Like he owned the building. Moose noticed his wrists. Big wrists. Too big. They hardly looked real.

As the thick-wristed man walked toward him, his face unreadable, Moose noticed that his eyes had that flat, dead kinda look, the classic thousand yards stare of the Vietnam vet. Trying to be casual, Moose shifted his body as he stabbed a button on the monitor array, simultaneously touching the concealed buzzer button.

That alerted the hidden sharpshooters. They were the first line of defense, but a last resort. The uniformed security were already percolating around the lobby, putting themselves in position to surround the strange guy in the T-shirt.

The cameramen, of course, would be piling into the elevators to record the slaughter. The bastards. But company priorities were priorities. Mulroy was under explicit instructions to hold fire until the videocams were in place and taping. Even the wall-mounted security cams had a direct feed up to master control.

Mulroy released the button, looking up from the main monitor.

"Can I help you, sir?" he asked the approaching man.

"No, but you can help yourself."

"Come again?"

"You can tell me where to find Jed Burner."

"Mr. Burner is not in the building."

"Fine. You can tell me where I can find him, then."

"I can't do that without knowing your business with Mr. Burner."

The security team was hovering just behind the thick-wristed guy. With Moose ready to vault over the security desk, he would have no place to run.

Then the guy made it easy for everyone.

"My business is my business," he said.

"In that case, I'll have to ask you to leave." And Moose motioned for security to close in. The guy's clothes were tight. Not much danger of concealed weapons. He was thin as a rail too. Moose relaxed slightly. The guards were enough. No need to jump in. Besides, he was getting too old for that kind of crap.

One guard hung slightly back, one hand on the butt on his holstered revolver, while the flanking pair moved up to take the man by the elbows. They used both hands, just as Moose had instructed them, so the man would be instantly immobilized.

The hands came up and Moose Mulroy blinked.

The two guards were suddenly clutching one another, and the skinny guy, not six feet away just the blink of an eye before, was no longer there.

Moose blinked again.

And the guy shot up from under the desk top. Like magic. Moose Mulroy found himself looking into two dead eyes that smiled with a faintly humorous light even though the rest of the face wasn't smiling at all.

Moose was well-trained in what he did. He went for his sidearm. He heard the snap and felt the pull of his leather holster as it was unceremoniously detached from his gunbelt by a pinkish blur at the end of a thick wrist. The holster flew across the lobby, taking his revolver with it as a second hand—feeling like warm steel—took his throat while the first hand spun him around.

Resistance was the first thought in Moose Mulroy's mind. He knew a little judo, a smattering of aikido, and a lifetime accumulation of rough and tumble.

Resistance never got past the impulse stage, however.

For the man suddenly had Moose by his spine and suddenly the only thoughts in Moose's thick skull were those of pleasing the skinny guy with the irresistible hands.

Now Moose Mulroy understood that a human hand cannot reach in through flesh and walls of back muscles and seize a man's spinal column like it was a tree branch. He knew it, would have sworn to the impossibility of it. On a stack of bibles.

But standing at his security desk, looking at the two security guards doing a four-handed handshake while the third tried to separate them like Moe in a Three Stooges skit, Moose Mulroy knew without a doubt that a hand had wrapped around his spine. He could feel the fingers even through walls of muscles that felt dully painful—just the way they did that time in Pleiku when he had been bayoneted by a Vietcong sapper. It hurt. It hurt bad.

And the truly terrifying thing was that there was nothing Moose Mulroy could do about it.

The man spoke calmly into his left ear. "Say the magic words and keep your spine."

"Glad to," Moose grunted.

Before the man could instruct him further, the elevator doors opened and two sets of camera crews pounded out. They pointed their camcorders at Moose Mulroy standing there helplessly.

My job is history, Moose thought.

Aloud, he managed, "Get those cameras away from here! This is a hostage situation."

Wrong thing to say. The cameraman inched closer. The idiots obviously thought they were bulletproof.

Other security were arriving now. One guard asked a question.

"What do you want us to do, Moose—I mean, Mr. Mulroy?"

"Just relax. Nothing bad will happen if everyone relaxes." Moose directed his voice toward his captor. "Isn't that right, pal?"

"Depends on my mood," said the man in an unruffled voice. "I'm looking for Jed Burner."

"Not in the building," someone said. "Honest."

Then a desk phone rang. The man reached down and picked it up. He moved his body only slightly, but the hand holding onto Moose's spine moved with him. Moose moved too. He also saw stars. Electric green ones.

The receiver came up to Moose's ear. "Yes?" he grunted.

"Mr. Mulroy! Mr. Burner's helicopter just landed and there's something going on. I hear shooting."

"I'm a little busy right now," Moose grunted. "Can't someone else take it?"

Then through the earpiece came a shriek. It was no ordinary shriek. It sounded sharp enough to cut diamonds.

For the first time, a worried note crept into his captor's tone. "That isn't who I think it is?" he muttered.

"If you're thinking it's Haiphong Hannah, your thinking is right on the money."

"Actually, I was thinking it sounded just like Cheeta Ching."

"That's possible, too. She blew in twenty minutes ago, all hot and bothered and looking for Burner."

"Damn," said the voice in Moose's ear, and suddenly Moose found himself walking backward toward the elevator, a human shield. It was his worst nightmare.

Security paced him every step of the way, hands on gun butts. No one was dumb enough to draw iron. And Moose fervently hoped no one would. He liked his spine—even though at this exact moment it felt like an arcing electronic cable in his back.

"You're my office guide," the voice said.

"We got pages for that kinda work."

"You just volunteered."

Then, they were in one of the elevators and the doors were closing on the frightened faces of the security team and the glassy fish eyes of the clustering videocams.

As the lift shot up, Moose grunted out a halting question.

"You here to kill somebody?"

"Maybe."

"If it's Haiphong Hannah, you'll get no argument from me."

"Right neighborly of you," said the voice of the man who owned Moose's spinal column. He showed his appreciation by giving a brain-darkening squeeze.

When Moose Mulroy regained consciousness some hours later, he was surprised to find himself alone and in one piece. The first thing he did was tear off his shirt and run screaming into the men's room.

The long mirror showed that a fist-sized area between his shoulder blades was a mass of purplish black, edged in green. It was the biggest, ugliest bruise Moose Mulroy had ever seen.

Otherwise the skin was completely unbroken. There wasn't a drop of blood. It made no sense, but for a month afterward Moose could still feel those strong

fingers wrapped so tightly around his spine the finger-
tips must have met.

Ultimately Moose Mulroy had a lot of time to con-
template it all, because he found himself unemployed
and on the street. He considered himself lucky.

Lots of folks ended up dead.

13

Remo Williams released the security chief on the thirty-fourth floor, the top floor. The man made a pile in one corner of the elevator as Remo came out of the lift with every sense alert.

He found himself surrounded. By videocam lenses.

A man waved at him from behind his camera.

"Just pretend we're not here," he said in a friendly voice.

"That's right," chimed in a second. "We're just here to record events as they happen. Pay no attention to us."

"Do whatever you were going to do," encouraged a third cameraman.

And so, forefingers extended, and Remo began to methodically shatter each camera lens.

"Hey! You can't do that!"

"This isn't how it's done!"

"We're the media!"

Remo growled, "And here's the message: Get out of my way."

Their eyes blackening from sudden impact with recoiling viewfinders, the camera crews begrudgingly fell back.

There was only one security guard. He had his Glock up in a two-handed marksman's grip, the muzzle pointed at Remo. For a twelfth of a second.

Walking on the outside of his soles, Remo feinted, moved in, and used the man's own hands to crush the plastic gun into so much sharp black plastic shards.

He left the guard moaning and wringing his blood-ied hands.

Heads poked out of half-open doors all along the corridor.

"Which way to the roof?" Remo asked.

Most of the heads withdrew like frightened gophers.

A hand snaked out and pointed helpfully in the di-rection of the ceiling. "Up. The roof is up."

"I know that, you dip. What I don't know is how to get there."

"Fire stairs. Straight ahead and turn left."

Then, a bullet ripped down through the ceiling tiles and forced the remaining heads to withdraw behind slamming doors.

Remo shot forward. A woman screamed. The high, piercing sound was joined by another scream. Both screams were ear-punishing. Yet they blended into one anguished otherworldly shriek as if vented by identical twins, dying in harmony.

Remo floated up the stairs, leaping over the sprawled bodies of security guards who had died defending their posts, and reached the roof.

It was a nest of satellite dishes. In the center of the nest, like a dragonfly, sat a luxury helicopter.

And standing in the shadow of the drooping heli-copter blades was a small knot of people.

The knot consisted of two parts—a man and a woman, and another man with a woman.

The nearest pair whirled, and Remo recognized the flat, pasty face of Cheeta Ching. She was so frightened her face was shedding flakes of pancake makeup like dandruff.

"Ronco!" she cried. "Help me!"

"Ronco?" Remo said blankly.

"Stay back," the man with the gun said, pushing the barrel into Cheeta Ching's temple. He was tall, his features masked by oversized sunglasses and a big hat. He was using Cheeta Ching as a human shield, but Remo could see that his lower legs, visible behind Cheeta's, were bare.

"What makes you think that'll stop me?" Remo asked.

"Ronco! How could you!"

The gunman transferred the pistol muzzle to Cheeta Ching's bulging stomach. "Or I can waste the brat."

Remo stopped dead still. The baby was another matter.

"Just hold that pose," said the gunman, walking backward.

The other pair had frozen at the open door of the helicopter, Jed Burner turned and gave Layne Fondue a hard shove. On all fours, she scrambled into the helicopter.

Then the gunman resumed backing away, pulling Cheeta with him. Her almond eyes were wounded.

"Ronco!" she pleaded. "Don't let this happen!"

"Ronco," warned the gunman, "don't be a chump."

Remo stood, rotating his thick wrists absently. His face was stone.

The gunman reached the waiting helicopter and abruptly sat down on its sill. Remo saw his legs clearly. He was wearing a plaid kilt of some kind.

But Remo was keeping his eyes on the man's hands. To pull Cheeta Ching into the helicopter in her condition was a two-handed job. To pull it off, the gunman would have to point his weapon away from his captive.

Crossing the roof while the gun was pointing elsewhere was possible, Remo knew. But the weapon would have to be at least three feet from Cheeta for it to work. Any closer and it was even money Cheeta would catch a bullet.

Imperceptibly, Remo came up on his toes, ready to strike.

Then, behind him, KNNN cameramen poured out of the roof hatch, along with a pair of reporters clutching hand microphones. Fanning out, they called excited questions to no one in particular.

"Is this a kidnapping?"

"If so, who's being kidnapped?"

And the gunman whipped his muzzle back to Cheeta's belly.

"You!" he shouted, yanking Cheeta into the helicopter. "Keep them away or the slope gets a .45 caliber abortion right here!"

That decided it. Remo pivoted and began tripping legs. He caught videocams as they slipped from clutching fingers and smashed them under his feet. He made sure to pop cassette ports where he could and pulverize the cassettes, so that his face could not be broadcast.

The helicopter began to wind up.

"Nobody go near that bird," Remo warned, crushing a cassette to powder in a cameraman's face.

And no one did.

Blowing air and city grit, the Superpuma lifted off and racketed out to sea.

Remo watched it go. "Damn," he muttered. "Chiun is going to kill me."

A reporter shoved a microphone into his face and asked Remo a breathless question.

"Can you tell us what's going through your mind right now?"

Remo answered the question by using the mike to perform a radical tonsillectomy on the questioner.

The others withdrew.

"Pretend we're not here," one suggested.

"Pretend *you're* not here," Remo growled.

The KNNN news gatherers who could still walk under their own power hastily helped the others down the roof hatch.

Remo ignored them. His features grim, he watched the helicopter become a dwindling speck of light in the night sky.

When the sound of its rotors no longer reached his sensitive ears, Remo slipped jumped down the hatch and found an empty office, where he called Harold Smith.

"Smitty. Bad news."

"What is it, Remo?"

"I got here too late. Burner and Haiphong Hannah just took off with some guy in a kilt. They got Cheeta. She's a prisoner."

"What was Cheeta Ching doing there?"

"Who cares? Listen, if Chiun finds out I've blown this mission, there's no telling what he'll do."

"How can we stop it?"

"Search me. But I'll find a way."

And he did.

Twenty seconds later, the building filled with the tormented wrenching of metal under extreme stress. The awful sounds could be heard coming from the roof. When a two-man security team ventured up there, they came down, weapons mysteriously missing.

"I think we should evacuate the building," said one.

"Evacuate?" the station manager blurted out. "Why?"

"The guy on the roof told us we should."

"What kind of a reason is that?"

Then one of the satellite dishes sailed past the long eastern window, on its way to the sidewalk many floors below.

Staff surged to the window. Another dish cartwheeled past.

The station manager cleared his throat and rumbled, "I move we evacuate right now."

The evacuation was swift, orderly, and successful. Everyone exited the west side of the building, because the dishes seemed to be falling on the east face.

Eyes straining upward, the entire staff of KNNN waited for the third and last satellite dish to fall.

Remo Williams finished dislocating the last satellite dish from its roof base. He did this with the naked edge of his palm. The base consisted of steel struts painted white. They were built for support, not resisting hands that could by touch alone seek out weak spots and snap them with lightning blows that separated the metal along molecular lines, leaving superclean edges, as if giant bolt cutters had been brought to bear.

Remo left the last dish when it fell. KNNN was no longer transmitting. He went downstairs to report to Dr. Smith.

The building seemed deserted. Remo's acute hearing detected no sounds of life. Air conditioners hummed. Water moved through plumbing. A mouse chewed at a partition.

But no human heartbeats came to his ears.

He picked up a phone at random, holding the one button down.

"Smitty, good news. I solved the problem."

"How?" asked Harold Smith.

"I knocked KNNN off the air."

Pause.

"Remo," Smith said tightly, "I hope you have done the correct thing."

"Maybe I did and maybe I didn't. But I bought us some time."

"No, I mean in reference to the blackout matter."

"I'm worried about Chiun. Screw the rest. Besides, isn't KNNN the source of the jamming?"

"That is my information, but we have yet to prove it."

"Well, I got the building to myself. At least until the local Marines are sent in. Just tell me what to do."

"Look for suspicious equipment."

"Hold the phone," Remo said, sweeping the control area with his deep-set eyes. "On second thought, this is a cellular. I'm going to carry you with me, Smitty. Try not to wriggle."

Remo walked around the sprawling control area. There were banks and banks of monitors, tape decks, and other broadcasting equipment Remo didn't recognize.

"I can't tell one thing from another around here," Remo told Smith. "Give me some clue."

"I cannot," said Smith. "I am not very familiar with broadcast equipment."

"Wait a minute. I just found something weird."

"Describe it."

Remo was looking through a long Plexiglas port. Inside was what appeared to be a video library racked in row upon row of shelving. There were two great tapedecks at the far end of the room.

And moving along a ceiling track, an aluminum robot arm. As Remo watched, it slid along, emitting a thin red laserlike beam. It was scanning the exposed sides of the racked cassettes. As the scanning beam came to a silver bar code label, it beeped, then stopped. The arm telescoped downward to grab the cassette between flat aluminum fingers.

Holding it firmly, it retracted, and tracked back to the dual cassette decks and with too-precise movements, inserting it into one deck. A red light went on as a matching red light in the other deck winked off. The second deck released its cassette and the arm swung in perfectly and seized it.

Slowly, it retreated along its track until it came to an empty slot. Smoothly, the cassette was returned to its receptacle.

"It's some kind of automatic cassette feeding thingy," Remo said.

"Thingy?"

"It's big, there's no one in charge and I don't even see a chair for someone to sit in."

"Remo, many cable outfits run automatic programming. The commercial tapes are programmed into a guiding guiding computer."

"That explains the bar codes."

"Bar codes?"

"Yeah. Every cassette is coded."

"I do not think that is what we are looking for," Smith said disappointedly.

"Maybe I should rough up some of the technicians," Remo suggested.

"Where are they?"

"Out on the sidewalk waiting for the third shoe to fall."

"Er, I fail to understand."

Then above him, Remo heard the clattery rattle clatter of helicopter blades.

"Don't look now," Remo said guardedly, going to a window, "but either the bad guys are back for more hostages or the local SWAT team just arrived."

"Remo, can you leave the building unseen?"

Remo opened a window and looked down. The streets were choked with people looking up.

"No," Remo told Smith.

Smith groaned.

"Can you leave it safely?" Smith asked.

"Probably."

"Do so. If KNNN is off the air, you may have crippled any jamming capability they might possess. It is time to regroup."

"Gotcha," said Remo, dropping the phone.

He made for the elevator, and before he could press the call button, every door on every elevator opened simultaneously and out came floods of cameramen. They were looking through their viewfinders and didn't notice Remo at all.

Remo whistled. A baker's dozen lenses swept in all directions. They pointed up, down, up the corridor, down the corridor—in every direction except where Remo was standing.

So Remo shouted, "He just headed down the stairs to the lobby."

A man took up the cry. "He's headed for the lobby!"

Instantly, the cameramen ducked back into the waiting elevators, unaware that Remo was snugly in their midst.

No one noticed that Remo was riding to the lobby with them. They kept their videocams on their shoulders, their eyes glued to eyepieces, fingers on triggers—ready to record whatever sight the opening doors revealed.

They revealed, Remo discovered to his displeasure, a phalanx of Atlanta Metro Police in full riot gear.

A cameraman shouted, "He headed back this way!"

Bending his knees so no one could see his face, Remo rammed a pointing finger out of the clot of bodies and said, "There he goes now!"

Immediately, the elevators emptied. The lobby was soon boiling with riot helmets and videocams bumping blindly into one another.

Remo said, "What the hell," and abruptly pressed the Up button.

The lift took him back to the top floor, where he made his way to the roof stairs in time to meet landing police helicopters.

They were festooned with lights and M-16 rifle barrels prodded from the open sides of the bubbles. One sweeping light found him, and he heard someone yell through a bullhorn, "Don't move! We have you dead to rights."

Remo moved anyway. The light tried to follow him. Each time, he eluded it. Once he inserted his hands into the beam long enough to make a hand shadow of a bunny rabbit nibbling a carrot.

That brought a fusillade of bullets, and enough noise and confusion that Remo was all but invisible on the darkened tower roof.

Moving with a self-assured calm, Remo took hold of the tipped-over satellite dish. It was as big as a swimming pool, but light in proportion to its weight. Not that its weight would have mattered to Remo.

But there was a steady breeze out of the west and the dish was unwieldy. Using his sensitive fingers to find its center of gravity, Remo flexed his wrists. The dish, responding to an innate balance that was in all things, came up in Remo's hands and he caught the breeze. That helped.

Remo walked to the helipad, not exactly propelling the dish so much as guiding it, like a great round aluminum sail.

The police choppers were hovering there, preparatory to landing.

Holding the dish over his head like a shield, Remo began fending them off.

The ringing clash of the dish against landing skids spooked the first chopper pilot. He swung away. Remo slid under the next one and caught the tip of a skid with the joined points of the dish's emitter array. Walking backward, Remo guided the chopper along like a stubborn kite, then whipped it free.

The chopper made crazy circles while the pilot attempted to being the ungainly bird under control.

The third chopper pilot, seeing his comrades in distress but not what was causing it, orbited the tower warily.

At the roof edge, Remo gave the dish a flip. His motion was short and economical, but the twenty-foot dish flipped out into space, hanging emitter side down like an umbrella with a snapped-short handle.

Remo leaped into space and grabbed the emitter in both hands. The dish, which had been hesitating in midair, began to slide downward.

It was not as good as a parachute, but it had nice gliding characteristics. Remo swung his feet, slipping a little air and the dish skipped past a nearby office tower.

People in the lighted office windows waved to him. Remo ignored them. He was focused on his breathing. It took a lot of concentration to think like a feather.

As the SWAT helicopters gingerly settled to the roof helipad on bent skids, Remo rode the dish over a mile outside the city, steering it toward the scent of fresh water that promised a safe landing. When he spotted the glint of moonlight on water, he dropped toward a soft, if wet, landing.

When a caterwauling contingent of the Atlanta Metro Police arrived, all they found was the bent dish, floating in East Lake.

Remo Williams floated beneath the cool water, holding his breath, untouched by crisscrossing police helicopter searchlights, and wondered what the Master of Sinanju would say to him when he learned that Remo had allowed kidnappers to abduct the mother of his child when she was about to give birth.

As he waited for the helicopters to give him up for dead, Remo's lean body gave a great shudder that had nothing to do with the deep chill of the lake water and everything to do with the cold thoughts in his brain.

14

News moves instantly in the age of satellite communications.

In New York, the three major broadcast networks learned of KNNN's loss of signal at exactly the same time.

So much had KNNN changed the way the world got its news that in every control room of each network there was a man whose job it was to monitor KNNN round the clock for breaking news. There were on the payrolls as "market research monitors."

At MBC, the monitor saw his KNNN satellite feed go down.

At BCN, the monitor gasped as the pair of KNNN anchors became a black square with the words NO SIGNAL in the upper right-hand corner.

At ANC, they saw the same thing.

At the three majors, the cry was the same.

"It's happening again!"

But it wasn't. Line monitors were checked. And rechecked. All other transmissions were up.

"It's just KNNN," the news director at BCN said, relief washing along his vocal cords.

Then it struck him.

"Get a team down to Atlanta. This is news!"

Planes were charted. Equipment was hastily rushed to waiting hangers. Flyaway satellite dishes were hauled out of storage.

And in less than an hour, with a full Georgia moon

washing West Peachtree Avenue, the remote microwave vans started pulling up. Masts were erected. And
videocams were busily recording the sight of two
mighty satellite dishes lying in the street as the KNNN
anchor teams milled about, dazed expressions on their
faces as they interviewed themselves on tape for later
broadcast.

The first to arrive was Don Cooder of BCN News.
He stormed into the crowd wearing his lucky safari
jacket. Usually, it was something he saved for reporting coups and civil wars, but since this was, pro-
fessionally speaking, enemy territory, he thought
wearing it was a good idea.

"I'm looking for Jed Burner," he said, biting out
his words.

"No one's seen him."

"A KNNN anchor, then. Is there an anchor who
hasn't been interviewed yet? I'm offering a BCN
exclusive!"

From the crowd, a half dozen hands jumped into
the air.

"Me! Me! I haven't been on the air in three hours!"

"No, me. I'm more photogenic!"

"One at a time! One at a time," Cooder said hastily. "Everybody will get his or her chance." Cooder
stopped, turned to the videocam and pitched his voice
an octave deeper.

"This is Don Cooder, speaking to you from in front
of KNNN Headquarters here in Augusta, Georgia."

"It's Atlanta!" a voice called out.

As if he hadn't heard, Cooder pushed on. "For
those just tuning in, here are the facts as we understand them to be: Hours after broadcast TV is blacked
out from the Manitoba to Monterrey, calamity befell
Kable Newsworthy News Network's once great em-
pire—"

"What do you mean 'once great?' " a voice
snapped.

"You're off the air," Cooder snarled.

"But we'll be back."

Cooder whirled. "Do you mind?"

"Hey, Mom!" someone yelled, waving past Cooder's turned back. "I'm fine! Don't worry about me. It was just the satellite dishes."

"Who's doing this stand-up, you or me?" Cooder snarled.

It was the wrong thing to say. KNNN anchors exchanged glances and suddenly Hurricane Don Cooder, veteran of the natural disasters, civil rights coverage, Vietnam, and Tiananmen Square, was fighting for his own microphone in full view of his faithful audience.

"Let go of my mike or I'll brain you with it!" he snarled.

"Cut Cut!" the remote producer yelled frantically.

Hearing the sound of his colleague in distress, Dieter Banning came running to the rescue, his London Fog trenchcoat skirts slapping at his legs.

"Get that fucking camera on him!" he yelled to his cameraman.

"What about you?"

"Never fucking mind me! I'll do a damn voice-over."

The videocam light blazed into life, and Dieter Banning's frantic voice was suddenly crisp, cool, and mannered as that of an English valet.

"The scene here in Atlanta tonight is reminiscent of Beirut," he said as Don Cooder, gaining the upper hand, proceeded to pummel his rival into submission. "As so often happens in the wake of such things, the fabric of ordinary society quickly breaks down. To American viewers this may seem like nothing more than a boisterous argument, but I assure in the more civilized corners of the world, say, London, or Ottowa, the sight you are now watching would be met with anguish, shock and utter shame. . . ."

Tim Macaw was trying to get the facts. That was all he wanted—the facts. Without facts, he had no story. It was good to have pictures, essential in this age of electronic journalism, but if you don't have the facts, pictures were so much electronic confetti.

"Does anyone know what happened here?" he cried out, pushing into the crowd.

"KNNN is down."

"Can anyone confirm that?"

"Sure. Me," said a helpful voice.

"Me, too," said another voice.

"Good. Good. What caused it?"

"Someone ripped the satellite dishes off the roof."

"Who?" Macaw asked.

"Nobody knows."

"What is this all about?"

"Nobody knows."

"Where is Jed Burner? Has anybody seen Jed Burner?"

"He disappeared just before it happened."

"Oh. Does anyone else know this?"

"Search me."

Tim Macaw, sensing a story, turned to his remote producer.

"They're saying Jed Burner has disappeared. Has anyone broken the story yet?"

"No, Tim."

"Well, can we confirm it independently?"

"How? Usually we confirm these things by turning on KNNN. Can't now."

"Right. Damn. What do we do?"

"If we air and it's wrong, we look stupid."

"But if it's right, and we don't get it out there, one of the other networks will own the story."

"It's your call, Tim."

Shoulders slumping in defeat, Tim Macaw moaned, "What do print guys do in situations like this? Damn."

On one corner a black man in black Cons and a backward cap was doing a rap before the TV cameras.

> KNNN is out of shout,
> Global news is down for the count.

Nobody knew who knocked it flat,
Check it out—Vox TV is where it's at.

Shifting into a mellow announcer's voice, he added,
"This is Vox TV's *Rap News*. First with the news that
today's young people can understand. Now we return
to *The Stilsons*. Tonight, Fart microwaves baby Sue
and Gomer mistakes her for . . ."

In his Folcroft office Harold W. Smith changed
channels the old-fashioned way. By hand.

It was total chaos down in Atlanta. The media had
jumped on the least important part of the story—the
disabling of KNNN's broadcast ability. The abduction
of Cheeta Ching, ostensibly by Jed Burner, Layne
Fondue, and an unknown confederate, had yet to
break.

With luck, the news would not air until Remo had
broken the bad news to the Master of Sinanju.

As for the mysterious Captain Audion, Harold
Smith knew that whatever his carefully laid plans had
been, Remo had thrown a monkey wrench into them
by disabling KNNN.

He turned down the sound and went back to his
computer, from which he was monitoring the land,
sea, and air search for the missing KNNN Superpuma
helicopter, initiated in utter secrecy by the President
of the United States himself. The new chief executive
was only too happy to pitch in and do his part.

He had been watching KNNN when it went down—
and Harold Smith was the first person he called.

15

Remo Williams didn't know what to do.

After he had eluded the Atlanta police, he had checked into a Decatur motel, showered, and walked the floor with the TV on.

Like a pack of sharks smelling blood in the water, the networks were providing continuous coverage of "The KNNN Knockdown," as BCN was calling it. Anchors interviewed anchors, who returned the favor. It was a feeding frenzy of interviews, and nowhere was the opinion of an ordinary citizen heard.

A Martian would have thought a religious temple had been desecrated.

There were standups, two-shots, and endlessly repeated film clips of the downed satellite dishes, frightened KNNN staffers, not to mention assorted fistfights. Interspersed with commercials that were three times more interesting than the coverage itself.

Remo had enjoyed none of it. Except the footage of Don Cooder and a nameless KNNN anchor wrestling for possession of a live mike.

The spectacle of Don Cooder under great stress reminded Remo of the time two years back when Cooder had talked a dippy physics student into building a live neutron bomb for a segment of *24 Hours*, ostensibly on the easy availability of nuclear technology, but actually as a gigantic ratings ploy. Someone had stolen the bomb and detonated it. Chiun had been on ground zero when it happened, with Remo a helpless witness.

Chiun had survived. A miracle. The Master of Sinanju had burrowed underground to safety, but no
one knew it. Not even Remo, who had mourned his
Master for many long months, until Harold Smith had
located the comatose old Korean under a California
desert and resuscitated him.

In the aftermath of the incident, Remo had begged
Smith to let him take down Don Cooder. Smith had
refused. Remo had never been satisfied with his rea-
soning. So the sight of Cooder making a fool of himself on live television gave Remo a little solace. But
not much.

As he paced, switching channels in the hope of getting some word of Cheeta Ching's whereabouts, Remo
wrestled with what he would tell Chiun if the worst
came to pass.

For nine months, the impending birth of the baby
had haunted Remo. Chiun's insistence that Cheeta
and the baby come to live with them threatened their
long association. Now this.

There was no way Remo could tell Chiun the truth
without destroying their relationship.

In the blackest part of the night Remo had called
Harold Smith.

"Smitty. Any news on Cheeta?"

"A full-scale search has turned up nothing."

"What are they doing," Remo said heatedly, "playing with themselves? Tell them to get on it."

"Remo, it is the middle of the night, Georgia is
very big and the helicopter is very small. It could have
set down anywhere."

"Or crashed," Remo said dully.

"Or crashed," Smith agreed.

"I never thought I'd see the day I cared whether
Cheeta Ching would live or die. This is a mess."

"Perhaps."

"What do you mean, perhaps?"

"You have knocked KNNN off the air. Jed Burner
has fled for parts unknown. It may be the end of the
crisis."

"Not *my* crisis. I'm holed up in a motel room and I'm thinking of staying here until this blows over."

"You might as well go home, Remo. There is nothing more to be done in Atlanta."

"So what do I tell Chiun?"

"The truth."

"He'll kill me."

"I rather doubt that," Smith said dryly. "The bond between the two of you is very strong."

"Yeah, well I definitely noticed it getting looser and looser the closer Cheeta got to her due date."

"Remo, your face was seen by unknown numbers of KNNN staffers. I would prefer you out of Atlanta and where I can reach you."

"I'll think about it," Remo said, hanging up.

A lot Smith knew. For twenty years, Remo had worked for the old skinflint. There were times when Remo thought he understood Smith, and there were times he despised the man. These days, their relationship was neutral. But Smith didn't appreciate the elemental moods of the Master of Sinanju, how he could turn on Remo over matters of honor or pride.

Remo Williams, the second greatest assassin on the face of the earth, was normally without fear. As he checked out of his motel, he was afraid for his future and desperately trying to come up with a convincing lie that would salvage it.

And as he inserted the key into his front door lock, two and a half hours later in Massachusetts, he was still wracking his brain.

Maybe, he thought, *I'll tell him Smitty wants us to fly to Peru and dismember Maoists. Chiun would like that.*

The Master of Sinanju was in the kitchen when Remo stepped in. He was making tea. He was humming. This was going to be rough, Remo knew.

Remo stepped in, and Chiun looked up.

The Trinitron stood on its island, black and mute.

Momentary relief washed over Remo. Chiun couldn't have gotten the news.

Remo opened his mouth, trusting to the first lie that emerged.

Instead, he found himself speaking the truth.

"I blew it, Little Father," he said contritely. "I'm sorry."

"This is understandable," Chiun said, setting out a celadon cup.

"It is?"

"You did not have your teacher to guide you to success."

Remo blinked. "That's right, I didn't, did I?" It hadn't occurred to him. But there it was. An escape hatch.

"Have you broken the news to Smith?" Chiun asked, taking a second cup from the cupboard.

"Yeah."

"He is angered?"

"Actually, he thinks I solved the TV problem even if the bad guys got away."

"A partial success whispers of completeness in a coming hour," said Chiun, pouring the tea into both cups.

"Smith has practically the entire Air Force, Coast Guard and Navy looking for the guy now."

Chiun frowned. "He swam from you?"

Remo shook his head no. "Helicopter."

"Ah. Then you have an acceptable excuse, for we do not fly after helicopters. It is not in our job description."

"Yeah, yeah. Right. Maybe we should turn on the TV now," he added, thinking maybe it would sound better coming from someone Chiun couldn't reach out and strangle.

Chiun frowned. "The squawking of rude readers of the alleged news of this province would spoil such a morning as this."

"There might be news of Cheeta, you know?"

Chiun's wrinkled features quirked. "Is it not too early for the heads that talk?"

"When I left Atlanta, they were all over every channel. They think KNNN going down is big news."

"Then by all means, Remo. Turn on the television device. I have poured you a cup of tea."

"Thanks," said Remo, hitting the on button. The set warmed up, and Remo felt his heart climb into his throat. The last time he had left Chiun, he felt angry and hurt. Now all he wanted was not to be the one to break the bad news—whatever it was.

The set winked into life. And almost immediately winked out again.

"What's wrong with this piece of junk?" Remo said, giving it a whack.

"I do not know."

"Have you been playing with the contrast knob again?"

"You make the pictures too light," Chiun sniffed. "It is bad for the eyes if they are not made to work."

"Well, I don't like it dark," said Remo, turning the contrast knob. The picture lightened. In one corner. There, emerging from the shifting from high contrast to lower contrast, were two mocking white letters:

NO SIGNAL.

"Damn!" said Remo.

Chiun looked up from his tea. He frowned.

"I thought you rendered the fiends impotent," he said.

"I did. I thought I did. Wait a minute, maybe this is a recap of the blackout footage." Remo changed the channel. The other channels were also black. They weren't hooked up to cable, so there was no way to tell what was happening there.

"Not now!" Remo moaned.

Chiun padded up to the screen, his tea forgotten. His facial wrinkles were gathering like storm clouds.

"Is it not a rerun?" he muttered darkly.

"Well, it is and it isn't," said Remo, running up and down the stations. "The out-of-state stations were just as black."

Then the telephone was ringing. Remo took it.

"Remo," said Harold Smith. "It has begun again."

"Yeah, and the timing couldn't be worse. I just

turned on TV so Chiun and I could catch up on breaking news and the screen went dead."

"Remo, it is clear that Jed Burner's KNNN broadcast equipment is not responsible for this."

"Maybe not. But he's involved in this somehow, he and Haiphong Hannah. He's gotta be."

"That remains to be seen," said Smith.

"If he isn't, who else could it be?"

Suddenly, the TV began speaking in an electronically filtered voice.

"Do not adjust your set. The networks have refused to accede to my modest demands. So I am declaring a moratorium on all TV for the next seven hours. Or until my demands are met. I now return you to the Electronic Dark Age of"—an echo chamber effect cut in—*"Captain Audioooonnnn."*

Then with Remo watching, the Master of Sinanju turned and hissed, "This is all your fault!"

"Huh?"

"You have failed," Chiun said loudly. "And because of your failure, I am deprived of all tidings of Cheeta Ching."

"I'm sorry, Little Father. Maybe Smith can point us in the direction of the problem. You and I working together, we can probably solve this in a day."

"No. My place is at Cheeta's side. I must go to her at once."

"Oh no," Remo groaned, watching the Master of Sinanju hurry from the kitchen and float up the stairs to pack.

"Smitty," Remo hissed into the receiver. "You hear that?"

"I did."

"What do we do?"

"I do not know," Harold Smith said in a hollow voice. "But you must stay with Master Chiun and keep him from coming into contact with Don Cooder. The results could be catastrophic."

"They could be worse than that," Remo muttered, thinking that if there was anyone on earth the Master of Sinanju would like to snuff, it was Don Cooder.

16

Don Cooder entered the newsroom of BCN's New York headquarters, bloodied but unbowed. He was holding a raw steak over one eye. London broil.

"Admiral on the bridge!" the floor manager called, after giving a sharp blast in the bosun's whistle.

"Let no one doubt Don Cooder's manhood after this day," Don Cooder said.

"Don!" the news director called, white-faced.

"No matter the danger, no matter the risks, if it needs reporting, Hurricane Don Cooder will report it," said Don Cooder.

"But Don."

"No buts! I know what you're going to say. Stow it. I may be head anchor, but in these veins flows the blood of a natural-born reporter. I can't help it. At times like these, I'm like a hound dog with a treed coon under a full moon. Call me country, but country is what made Don Cooder the knight of the remote newscast that he is."

With that, Don Cooder stormed in the direction of his office.

The news director was holding his arm leveled at the line monitor, where the tiny white letters NO SIGNAL glowed faintly against the blacked-out screen.

"Does anybody want to tell him?" he said in a dispirited voice.

"What's the use? Until we're up again, what's the use?"

"What if we don't come up again?"

"I don't want to think about it," said the news director, his eyes dull and defeated.

"Hey, check this out. MTV is putting on a news bulletin."

Every man in the newsroom rushed to the bank of monitors.

A young girl in purple and silver hair was speaking in a spritely voice.

"Can you, like, stand it?" she was saying. "The networks are, like, having really, really major technical difficulties again. But chill out. You still have your MTV. So here's Fed Leppar with *Petaluma*."

On came a music video that compressed more scenes than *War and Peace* contains into 120 seconds of quick-cut disconnected plotlessness.

The news director snapped. "That's it! Nothing about the ransom demands? What kind of news bulletin is that?"

"Right now, the only game in town," said the floor manager, his eyes flicking along the other monitors.

17

As the cab whisked them from Newark Airport to the BCN studios in the heart of Times Square, Remo Williams grew worried.

What would Chiun say when he found out the truth? Would he fly off the handle? Would he blame Remo? It was impossible to tell. Remo had seen the Master of Sinanju under every conceivable situation during their long association. But this—*this* was different.

Remo decided he would have to get control of the situation before it got out of control.

"Look," Remo told Chiun as Seventh Avenue flashed past. "We can't just barge in on Cheeta."

"Why not? She will be pleased to see me."

"Last time, she kept asking after me, remember?"

Chiun sniffed disdainfully and stared out the cab window. It was a sore spot with the Master of Sinanju. His infatuation with Cheeta Ching, even after her pregnancy, had not been completely reciprocated. On the few occasions when their paths had crossed, Cheeta had shown a strong interest in Remo—although she seemed unable to get his name right. Remo had chalked those incidents up to the super-charged pheromones his Sinanju-trained body constantly released. Still, for a woman carrying Chiun's child, her behavior was bizarre.

"And we're on assignment," Remo added.

"*You* are on assignment," Chiun sniffed. "I am on maternity leave."

"In your case, it's paternity leave, and did you clear this with Smith?"

"Emperor Smith understands these matters," Chiun said loftily. "He too is a father."

"In that case," Remo growled, "he understands a heck of a lot more than me. Anyway, we gotta treat this like an assignment. We can't blow it."

"I am not the blower of assignments in this vehicle," Chiun said.

"I won't argue with that—"

"Because you cannot," Chiun snapped.

"Okay, but chances are we're going to bump into Don Cooder."

Chiun's eyes narrowed and a slow hissing escaped his lips.

Remo said, "He's off-limits. Smitty said so."

"I will do what I must," Chiun said stiffly.

Inwardly, Remo groaned. His palms were actually sweating. He couldn't remember the last time they had done that.

The cab dropped them off at the studio entrance, and Remo got out first. He took the lead, Chiun following closely behind, his footsteps more quick than they normally were.

As they approached the security desk, Chiun called out, "What news of Cheeta?"

Remo's heart sank.

The answer came back. "None."

Chiun's features brightened. "Good. Then I am not too late for the joyous event."

Remo pulled a card out of a wallet that was stuffed with them. "Remo Neilson, FCC," he told the security guard. "I'm here about the blackout."

"That so? Any idea what's causing it?"

"We think it has something to do with hairspray buildup in the transmission equipment," Remo said with a straight face.

"Wow! Does that mean the anchors will have to shave their heads?"

"That's up to Congress," said Remo. "Point us to the guy in charge."

"You mean Don Cooder?"

"Who put *him* in charge?" Remo demanded.

"His agent." The security guard pointed. "Down the hall, take a right. then another right, then another right and again a right—"

"That's four rights, right?"

"Right. All the offices are strung around the newsroom. It's screwy, but that's the news."

Remo said, "Let's go, Little Father."

The guard looked at Chiun uncertainly, "He with the FCC too?"

"Korean version. We think this has international ramifications."

"No kidding? Damn shame they can't put the story out over the air."

The security guard allowed them to pass and Chiun got in front, his clenched hands held before him like an anxious hen.

"Cheeta will be overjoyed to see me," he squeaked.

Remo caught up and whispered, "Remember—let me do all the talking."

There was a palpable aura of depression in the corridors. Normally, Remo knew, a news operation was a bustling place. Here, staff moved slowly, faces white, eyes dispirited.

They passed the newsroom, visible through a curving pane of glass. It was dark, lit only by a handful of TV monitors. Only a few were working. A bunch of people were watching one in particular. Remo recognized the MTV logo up in one corner.

A man with rolled-up shirtsleeves ran in, waving wire service copy.

"Three more people have died of that new HELP virus out in California!" he shouted.

"So what?" a colorless voice shot back.

"But it's news!"

"If we can't put it out, it's trivia."

Remo and Chiun moved on.

A young woman in Levi's stepped out of an office, hugging a sheaf of papers to her chest.

The Master of Sinanju beamed. "Direct us, O television person, to the illustrious Cheeta Ching."

"I don't know where she is," the woman said. "Please excuse me. I have to get these to Don Cooder. It's his overnight ratings."

"We're going that way," Remo said helpfully. "We'll take it."

The girl hesitated and clutched her rating reports more tightly.

Remo smiled his disarming best and flashed his FCC card.

"It's okay. I know the numbers before anyone does."

"I guess it's all right . . ."

Remo took the reports and asked, "Which way to Cooder's office?"

The girl pointed down the corridor. "Take a left, then another left, then—"

Remove rolled his eyes. "Just give me a number."

The girl raised four fingers and said, "Five."

"His name on the door?"

"Of course," she said, walking off. "It's in Mr. Cooder's contract."

Remo took the lead, wondering what was going on. No one seemed aware that Cheeta Ching had been kidnapped. As he tried to figure out if this was good or bad, he began counting lefts.

The door marked DON COODER was at the fifth left. There was a star on it.

Beside it was a door marked CHEETA CHING. It had a star on it too—a smaller star.

The door was locked. As the Master of Sinanju cleared his throat nervously, Remo knocked.

There was no answer. Chiun put an ear to the panel, face collapsing.

"Guess she's hasn't shown up for the day," Remo said innocently.

Chiun stood looking at the door, frowning.

"She is an early riser. Why is she not here . . . ?"

"Maybe Cooder can tell us," Remo said quickly,

thinking any port in a storm. He rapped on Cooder's door. "Remember, behave."

"I have given my promise . . ." Chiun said thinly.

"Get lost!" a voice snarled from behind the door.

"Ratings reports," Remo shouted. "Get 'em while they're hot."

The door flew open and the wild-eyed face of Don Cooder appeared. "How'd I do on the flyover?" he asked, reaching out like a starving man to snag the reports. Remo backpedaled, simultaneously flashing his FCC ID card.

"In the tank," he said, holding the ratings out of Cooder's clutching grasp. "Gotta talk to you about this TV blackout."

Don Cooder flashed his trademark smile. It looked as if every muscle in his body except his lips were concentrated on forming that thin-lipped grimace. "Is it important? I'm powerful busy."

"How important is the fact that all TV is blacked out?"

"It is?"

"Don't you know?" Remo asked.

"Right now, it doesn't matter."

"Why not?"

Cooder checked his watch. "I don't go on until 6:30."

"That's one way of looking at it. Look, we want to talk to you about this blackout thing."

"All right. As long as it's off the record. I hate being interviewed. People always ask me about my ego—make that alleged ego."

They stepped into an office that made Remo think of an overgrown child's den. The wall were covered with posters of famous movie cowboys. Remo recognized one. It showed Tom Mix, six feet tall and all his bodily wounds marked and labeled.

On a long table sat was a battered old typewriter side by side with an amber-screened computer terminal. There was a tiny brass plaque under the typewriter which said, Don Cooder's First Typewriter.

Attached to the terminal was a silver foil sticker that said, WE HANG DATA THIEVES IN THESE PARTS.

Beside this stood a pedestal on which a copy of the Bible lay open.

Cooder took a seat behind his desk and adjusted on his smile. It still didn't fit.

"What can I tell you, Mr.—?"

"Neilson. Remo Neilson."

"And I am Chiun," said the Master of Sinanju in an arid voice.

Cooder blinked. "Chiun, Chiun, Chiun. Where have I heard that name before?"

"One hears the name Chiun in many places," the Master of Sinanju returned coolly.

Cooder crossed one leg over the other and took hold of a dangling boot. "I'm sure one does, but for some reason, I know that name."

The Master of Sinanju lifted a finger and pointed the long colorless nail at the open copy of the Bible.

"Amos 5:26. You may look it up."

"No need. I know the Bible by heart, practically. Let me see . . ." Cooder closed his eyes. " 'But ye have borne the tabernacle of your Moloch and Chiun, your images, the star of your god, which ye made to your selves.' "

"Huh?" Remo said. "*That's* from the Bible?"

"You may look it up if you wish," Chiun said blandly.

"I will," said Remo, going to the pedestal. He flipped pages until he got to the Book of Amos and read along, a frown came to his strong face.

"Hey! It's here!"

"Of course," said Chiun, eying Cooder coldly.

"Your name! It's in the Bible. How did it get there?"

"It was put there," said Chiun, eyes still locked with those of Don Cooder, "by the first of my ancestors who bore the proud name of Chiun."

Cooder was looking visibly impressed.

"I'm a religious man," he said. "Not many know it,

but it's true. Happy to talk to someone with a name out of the Good Book." His squinty eyes flicked to Remo. "What did you say your name was?"

"Remo," said Remo, looking away from the Bible.

"Well, not all the good names found their way into the Good Book," and he laughed like a nervous spinster. "Now how can I help you God-fearing folks?"

"We're looking into the blackout situation," said Remo, stepping away from the Bible.

"Why ask me? I just read news."

Chiun interrupted. "What is that?" he asked, pointing to a carved wood statuette that occupied a prominent spot on Cooder's desk. It was of a woman in a long concealing garment and head covering.

"That? That's an embarrassing question to ask a Texas Baptist like myself. It just happens to be a saint."

"Looks like a nun," said Remo.

"That's right. You must be a Catholic boy."

Remo said nothing.

"This here's Saint Clare of Assisi," Cooder explained. "Probably kin to Saint Francis. Saint Clare is the patron saint of television, believe it or not. So designated by Pope Pius XII back in '58. I did a feature on her once. The Pope, God rest his soul, up and decided television was too powerful not be watched over from above." Cooder frowned. "Saint Clare must have been looking the other way when the FCC gave Jed Burner his broadcast license."

"You think Burner is behind this?" Remo demanded.

"Sure. He's got the most to gain. People can't watch free TV, they have to get cable. Makes sense, doesn't it?"

"It did until KNNN went down," Remo pointed out. "They're off the air and so are you."

"Don't ever go into journalism, friend. You wouldn't last a minute in this man's game. It doesn't take a rocket scientist to see that Burner has his jamming equipment tucked away somewhere."

"Yeah. Well, I know enough to know that the jamming isn't coming out of Middle America."

"No?"

"It's coming out of Canada."

"What makes you say that?"

"That graph you showed last night. The center is Canada, not the U.S."

"You sure about that?" said Cooder, absently picking up the statuette of Saint Clare and rubbing her wimple with his thumb.

"Positive."

"You know, I'm glad you told me that."

"Why?"

"It kinda points me toward tall cotton."

"Huh?"

"Meaning I think I know who might be back of this jamming jamboree."

They waited for him to say it, and why he didn't, Remo asked, "Let's hear it."

"Can't. I have to protect my sources."

"Sources?" Remo said hotly. "I just gave you the major clue. You just said so."

"And I'm protecting *you*."

The Master of Sinanju slipped up to Don Cooder and, without exerting his frail-looking form, extracted the statuette of Saint Clare from Cooder's strong fingers. He held it up.

"The workmanship is good," Chiun said absently.

"Hand-carved. Did it myself," Cooder said proudly. "I used to whittle some in my short-pants days."

Then the Master of Sinanju closed both thin hands over the statuette and began squeezing. The statuette was of hickory. It made cracking and splintering sounds. The head of Saint Clare popped off and landed in Cooder's astonished mouth.

By the time he spit it to the floor like a hard plug of tobacco, the Master of Sinanju was pouring the remains onto the desk. It slipped from his fingers like sawdust. It *was* sawdust.

"I know that old trick," Cooder said, regaining his composure. "You slipped the real one up your sleeve."

"Uh-uh," said Remo. "What you see is what you get."

"I don't cotton to being threatened."

Remo folded his arms. "Cotton to it."

"Well," Cooder drawled, "since you two have high-carded me, I guess I can let slip a whisper." He lifted his hands. "As long as it doesn't go any further now."

Remo and Chiun glared and said nothing.

"I'll take your silence as acquiescence," Cooder said quickly. "The Canadians are back of this."

Remo blinked. "How do you figure that?"

"Ever been up there? They hate our TV. Always have. Spend half their days complaining about U.S. TV signals getting up there and polluting their culture. You want my advice? Start with Canada. But don't quote me."

"That's ridiculous," Remo said.

"Or," added Cooder, "you might check out own front yard for saboteurs."

"Meaning?"

Cooder dropped his voice to a conspiratorial whisper. "I hate to speak ill of a fellow colleague, but war is war. Dieter Banning is as Canadian as they come."

"Banning? His network is off the air too."

"I'm not blaming my good friends over at ANC, mind you. I'm saying that they may have a skunk in their woodpile. Catch my drift?"

"Skunks stink," said Chiun.

"That's it exactly. You two follow the smell and you'll break this plot as wide open as all outdoors. One thing though."

"Yeah?"

"If you crack it, I get an exclusive."

"No," said Remo.

Cooder lost his smile. "Not very neighborly of you," he muttered.

"Write a letter to the FCC."

"Count on it."

"Come on, Chiun."

"One question I would ask this man," Chiun said.

"Shoot."

"Where is Cheeta Ching?"

Cooder frowned, "Knowing her, probably looking for a cardboard box or something to have her kid in. Meow."

Chiun stiffened and only Remo's urging got him through the office door before the worst happened.

Out in the corridor, Remo turned to the Master of Sinanju and asked, "What do you think, Little Father?"

"I think there must be someone in this building who knows where Cheeta may be found," Chiun said bitterly.

Remo hesitated. "You heard Cooder," he said. "She's probably in some hospital. And I meant that stuff about Canada."

"Cheeta would not go away without contacting me."

"Forget Cheeta. Canada. What about Canada?"

They were standing outside the closed door to Cheeta Ching's office. Behind the door, a phone tweedled.

"Cheeta!" Chiun gasped. "Perhaps that is her!"

"Wait a minute, don't—"

The Master of Sinanju whirled, a fist like calcified bone sweeping for the doorknob. The knob recoiled from the impact, banging across the floor as Chiun pushed the maimed panel inward.

He rushed for the tweedling phone, his skirts flying.

Remo pulled the door closed after him, hoping against hope no one would notice the missing lock.

He was leaning against the door when Chiun snapped up the receiver and drew it to his face.

"Cheeta!" he cried.

Then, before Remo's eyes, the Master of Sinanju's parchment features turned the crimson of burning paper. His tiny mouth made a shocked O.

With frantic gestures of his free hand, the Master of Sinanju waved Remo closer.

When Remo reached his side, Chiun slapped the squawking receiver into his hand, hissing. "I cannot speak with his man!"

"Who—" Remo asked Chiun.

"This is Cheeta Ching's husband," a grumpy voice demanded. "Who am I speaking with, please?"

"FCC," said Remo.

"Put my wife on."

"She's not here."

"Well, where is she? She didn't come home last night. Is she on assignment?"

"Search me," said Remo, abruptly hanging up.

"Remo! Remo, did you hear?"

"I could hardly help it," Remo said dryly. "You stuck me with your dirty laundry again. That was Cheeta's better half."

"I know who it was!" Chiun snapped. "It is what he said that is important. Cheeta is missing!"

"Don't jump to a rash conclusion, Little Father," Remo said hastily. "It might not be like that at all."

"We must find her!"

"How?"

The Master of Sinanju froze. His shoulders slumped and his lifted hands came down. "We must search for clues. Hurry, Remo, help me search."

Reluctantly, Remo started checking around the office.

On the carpet by the door, he found an amber vial of pills, sealed with a white child-proof cap.

"Check this out," he told Chiun.

The Master of Sinanju was suddenly at Remo's side.

"What is it?" he squeaked excitedly. "What have you found?"

"Prescription pills. Made out to Cheeta."

"What do they say?"

" 'Take every four to six hours.' "

Chiun's pale eyebrows knit together. "Why would Cheeta eat mere pills? She is a Korean. Koreans do not need medicines. We eat rice three times a day."

"I don't know," Remo said, "but Smith might. Let's check it with him."

18

Harold Smith was fielding phone calls when the cable installation serviceman showed up at his Folcroft office.

"The man from the cable company is here, Dr. Smith," his secretary announced through the intercom.

"Excuse me, Mr. President," said Harold Smith, hanging up the red receiver and sweeping the phone into the open drawer of his desk. He closed the drawer, locking it.

Into the intercom, he said, "Send him in."

The man wore a blue repairman's uniform and asked, "Where is it?"

"Right here," said Smith, indicating the portable black-and-white TV set on the desk.

The installer stared at the set with disbelieving eyes.

"You want me to hook you up to *that*?"

"Yes. And please start immediately, I am quite busy."

"But it's black and white. Who springs for cable and watches it on a dinky little set like that?"

"If you do not mind, I have much to do," said Smith in a irritable voice.

"You're the boss," the installer said good-naturedly.

Smith stood up. "I will be having lunch. If any of the desk phones ring, just let them ring. Under no circumstances answer them."

"Natch."

Smith left the man stringing wire off a steel spool

and informed his secretary that he was eating lunch out this afternoon.

Smith went down to the commissary and purchased a cup of prune-whip yogurt. He paid for his lunch in exact change from a red plastic change holder, took a white plastic spoon, and went outside to his station wagon.

Driving past the gates, Smith took the single approach road and pulled into a secluded spot overlooking Long Island Sound. Opening his suitcase, he extracted the receiver and reconnected with the White House.

"I am sorry, Mr. President. The cable installer arrived early. I could not speak. Please continue."

"The Federal Communications Commission tells me they couldn't trace the audio signal," the President said, "and until it comes back, they're helpless. This is real frustrating, Smith. I have a flock of SAC bombers jammed with tracking equipment and they might as well be paper kites. Any help on your end?"

"I share your frustration, Mr. President, but until Audion puts out a traceable audio there is nothing that can be done on this end."

"I was afraid you were going to say that."

Harold Smith hung up the phone and opened his cup of yogurt. He had just pushed the white plastic spoon into the cold purplish gray mass when the computer phone rang again. This time, it buzzed. That meant Remo and not the White House calling back. "Yes, Remo?"

"Smitty, I'm in a pay phone. Chiun can't hear me."

"What is the situation?"

"Weird. Nobody at BCN seems to know Cheeta is missing."

"Good."

"And Chiun and I talked to Don Cooder."

"Was that wise? Given their past history?"

"Chiun was so stuck on finding Cheeta, he didn't cause any more of a fuss than usual."

Smith released the air in his lungs slowly. It would

have passed for a sigh if it weren't for a certain nasal whistling quality.

Remo added, "Cooder has a harebrained theory."

"Yes."

"He thinks Dieter Banning is behind this."

"Banning? The ANC anchor?"

"I told him the center of the jamming area looked like Canada to me and—"

"Canada?"

"Yeah. BCN showed a graphic. The center looked like Canada to me."

"Where exactly?" Smith asked.

"Search me. Canada might as well be Antarctica for all I know about it."

"Remo, I just got off the phone with the President. The FCC has so far been unable to get a fix on the audio transmission. I wonder if it is because the signal is not of domestic origin, as supposed."

"Would the Canadians be jamming our TV?"

"Canada has always been sensitive to U.S. cultural contamination. Particularly in the area of broadcast signal spillover. Their Federal government is engaged in a program of converting their television broadcast system to cable in the hope of regulating—in effect, prohibiting—U.S. television programs from reaching their citizenry."

"What's wrong with our programs?"

"They complain about the violence and corruption."

"They don't have violence or corruption up on Canada?" Remo asked.

"They have a different culture than we do," Smith said.

"I didn't know that had *any* culture."

Smith's voice grew sharp, "Remo, why does Don Cooder suspect Dieter Banning of complicity in this matter?"

"He thinks Banning is a Canadian agent. Is it possible?"

"I cannot say, but Don Cooder is well-known for his reliable news sources. He could be right. Remo, look into the Banning connection. It is all we have until we get a precise fix on the pirate signal."

"Okay, but I can't count on Chiun. He's making noises about looking for Cheeta in every hospital in the city."

"Your priority is the assignment. Perhaps one will lead to the other."

"One other thing, Smitty."

"Yes?"

"I found some prescription pills in Cheeta's office. Looks like she dropped them on her way out the door."

"What is it called?"

"Terbutaline Sulfate."

Smith logged onto his portable pharmacopoeia database and input the unfamiliar words.

"Remo," he said, "Terbutaline Sulfate is normally prescribed to delay labor, where there is risk of a premature birth."

"According to the label," Remo said, "the prescription was refilled just last week."

"I am not sure I understand," Smith said slowly. "Miss Ching is now in her tenth month."

"Well, I do. Cheeta's been trying to keep the kid in until sweeps month."

"Preposterous. What kind of mother-to-be would—"

"A ratings hound," snapped Remo. "And if all that's holding her back are these pills, then Cheeta could drop the big one any second now, and our troubles come in triplets."

"Remo, look into the Banning angle. Make no moves without further consultation. I will pursue my own leads."

Harold Smith hung up and returned to his yogurt, a pained expression on his lemony face. He was not thinking of the developing crisis, or of Cheeta Ching's impending childbirth. Harold Smith was thinking of the cable installation fee that would have to come out of the CURE operating budget. It was a small expenditure in the larger scheme of things. Still, it rankled his thrifty soul.

Licking the last traces of yogurt from the plastic spoon he fully intended to wash and surreptitiously return to the Folcroft cafeteria dispenser, Smith made a mental vow to cancel his subscription to cable as soon as this crisis had passed. He hoped to solve it in thirty days. The entire fee was refundable if cancelled in the first month.

It made him feel much better as he piloted his station wagon back through the watchful stone lions that guarded the gates of Folcroft Sanitarium.

19

Remo Williams stepped from the phone booth near Times Square. It looked like a ghost town of boarded-up theaters, storefronts and deserted buildings.

There was no sign of the Master of Sinanju. Anywhere.

"Damn," he said.

Remo had left Chiun at a line of cabs, telling him that he would only be a minute. Chiun had agreed without the usual argument, because the location allowed him to watch the BCN studio entrance, in case Cheeta Ching showed up.

Remo had felt guilty over prolonging the deception, and was half-resolved to break down and tell the truth about Cheeta's abduction, but now . . .

"See anything of an old Korean in a kimono?" Remo asked a cabby leaning against the hood of his taxi and wolfing down a pastrami sandwich.

The cabby stopped in midchew and said thickly, "I thought only geisha girls wore kimonos."

"Answer the question."

"Sure. He was watching the bulletin with the rest of us, gave a yip and grabbed the first cab."

The cabby was pointing to the large TV screen on One Times Square Plaza, which, like all the rest of broadcast TV, was as black as a hung crepe except for the tiny NO SIGNAL Chyron.

"Bulletin? The screen's blacked out."

"This wasn't a regular bulletin," the cabby explained. "It was more along the line of a ransom demand."

"Ransom?"

"Wait, here it comes again."

The screen suddenly flared to life.

And looking out over Times Square was the flat, scared-white face of Cheeta Ching. Her hair was a Medusan mass of split ends and her red mouth was moving, but no sound was coming out.

"She's saying that she's having—whadyacall'em—Braxton-Hicks contractions," the cabby explained.

"You can read lips?"

"Naw. The sound was coming in over the dispatch radio, last time. Whatever's messing up TV reception, it's put the radios on the fritz too." The driver obligingly got behind the wheel and turned his radio up.

"—sist that my network agree to all of this lunatic's demands at once," Cheeta was saying in a shrill, helpless tone. "I can't have my baby now. I look a wreck and I don't have my midwife and—"

The screen turned blue and the blue framed a graphic of a stainless steel nautical anchor in a triangular Warner Bros's-style crest.

"We interrupt this interruption of broadcast service," the sonorous voice of Captain Audion broke in, *"to announce an escalation in our earlier demands."*

The screen was again black.

"The price per network is up to fifty million, but for BCN, I'll throw in Cheeta Ching for an extra ten."

"I'd pass," the cabby opined. "That broad ain't worth last month's rent. Did you see her hair? It's terrible what they pay these people, and they can't even groom themselves right."

"That the message my friend heard?" Remo demanded.

"Yeah, I had my radio up full blast on account of everybody and his brother wanted to hear what she was saying. Fat lot of good it did me. Not one fare."

"Any chance you overheard where my friend went?"

"Sure. He told the first guy in line to take him to the ANC studio."

"You the second guy in line?"

The cabby gestured through his windshield. "You see anybody in front of me now?"

"Then you get to take me to ANC," said Remo, reaching for the passenger door handle.

"Okay, just let me finish my pastrami."

Remo reached over the roof of the parked cab and took hold of the roof light. He disengaged the fixture and handed it to the driver through the open window.

"What's this?" the cabby muttered, pastrami shreds dribbling from his lips.

"An example of what will happen to your head if you don't get your ass into gear," said Remo, dropping into the back seat.

He slammed the door shut as the cab left the curb.

There was only one reason the Master of Sinanju would race off to ANC without him, Remo knew.

Chiun was going to ransom Cheeta Ching by wringing the truth out of the person he believed was her abductor.

Dieter Banning.

20

Everyone agreed that Dieter Banning was the most erudite, well-dressed, and polished anchor on American TV.

The truth was that Dieter Banning's early reading consisted almost exclusively of American comic books. Although his resume included Carleigh University in Ottowa, he had in fact enrolled in their night school. He lasted a single week, quitting because, in his words, "There weren't enough pictures in the texts."

He bought his clothes in bulk from a London discount house. But because they were British, he made the annual best-dressed lists.

No one questioned his lack of credentials, because Dieter Banning looked like an anchor should look, spoke the way an anchor was expected to speak, and did it all in an impeccable clipped accent that seemed above reproach.

But most of all, Dieter Banning had the credibility of a man who had the courage to wear his own hair on network TV.

Few viewers would have acknowledged it, in an age of toupees, blown-dry shag cuts and hair weaves, but news viewers subconsciously trusted Dieter Banning because he had the courage to let his thinning hair go out over the air unembellished and unaugmented.

"I'm a journalist, not a fucking Macy's mannikin," he had retorted when the unfamiliar American word "Rogaine" was uttered by the president of the news division. The occasion was Banning's forty-second birthday and the renewal of his first two-year contract.

"Need I remind you, Dieter, that there's an appearance clause in your contract?"

"Take it out, or I walk."

No one in network television had ever heard of such a thing. Dieter Banning was being paid a cool 1.7 million dollars a year to read off a teleprompter five nights a week and he was actually balking at a little career-enhancing cosmetics.

"You," said the news manager, "are either the next Edward R. Murrow or an utter fool."

Dieter Banning simply stared at his *lobster Fra Diavolo* and said nothing. He found that worked well with Americans. They usually filled the silence with some babble of their own, usually their worst fears.

His employer did not disappoint him.

"Okay, the clause goes. But the ratings better not erode or we're revisiting this whole discussion next renewal."

"Fine," said Dieter Banning, wondering who Edward R. Murrow was. The name had a vaguely familiar ring. Perhaps Murrow was one of those "deputy dogs" who did the weekend reports.

The next day, everyone in the newsroom had nice things to say about his hair.

"New haircut, Dieter?"

"Perhaps," said Dieter, who had dug out an old photo of Edward R. Murrow and fought his hair into a close approximation of the late TV journalist's understated hairstyle.

No one ever commented on the resemblance. But Dieter Banning's ratings went steadily up in the coming months, until his was the undisputably top-rated newscast. While other anchors primped, moussed, augmented and fried their follicles with industrial-strength blow dryers, Dieter Banning's low-maintenance coif was sending out a nightly subliminal message that whispered "Trust me," and almost everyone credited his well-bred manner of speaking.

Dieter Banning had been at his desk when his network went down for the second time in twelve hours. The ANC program director barged in.

"Dieter. We're down again."

"Son of a bitch!"

"It's that Captain Audion again!"

"Shit!"

"All the other networks are black too."

Banning shrugged and said, "Shit happens."

"What do we do?"

"Well," he said with wry unconcern, "we were promised a seven-hour blackout, so I imagine that gives us seven hours to prepare our evening broadcast."

"But the network is losing a fortune. The brass is foaming at the mouth."

Banning smiled coolly. "Get pictures."

Dieter Banning was still at his desk when the excitement started three hours later.

"Is there a problem?" he asked a passing clerk. People had been racing by him for the last last five minutes, howling and frantic, and Dieter Banning thought their stark faces looked more drained of blood than usual. They were often that way, these Americans. Temperamentally unable to handle the pressure of daily news gathering. Here it was nearly noon, and Dieter Banning had already written his five-line lead for the 6:30 feed. He was quite proud of it. The prose almost scanned.

"We're under attack!"

"Oh, don't be so bloody melodramatic," Banning rejoined. "So, Middle America is bereft of a few lame game shows and downmarket tabloid programs and soap operas. The world still spins on its axis, eh?"

"You don't understand. Two security guards are dead! And an FBI SWAT team has been called in."

Dieter Banning blinked, and stood up, his face paling. His legs, under his kilt, paled too.

"Attack! By whom?"

"No one knows."

"We are a news gathering organization. Shouldn't someone know by now?"

Then a voice shouted, "Here he comes!"

ANC security was provided by Purolator guards. The marble lobby was usually thick with them, day and night. A nightly newscast was a convenient target for any desperate attention-seeking person with the firepower to bluff his way to the anchor desk. It had happened. Not at ANC, but at other networks and not a few local stations.

There were contingency measures in place if a terrorist or other criminal attempted to hijack *Worldly News Nitely*.

The first was simple: Shoot the terrorist dead. Dead terrorists don't commit much mischief, and rarely sued.

Obviously, this terrorist was resisting being shot. Pity.

The second line of defense was to go black. There was a master switch that would shut down all transmissions, both broadcast and cable, and replace it with a technical difficulties sign. This would buy time for negotiations, not to mention insuring that ANC got the exclusive footage.

Here at least, luck was with ANC. They were already black.

The third contingency plan was to go to the bunker. The ANC studios were a designated community fallout shelter, and the basement was well stocked with provisions in the now-unlikely event of a thermonuclear exchange. It boasted a door that could have been hung on a bank vault.

It's clearly time, Dieter Banning decided as security guards began giving back, firing wildly, before the unseen intruder, to seek out the bunker.

"Excuse me," he asked a cowering intern, "which way to the bunker?"

The cowering intern said nothing. Possibly the gunfire was drowning out his inquiry, so Dieter Banning restated the question in his brand of perfectly enunciated Americanized English.

"Excuse me you stupid bitch, but where the hell can I find the fucking bunker!"

The woman burst into tears and pointed toward a fire door. "Follow the yellow arrow," she sobbed.

"Thank you," said Banning, hurriedly exiting the newsroom. He found the yellow arrow, which led to another yellow arrow, which pointed down a seldom-used flight of steps. At the bottom of the steps there was another fire door.

Dieter Banning almost lost his kilt at the door. The kilt pin snagged the latchbar. He pulled free and went on. It was one of the biggest secrets in the news industry that the ANC anchor desk hid the clan tartan worn by the male Bannings of Ottowa since they came to the New World in 1853.

The bunker was around the first bend in the corridor, a yawning cavern of stainless steel and white-painted brick.

It was empty, so Banning stepped over the sill and pulled the ponderous door behind him.

It was quite dark, but after a moment's fumbling he found a light switch.

Outside, someone was pounding on the door.

Banning gave the wheel a spin, securing the door from intruders. To be polite, Banning called through the door.

"Yes. Who is it please?"

"Ned Doppler. That you, Dieter?"

"Do you have bunker privileges, Ned?"

"It's in my contract."

"Got it on you?"

"No."

"Then you cannot easily slip it under the door, can you?"

"Dieter, you sissy prick! Open this door. It's a slaughterhouse up there."

"If it becomes a slaughterhouse down here, you *will* give a yell, won't you?"

Then another voice came through the door, high, ringing, angry.

"I seek the fiend who calls himself Dieter Banning."

"Here's in there," Ned Doppler said instantly.

Banning snarled, "Traitor!"

"Why don't I leave you two alone?" added Doppler, his footsteps going away.

"I think it only fair to warn you," Dieter Banning called to the person outside the vault door, "I have no intentions of coming out."

"In that case," the voice replied coldly, "I am coming in."

Dieter Banning gave a little laugh. It sounded so hollow in the great vault he got a little worried in the silence that followed the last lingering echo.

The next sound brought Banning's manicured hands clapping over his ears.

They were shrieks, howls and other sounds. Metallic sounds. Human beings weren't making them. Machines were. They must be. But what kind of machine sounded like an ocean liner going through a Veg-o-matic?

When the great door showed cracks of lights around the rounded seams where it met the door casing, Dieter Banning knew the sound was that of the bunker door being breached.

Then the vault door fell and the gaping hole framed the sight of the person who wanted Dieter Banning so badly he had blown through ANC like a frenzied tornado.

A tiny Asian man with fingernails like talons.

"You will reveal the truth about Cheeta Ching," the attacker told Dieter Banning, "or you will die on the spot where you stand!"

"Glad to. Cheeta Ching is in collusion with her husband to delay the baby until sweeps month. I plan on breaking the story the day she gives birth."

The tiny Asian's facial wrinkles compressed in stages, like a mainspring being wound to the snapping point.

Then, the mainspring sprung.

"Oh, bugger," Dieter Banning muttered, "I'm fucked."

And he felt a sudden hot weight in the seat of his pants that he couldn't explain unless—ridiculous thought—he had lost all bowel control.

21

Harold W. Smith returned to his office exactly thirty minutes after he left it.

"He's still here, Dr. Smith," said Smith's secretary.

"Thank you, Mrs. Mikulka."

Frowning, Harold Smith entered his office. He disliked leaving it alone, but he felt confident that the cable installer would come across nothing untoward. The only unusual items in the entire office were the red telephone, safely locked in a drawer, and the CURE terminal, which Smith had sent slipping into its secret desktop reservoir.

Smith stepped into the room to find it unoccupied.

"My God!" he said hoarsely.

A waving hand lifted a screwdriver above the level of his desk.

"Be done in a second," a disembodied voice said.

Smith came around the desk and peered into the foot well. There, the installer was on his hands and knees, tacking the cable down with a staple gun.

"Is there a problem?" Smith asked.

"Naw. Usually, people put their TVs against an outside wall and it's just a matter of plugging her in. I didn't think you'd want a loose cable at your feet so I'm tacking it down. That's okay, isn't it?"

"That will be fine," said Smith. Hovering over the man, he felt awkward. His chair had been pushed off to one side. Unable to sit at his own desk, he stood with his gangling hands hanging loose-fingered out of his coat sleeves.

Presently, the repairman stood up and reached for the tiny TV set on Harold Smith's desk.

"Let's see how she fires up," he said, hitting the on switch of a cable box that perched atop the too-small set like a pit bull on a possum.

The screen came on. It was black. Two words, NO SIGNAL, glowed in thin ivory letters.

"Funny."

"What?" Smith asked.

"I got it turned to MBC."

"MBC is blacked out," Smith pointed out.

"Yeah, so I heard. But you're hooked up to cable now."

"Yes?"

"The signal the cable company transmits isn't picked off the air, you know. We'd have a piss-poor signal quality if we did it that way. We get it off a microwave transmission. New York Skypath. Direct." The man began switching channels. "Whatever's jamming the airwaves shouldn't affect you now that you're cabled up. But look at it. Everything network is black. Except KNNN. And they're broadcasting snow."

"Can you explain how it is possible to intercept both broadcast and cable-fed network signals?" Smith asked.

"It's not."

"Yet it is happening."

"No, it's not."

Smith's lemony face quirked. "Excuse me?"

"That 'No Signal'? Normally, you see that when a network isn't getting its signal from the affiliates. Usually it's a bad microwave path or something. Follow me so far?"

"I believe so," said Smith, giving his rimless glass a thoughtful adjustment.

"Okay. Let's say the networks are down. That still leaves the affiliate stations. It's their signal you receive. When an affiliate goes down, you don't get anything like this. Snow, sure. Color bars sometimes. Usually, they throw up a station ID card or a technical difficulties graphic."

"What are you saying?"

"What you're seeing isn't jamming. Can't be."

"Then what is it?"

The cable installer made faces at the screen.

"The only way I can figure it," the cable installer said slowly, "is that somebody's broadcasting black."

"Broadcasting black?"

"We're not looking at a 'No Signal' here. We're looking at a signal that *says* 'No Signal.' "

Smith's voice betrayed a growing excitement. "That means it could be traced?"

"Sure."

Harold Smith was a reserved New Englander. People thought him cold, aloof, and as warm as shaved ice. Expressions of emotion were rare with him, and limited to the occasional exclamation.

On this occasion, Harold W. Smith took hold of the repairman's right hand in both of his and pumped it furiously.

"You have been very helpful," he said. "I cannot thank you enough."

The installer brightened. "Glad to help. Say, while I'm here, I could cable up this whole facility in jig time. We offer a bulk discount . . ."

Smith abruptly released the man's hand. His voice temperature cooled audibly. "Thank you, no. Now if you will excuse me, I have some telephone calls to make."

The cable installer hastily packed up his equipment. "Well, don't trip over the furniture in your hurry to give me the bum's rush. Cheeze . . ."

22

A block from the ANC studio, Remo was forced to abandon the cab. The police had the area cordoned off with blue and white squad cars and NYPD sawhorses. A dozen ambulances waited in side streets their backs open and filled with body bags, which weren't full but not exactly empty either. There were sharpshooters on every roof, and a lone police helicopter orbited the scene nervously.

News crews were crushing against the cordon. There were enough of them to cover a civil revolt, and Remo wondered how they had got the word so fast. Then he noticed the ANC logo on literally every camera. Obviously, the crews had evacuated the building and begun recording. Some lenses were trained unwaveringly on the studio entrance. Others were covering the cordon. Still others filmed the first two teams. There was enough coverage, Remo thought, to support a 3-D hologram of the event.

Off to one side, Remo recognized Ned Doppler banging a handheld microphone against the hood of a police car, complaining, "The dip switch is gone on this thing!"

"What's the big deal?" someone asked. "We're blacked out, and can't broadcast live."

"We cares about a live standup? This is for *Nightmirror*!"

"So what's the rush?"

"I want to tape a standup on my brush with death while everything's fresh in my mind!"

Remo moved on.

A man in plainclothes tried to prevent him from entering the cordon. Remo flashed an FBI ID card and said, "Remo Reynolds, Special Agent."

The man responded by flashing a similar card of his own and said, "John Bundish, Division Chief, and I never heard of you."

"I'm up from Washington. Looking into the TV blackout."

Division Chief Bundish looked him up and down. "They dress that casual down in D.C. now?"

"Undercover. I'm pretending to be a makeup man. Listen, what's going on?"

"Crazy man busted in and is demanding that Cheeta Ching be brought to him. Guess he got his networks mixed up, or something. We got a call into BCN, but they don't know where the woman is. Meanwhile, the bodies keep piling up."

"Who's dead?"

"Who isn't is the question. We've got dead security, wounded technical staff, you name it."

"Damn!"

Division Chief Bundish noticed Remo's Italian loafers.

"Let me see that ID of yours again," he demanded.

Remo put a friendly arm on his shoulder and propelled him away from the crowd. "Let's talk in that alley over there."

Division Chief Bundish found his feet moving toward the alley despite his brain's attempt to resist.

In the alley, Remo confided, "Listen, I know who's behind all this."

"You do?"

"Yeah. North Korean terrorist. Name's Wing Wang Wo. A killer. A cold assassin. They call him the Korean Dragon. Someone's going to have to talk him out of the building before more people get killed."

"Hostage negotiation team is on the way."

"Yeah, but I'm here now."

"No chance. I'm in charge."

"You sure that's your final answer?"

"Positive. You see all those cameras out there? I can't have you representing the Bureau dressed for shooting pool. The least you could have done is thrown on a regulation windbreaker."

The man had a point, so Remo dropped him where he stood in his brown wingtips. They were about the same height and weight, so Remo stripped the man of his outer clothes and put them on.

Remo flashed his card at the first cop he came to and asked, "Who's in charge here?"

"Lieutenant Rebello over there."

Lieutenant Rebello scarcely looked at Remo's ID card. "We've got him barricaded in the basement fallout shelter. Everytime we send someone in—"

"Let me guess," Remo interrupted. "They don't come out."

A first-floor window broke and out sailed a riot-control helmet. It bounced upon impact, showing clearly that it still encapsulated its late owner's head.

A SWAT team in flak jackets raced up and gathered up the head—helmet and all—into a fire retardant blanket and rushed it to a waiting ambulance.

"They come back like that," the lieutenant said hoarsely.

"Got a bullhorn?"

A bullhorn was surrendered. Remo brought it up to his mouth, took a deep breath, and called, "You in there. This is FBI Special Agent Reynolds. *Remo* Reynolds."

"Liar!" a squeaky voice called out.

"You know who I am. The jig's up, Wo. I want you to surrender peacefully—or else."

"Or else what?"

"Or else, I'm coming in there after you."

"Do your worst, O FBI lackey."

A collective gasp went up. Assault rifles and side-arms were steadied over the hoods of the police-car cordon. Every trigger finger was white at the knuckles. The air filled with the simultaneous whir of video equipment.

Remo turned to the lieutenant and said, "Watch my back."

"You can't go in there. You saw what happened. And they were wearing full protective gear."

"I've done this before. And I speak fluent Korean."

And as the trigger-happy police watched, the FBI agent entered the marble ANC lobby and disappeared from sight.

"That's one brave agent," a cop remarked.

"That's one brave *dead* agent," Lieutenant Rebello said.

Ten minutes later, the well-dressed FBI agent emerged again, face grim.

"He's willing to surrender," Remo said.

"He is?"

"There's one condition."

"What's that?"

"Absolutely, positively no cameras."

The word went out. The cameramen were pushed back. A few news people cried out their first amendment rights and ended up in the backs of police cars, sitting on their handcuffed hands.

When that was done, Agent Remo Reynolds went back in.

Minutes ticked by. Huddling behind barricades, SWAT weapons pointed unwaveringly at the studio entrance.

Then, a figure emerged—short, wispy, swathed in a blue-and-gold native costume, hands raised in abject surrender.

"I am surrendering because I have met my match," he announced in a loud voice.

"Amazing," Lieutenant Rebello croaked.

The tiny Asian stepped out onto the sidewalk and said in a loud voice. "Fear not. I will harm no one because I have seen the error of my ways."

"Okay, take him," Rebello called. The police moved in, weapons raised and cocked. They looked eager to shoot at the slightest provocation.

"Don't," Remo said, stepping between the encircling gun muzzles and the Master of Sinanju. "I got him calmed down now. You'll only set him off again."

"He's surrendered, right?"

"He's agreed to surrender to the *FBI*," Remo corrected.

"I have watched their television program and it has struck fear my fearless heart," cried the old Korean in a high voice.

"Look," Remo said anxiously. "I gotta get him to FBI headquarters fast. I need to borrow a car."

Rebello waved his men back and shouted, "Get an unmarked unit over here!"

A nondescript sedan was brought up. Keys were surrendered.

The old Asian went meekly into the back. The door was clapped shut and FBI Agent Reynolds took the wheel, saying, "Thanks. You'll get a full report."

And as the way was cleared, the unmarked car disappeared from sight.

Lieutenant Rebello took a deep breath. "All right, let's sweep the building."

The FBI van arrived within fifteen minutes. The doors popped and slid open, and out came a team of agents in blue windbreakers with the letters FBI stenciled on the back.

"Who are you?" Rebello demanded of the agent who appeared in charge.

"Hostage negotiation team."

"You're a little late. Agent Reynolds took care of it. Talked the guy out clean."

"Reynolds?"

"Yeah. One guy. Never seen anything like it."

"I don't know any agent Reynolds."

"First name Remo. The guy was slick. Deserves a commendation."

The hostage negotiation team conferred among themselves. No one had heard of a Remo Reynolds.

"He must be with some other office," Lieutenant Rebello suggested in a tone that suggested diminishing confidence.

"We were told to liase with Division Chief Bundish."

"He was around her earlier. I haven't seen him since Reynolds . . ." Lieutenant Rebello swallowed. "That's right! Bundish. What the hell happened to him?"

Then, a voice called out, "Hey, there's a guy sleeping in this alley in his underwear," and Lieutenant Rebello's promising career in law-enforcement took a sharp, sudden drop into the toilet. In later years, he swore that at that exact moment he heard a distinct flushing sound.

23

Remo Williams ditched the unmarked car and street clothes on Park Avenue South, his face tight with anguish.

In his earlier life, he had been a cop. An ordinary cop. Nothing special. Except that he had been honest. He knew what it was to put on the blue uniform and stand between society and lawlessness. It was a long time ago, so long Remo had forgotten all but the rough outlines of those days when he had worn an extra twenty-five pounds and a face that had not been altered by plastic surgery and had espoused a simple, if naive, concept of justice.

What he had found in the basement of the ANC building had left him sickened: The sight of the Master of Sinanju standing red-faced and steely-eyed among a pile of headless corpses.

"Jesus Christ, Chiun!" Remo had exploded when he came upon the carnage. "What are you trying to do? Get us both killed?"

"It is not I who am at fault," Chiun had said tightly. "I have been attacked from the moment I set foot in this den of unrepentant Canadians."

"You killed cops. Honest, hardworking cops."

The Master of Sinanju looked down upon the piled dead.

"How do you know they are honest?" he asked.

"Skip it. Look, I gotta get you out of here in one piece. Those cops out there are hot to shoot you on sight."

Chiun drew himself up proudly. "I am not afraid."

"You'd better be. If they all come charging in—
hey, who's this?" Remo asked, noticing one body in
particular.

"Who is what?"

"This dead guy," Remo said pointing to a pair of
bare legs sticking out from under a pile of miscellane-
ous dead. The legs were half-covered in gray knee
socks, but they weren't what had caught Remo's eye.

He reached down and grabbed the body by the
ankles and pulled it free, fully exposing a brown tartan
kilt. Remo continued pulling and found that the rest
of the body was attired in a cheap coat and tie.

The body had no head.

"Where's the head to this one?" Remo had asked,
looking around for the missing item.

"Why do you wish to know?" Chiun had asked thinly.

"Because it's important," Remo snapped, lifting up
head after head and tossing them aside after a moment's examination.

"Why is it important?"

"Look, we don't have much time. The place is completely surrounded. There are sharpshooters on every
roof. There's no way out of here unless you come out
as my prisoner."

"Never! What would Cheeta think?"

"That's another thing. There are cameras everywhere. We can't just walk out in full view of everyone.
Even if we make it out alive, Smitty'll have us both
under a plastic surgeon's knife by sundown."

Chiun stamped a sandaled foot.

"I am not leaving until Cheeta is brought to me.
Such are my demands and I must abide by them or
be shamed."

"Will you cut the crap?" Remo had said, continuing
to look for a matching head. There were too many
heads. And they were too scattered about. It was as if
everyone had blundered into a head-husking machine,
which dropped the bodies where they stood but sent
the heads flying.

"Look," he said, giving up, "just do whatever I say and we'll work this out."

The tightness in Chiun's visage had loosened at that point. "I will go along," he had allowed, "but I will defend myself if provoked—even against the blue centurions of Emperor Smith."

"Okay, just sit tight," Remo had said. "I'll negotiate safe passage. And don't kill anyone else."

Remo had worked it all out, but he was still sick about it. In the earlier days of their association, these things tended to happen a lot. Bellboys maimed for nicking Chiun's luggage, telephone repairmen killed for interrupting his soap operas. Gradually, the Master of Sinanju had become accustomed to the odd ways of America—including the difficult-to-comprehend concept that ordinary citizens—peasants, he called them—were actually considered valuable and were not to be killed.

Such inconvenient incidents had long ago tapered off, but the occasional security guard, soldier, or police officer still managed to meet an untimely end. Usually when they caught Chiun in a foul mood.

This, however, was major even by Chiun's standards.

"Look, think hard," Remo was saying as he hailed a cab. "The guy in the kilt—who was he?"

"They were so many . . ."

"But only one in a freaking kilt. Now come on."

The cab slid to a stop. The cabby looked happy to see them. His radio was hissing static.

"Airport," said Remo.

"Which?"

"The nearest one. We're not fussy."

"Newark it is."

As they rode uptown, Remo asked in a tight low voice. "Now tell me who wore the kilt."

"It was that ballast," Chiun said.

"The what?"

"You know—the one who reads news."

"The anchor?"

"Yes. The deceiving Canadian anchor."

"You decapitated Dieter Banning?"

"He refused to confess his crimes. I demanded to know the whereabouts of Cheeta the Fecund, and he resisted, showering vile curses and imprecations upon my person. So I snuffed him."

"You put pressure on him first, right?"

"Correct."

"And he still insisted he had nothing to do with any of it?"

"He did not say that. He cursed me."

"You've been cursed at before. Usually you remove a few fingers. Sometimes a tongue. What's the big deal?"

The Master of Sinanju grew silent. His lower lip pouted out. "He spoke ill of Cheeta. He called her a slant-eyed goop."

"He ranked *her* out and *you* went ballistic?"

"I avenged the honor of a fellow Korean," Chiun sniffed.

"And lost the only lead we had."

"He was no lead. He had nothing to do with anything."

"Says you."

"No one holds his tongue whom the Master of Sinanju holds by the throat. You know this."

Remo said nothing. He did know it. No one could possibly resist the awful, agonizing pain Chiun was capable of inflicting. If Dieter Banning knew anything about Cheeta Ching, Chiun would have gotten it out of him. No question.

Ordinarily, that would have settled that. But Banning had been wearing a kilt when he died. And Cheeta Ching's abductor had been wearing a kilt too. What the hell did it mean?

At the Newark Airport, Remo called Harold Smith from a payphone. The Master of Sinanju hovered close.

"Smitty, Remo."

"What is the situation, Remo?"

"We ran into a little trouble."

"What kind?"

"You haven't heard?"

"No news is getting out."

"Well," Remo said, lifting his voice. "Chiun—who's here with me now—went on ahead to ANC without me. It seems Cheeta Ching has been kidnapped by Captain Audion."

Hearing this, Chiun raised his voice. "Remo was too slow, Emperor Smith. I dared not wait for him with Cheeta Ching in peril."

"Chiun blew into ANC and—"

"I was attacked the moment I entered the building," Chiun shouted. "I had to defend myself. The place is a viper's nest of Canadians. Vicious, anti-American Canadians."

Smith groaned. "There are casualties?"

"Piles of them," Remo admitted.

Smith groaned again.

"Chiun tried to get Dieter Banning to talk. Banning wouldn't. He insulted Cheeta. So Chiun wasted him."

"Remo, are you certain of this?"

"I saw the body myself. Of course, it didn't have its head, but it was wearing a kilt."

The Master of Sinanju held his breath.

No sound came from the receiver.

Then, in a low voice, Harold Smith asked, "A kilt?"

"Yeah," Remo said guardedly. "A kilt."

The Master of Sinanju looked from the silent receiver to his pupil.

"Why is this kilt important?" he asked suspiciously.

"Who said it was important?" Remo asked in a too-innocent voice.

"The tone of your voice."

Smith said, "Put Master Chiun on, Remo."

"A pleasure. Here. Smitty wants to talk to you."

The Master of Sinanju took up the receiver and said, "I am listening, Emperor Smith."

"There is a report that Cheeta Ching was abducted by a man who wore a kilt."

Chiun's eyes narrowed to slits. "A Scotsman?"

"He wore a kilt. That is my only information."

"Emperor Smith, you must find Cheeta. Her baby will be born soon. I must attend the birth."

"I am doing all I can. Please put Remo back on."

"Yeah, Smitty?" said Remo.

"Remo, are you certain that Dieter Banning is dead?"

"Yeah. Definitely."

"Either Banning is part of this conspiracy or he is not. I am going to get the word out."

"Yeah?"

"Perhaps something will happen."

"Okay, what do Chiun and I do in the meantime? We're pretty hot in these parts."

"Return to Folcroft. That way you will be convenient to New York if something breaks."

"On our way, Smitty. Thanks."

Remo hung up. The Master of Sinanju was looking up at him, his wrinkled face tight and searching.

"We're going back to Folcroft," Remo said.

"*You* are going to Folcroft. I seek Cheeta Ching, defamed by the base round-eye whites whom she had attempted to educate with her nightly songs of truth and purity."

"Look, we're at a dead end. If anyone can find her, it's Smitty. Let's give him a chance."

"Cheeta has pleaded for succor. The boy who is to be born is nigh—"

"Nigher than you think," said Remo.

"What do you mean?"

"That bottle of pills we found in Cheeta's office? They're to delay contractions. Cheeta's been holding back. Without her pills, the baby is due practically any minute."

The Master of Sinanju's anguished wail stopped pedestrian traffic in its tracks.

"*Aiieee!* Poor Cheeta. What will become of her?"

Noticing a prowling police cruiser through the terminal window, Remo said, "Right now, what will become of us is what worries me the most. Come on, we gotta find a rental car."

24

In his Folcroft office, Harold W. Smith called up the newswire services on his terminal.

There were sketchy reports of a massacre at the New York headquarters of the American Networking Conglomerate, but no confirmation of dead.

Logging off, Smith typed out a wire-service-style report that stated that ANC anchor Dieter Banning had been killed. He gave no other details.

With the deft clicking of keys, the report was simultaneously faxed to terminals at UPI, AP, a dozen major newspapers and news magazines, and the newsrooms of ANC, BCN, MBC, KNNN, and Vox.

Within seconds, pedestrians were reading it off the ticker at One Times Square.

At MBC, Tim Macaw ripped the fax out of his office machine and called his agent.

"They've lost Banning over at ANC," he said in a breathless husky whisper. "See if you can get me a sitdown with their news director."

Then he hung up, ran the fax through the office shredder and resumed touching up his boyish features with Gay Whisper pancake makeup.

The news director came bustling up with a sheet of copy.

"They're done editing your lead for the 6:30 feed," he said.

"Oh, good. Any problems?"

"Yeah, the woman-of-color editor said you can't say black. You gotta say Afro-American."

"That's ridiculous. It's a blackout. We can't call it an Afro-American-out. It makes no sense."

"Come up with a better word then. If we don't humor her, she's bound to go on another damn hunger strike."

"How about whiteout?" Macaw asked.

"But it's not white. We're not putting out snow. Besides, you know how she is about the word white. Last week, she complained when we used the word whitewash. Went into that whole Why-is-white-always-good-and-black-always-bad tirade of hers."

"Right, right. How does 'broadcast interruption' sound?"

"Already thought of that. The woman's editor says broad is N.G. Sounds sexist."

"Oh, that's right. She brought that up at the last hunkcasters conference." Macaw sucked on a tooth. "Can I call it a transmission failure?"

"The brass won't like that. MBC failing? Makes us look bad. Try technical difficulties."

"Won't the technical union have fits?"

"Damn. Good catch, Tim. Work on it. We've still got four hours until our signal's restored."

At the end of another hour, Tim Macaw thought he had two viable options: Signal-challenged transmission or De-emptive nontelecast.

At BCN, Don Cooder received the fax at his office desk. He had a Caller ID unit on his faxphone and he stabbed the button to see who had sent him a blind fax reporting the death of ANC anchor, Dieter Banning.

The digital readout read: 000-000-0000.

Cooder pressed it again and got the same string of ciphers.

"What kind of phone number is that?" he muttered.

Then he picked up his desk phone and stabbed out a number.

"Frank, I want a gut check on a fax that just came in . . ."

Harold Smith was listening to the President of the United States with one ear and the TV on his desk with the other.

It was not difficult to do. The TV was just hissing. The President was speaking in brisk sentences.

"The FCC are working hard on this thing, Smith. But they claim I'm asking the impossible. You can't trace a signal that isn't there."

"But it is, Mr. President."

"What is the source of this information?"

Thinking of the nameless repairman, Smith said, "That's classified."

The President cleared his throat unhappily.

Then Harold Smith groaned.

"What is it?" the President demanded.

"BCN is back on."

"But the seven hours aren't yet up."

Smith glanced at his watch. The seven hours were far from up. "Mr. President, check with your FCC commissioner. Find out if they were successful."

"I'll be back with you shortly."

Harold Smith hung up and turned up the TV volume.

The screen was full of snow. The snow had come on after a sonorous voice had intoned eleven simple words:

"We now return control of your television set. Until next time . . ."

Smith roved the channels. They were all full of snow, except the all-cable stations.

"What has caused Captain Audion to cease broadcasting?" he muttered aloud.

The red telephone rang once. Smith caught it.

"I'm sorry, Smith. They were still working on it when the signal stopped."

"They confirmed there was a signal?"

"A powerful one."

"Unfortunate," said Smith.

"There is one thing to report, however," the President added. "One leg of the triangle was plotted."

Smith perked up. "Yes?"

"The signal seemed to be coming out of Canada. Somewhere along North Latitude 62."

Smith pulled up a chart on his terminal.

"The high north," he reported. "Underpopulated terrain, all of it. A lot to search even if the Canadian Federal government were being cooperative."

"I've been ducking calls from the Canadian Prime Minister all day. He thinks this is some U.S. Early Warning Broadcast System test gone haywire."

"The Canadian prime minister is your problem, Mr. President. If the transmitter can be located, my people can destroy it. Until then, we can only await this madman's next move."

"The FCC are on standby."

"You might call the prime minister and give him the facts. It may be that the CRTC picked up something."

"CRTC?"

"The Canadian Radio-Televisions and Telecommunications Commission," Smith explained. "Their FCC."

"Oh. Will do."

Smith hung up. His sharp mind went back to the immediate question. Captain Audion had deliberately ceased broadcasting black. Why?

On his screen, Smith typed out possibilities.

POWER OUTAGE?

Good, he thought. Checking for power outages in Canada might narrow the locus point.

TO CONFUSE ISSUE?

Unlikely. Smith realized. Terrorists do not fold their hands before public deadlines.

FEAR?

Of what? Smith thought. It was too farfetched. Then it struck him.

KNOWLEDGE THAT TRIANGULATION HAD BEGUN?

"Possible," Smith muttered. "Just possible." He had two good leads now. He attacked the first and within twenty minutes had determined there had been no power outages in the vast Canadian landmass.

That left the other theory. Where did it go? A leak in the FCC? Or was Captain Audion himself FCC? Enormous technical knowledge and resources would be required to blanket the U.S. and its neighbors with a masking TV signal.

Or was it possible that the Canadians were indeed responsible for this outrage? Smith mused. It was looking more and more likely.

As Harold Smith mulled these thoughts over in his head, he noticed MBC anchor Tim Macaw on his TV. He turned up the sound.

". . . *At this hour, no one can explain the reasons for this unprecedented five-hour nonwhite transmission-impaired noncommercial interruption.*"

"The man is making no sense," snapped Smith, changing the channel.

Don Cooder was on BCN, his voice cracking with emotion.

"*Unconfirmed reports have it that ANC anchor Dieter Banning—a personal friend of mine despite our friendly rivalry for ratings—lies dead tonight, a victim of the faceless, voiceless, thoughtless unknown who calls himself Captain Audion. We here at BCN salute our fallen comrade in arms and say to this cowardly terrorist, the glassy eye of BCN is searching for you. Speaking for the management here, we will never accede to your ransom demand of our beloved Cheeta Ching. And in memory of Cheeta—not that we don't expect her to be returned safely to us—in lieu of our usual closing credits, we will run a retrospective of Cheeta's most recent work. Until our regular newscast tonight, this is Don Cooder, saying 'Courage.'*"

A commercial for a home-use pregnancy test kit narrated by Cheeta Ching came on, followed by another for woman's aspirin and a third in which Cheeta extolled the virtues of an intimate moisturizing product.

Only when the BCN copyright notice came on did Harold Smith realize the parade of commercials constituted the Cheeta Ching retrospective.

Face reddening, Smith switched channels. It was scandalous what went out over the air these days.

25

Cheeta Ching watched the parade of her commercials that followed Don Cooder's live broadcast in a room that was only slightly larger than the cot to which she had been handcuffed.

The room was lit by a 25-watt bulb on a frayed drop cord. The TV was a tiny portable set and no amount of adjusting could balance out the contrast. Either the tube was going or the power was dimming.

"You jealous bastard!" she shrieked at the screen.

Then she fell back on the bed and let out a shriek of another kind.

The Braxton-Hicks contractions were more closely spaced now.

A rude wooden door rattled, and a man shoved in.

"Y'all right?" a muffled voice asked worriedly.

"I have hot flashes, cold flashes, and heartburn I can feel clear up to my uvula," Cheeta spat. "I'm constipated, my ankles are swollen by preclampsia, and my contractions are making my tonsils pucker, so you'd better let me go, buster!"

"No chance."

Cheeta Ching sat up like the Bride of Frankenstein with a bowling ball lodged in her stomach. Her hair and eyes were wild.

The man in the doorway was dressed in a TV-screen-blue bodysuit with an silvery anchor stitched into a crest on his chest. Where his head should be was a large television set, topped by a pair of rabbit-ears antennae bent by contact with too-low ceilings. The screen was black and in the upper right-hand corner the words NO SIGNAL gleamed whitely.

"Who are you supposed to be?" Cheeta spat.

"Captain Audion."

"Captain Audacious, you mean." Cheeta fell back onto the pillow. "Uhhhrrr."

"Should Ah boil some watah, or somethin'?"

"They only do that in movies, you idiot! Get me a birthing chair!"

The light flickered momentarily and went out. When it returned, the wan glow was dimmer than before.

"Sorry," said the man with the TV-set head. "Power problem. Gotta go."

The door slammed, and as Cheeta Ching writhed on her cot, the mattress soaking up her cold sweat, her own voice was ringing surreally in her ears.

"Vagi-rinse. For the modern on-the-go woman who doesn't have time for yeast infections . . ."

"It wasn't supposed to happen like this!" she wailed.

26

Folcroft Sanitarium was all but dark when Remo sent his rented car through the open wrought-iron gates.

In the passenger seat, the Master of Sinanju sat in grim silence, his face stone, his hazel eyes cold agates that seemed hot around the edges.

Remo knew that look. Chiun was seething. Only the complete lack of a solid lead had enabled Remo to talk him into leaving New York.

"Smitty will know what to do," Remo said as he pulled into a visitor's parking slot and turned off the ignition. They got out.

"It will be too late," Chiun intoned, his voice sere.

"Look, I'm sorry about Cheeta."

"You are not," Chiun snapped. "You are jealous of Cheeta, and of the son whose undiluted Koreanness threatens you."

They were walking through the hospital green corridors now. The security guard had passed them upon Remo's flashing an AMA inspector's card. Although they often visited Folcroft, the guard did not recognize them because Smith often rotated personnel.

"I don't feel threatened by a baby," Remo snapped back. "It's just that having Cheeta and the kid move in with us would be a mistake. Big time."

"Now, it may not even be," Chiun intoned in a dead hollow voice. It suddenly rose to a bitter keen. "O where is Cheeta now? What anguish frets her perfect features? What thoughts can she be thinking, alone, abandoned, deprived of the wise counsel of the one who brought her to fruition?"

"Oh, brother," Remo said as they stepped off the elevator and onto the second floor.

"Who will cut the cord!" Chiun shrieked to the ceiling.

Harold Smith poked his gray head out of his half-open office, his face drained of color.

"What was that sound?" he gasped.

"Chiun was just wondering who will cut Cheeta's cord," Remo said dryly.

"Some witless white, no doubt," Chiun muttered darkly. Then, his voice calmer, he said, "Hail, Emperor Smith."

Distaste showed on Harold Smith's lemony face. "I wish you would not call me that, Master Chiun. I am not an emperor."

"Only your lack of ambition stands between you and the Eagle Throne," Chiun whispered. "Speak the word, and this mindless charade called the right to vote will be yours to abolish by royal decree."

Harold Smith returned to his desk and his computer.

"Any progress?" Remo asked, closing the door after him.

Smith shook his gray head. "The jamming signal went down before it could be traced. I am trying to ascertain why. So far, I have discounted a power outage at the transmission site, and other obvious causes."

Remo and Chiun took positions behind Smith and looked over his shoulder at the computer screen.

Smith pressed a key, bringing up a wire frame map of Canada. "The FCC was able to plot out the latitude of the pirate signal."

"So I was right," said Remo. "It *was* in Canada."

"Foreign enemies are usually the most dangerous," Chiun said thinly. "No doubt they covet your northernmost provinces, Smith."

"Canada is one of our closest allies," Smith pointed out, "and we share with them the longest undefended border in human history."

"You have never been at war with these people?"

"Not since the War of 1812," Smith said, pressing another key. A red line tracked across the map of Canada. When it completed itself, Smith added, "The transmitter is situated somewhere on that line."

"Can't we find it by air?" asked Remo.

"The line runs from the Canadian Northwest to the Canadian Shield. It's desolate country. Like looking for a needle in a haystack. Even if the Canadians would agree to U.S. overflights."

"They won't, huh?"

"They are currently blaming us for this transmission problem."

Remo frowned. "Satellite recon?"

"It will take time to reposition a KH-12 for this task. Normally, we do not spy on Canada."

Chiun lifted his voice. "Cheeta! Why are we not looking for Cheeta?"

"One will lead to another," said Smith.

"These evil Canadians are responsible for this outrage," Chiun said sharply, raising a shaking fist. "No doubt to avenge their inglorious defeat in 1812. It is our duty as loyal Americans to seize their ruler and hold him for ransom."

"Loyal Americans?" Smith said blankly.

"Let me guess," Remo added. "The ransom is Cheeta."

"Of course," said Chiun, his voice and face bland. "They will surrender her with great ceremony, as befits the high station of the hostages." The Master of Sinanju eyed Harold Smith. "I will be pleased to act as mediator, Emperor Smith. Perhaps certain untraceable poisons can be introduced into the Canadian ruler's food during the exchange banquet as a subtle hint that this outrage must be never repeated."

"No," Smith said flatly.

Chiun's sparse eyebrows lifted. "No?"

"Absolutely not. We do not know that the Canadians are responsible."

"The proof is in this telecast device," said Chiun, pointing to Smith's TV.

They looked. The *BCN Evening News with Don Cooder* was on. The sound was off. No one bothered to remedy that situation.

"Explain please," said Smith.

"It is known that the evil transmitter lies hidden in the wicked Kingdom of Canada."

"Canada is a democracy, but yes."

"You have told me that one of the abductors was a known Scot?"

"Yes. And Dieter Banning is a Canadian of Scottish ancestry," Smith corrected.

"A spy in your land," sniffed Chiun. "Whom I vanquished."

"That was unfortunate."

"Was it? Did the evil blackness not cease with his death?"

Smith blinked. He switched to ANC. Ned Doppler was reading copy, red-eyed and obviously close to tears. The screen was edged in black, no doubt the graphic department's idea of a tribute to the late Dieter Banning.

Smith made a thoughtful face. "That's right. It did. But why?"

"The answer is clear," announced Chiun. "The evil mastermind dead, his minions now cower, dreading your regal justice."

Smith shook his head. "Unlikely. Even if Banning was involved in this, his death would not result in . . ." Smith's voice trailed off.

"What is it?" Remo asked.

"I faxed news of Banning's death to every news organization, print and television. My aim was to elicit some response from Captain Audion."

"But instead Audion shut everything down," Remo muttered.

"I had been pursuing the theory that Audion was aware of our attempts to track down his signal, and cut transmission to avoid discovery," Smith said slowly. "Perhaps that was not the situation at all. Perhaps . . ."

Smith logged off his Canadian file and brought up a blank screen.

"We have two main suspects here," Smith said, "Jed Burner, president of KNNN and Dieter Banning, ANC's nightly anchor."

"Why are they called 'anchors'?" Chiun asked suddenly.

"Why do they always say 'nightly'?" wondered Remo.

"Not now," Smith said as he typed the names on the screen.

"Don't forget Haiphong Hannah," Remo inserted.

Nodding, Smith added Layne Fondue's name as well.

"According to your description of the events in Atlanta," Smith said absently, "Cheeta Ching was taken away by Burner, Fondue, and a disguised man wearing—"

"Don't say it," Remo said urgently.

"—a kilt."

"What is this? What is this?" Chiun squeaked, his voice shaking as his eyes went from Remo to Smith and Remo again. They stayed on Remo, cold and steely.

"I can explain," Smitty said hastily.

"It is not you who must explain your words, but Remo."

Remo swallowed.

"I tried to tell you back at the house," he said in a low voice.

Chiun's eyes narrowed to steely gleams. "Tell me *now*."

"Cheeta beat me to KNNN. I guess she was following the same lead Smith fed me. I got there just as they were bundling her into Burner's chopper."

"And you did not stop them?" Chiun said.

"The guy in the kilt had his gun on Cheeta the whole time."

"That would not have stopped a true Master of Sinanju, whose feet are swift as the snow leopard and whose hands are as the lightning whose thunder is not heard until the blow had been struck."

"He was holding the muzzle to Cheeta's stomach," Remo said.

Chiun's facial hair shuddered. His eyes grew heavy of lid, like a serpent. Remo felt the cold sweat return to his hands. He returned Chiun's unflinching gaze with an open unthreatening stare of his own.

"You did the correct thing," said Chiun in a remote voice, but turned his back on Remo. "But only because you have been trained by the best."

Remo let out a sigh of relief and wiped the back of his hand across his brow, leaving it more sweaty than before.

"Not that you are forgiven for not arriving early," he added coldly.

"Which I wouldn't have been if I hadn't wasted time trying to get you to come along," Remo shot back.

Chiun said nothing. Smith said, "Please describe the scene in Atlanta as you recall it."

Remo furrowed his brow. "I got past the guards, heard that Cheeta had beaten me to Burner and heard shooting. By the time I got to the roof, they were all hustling Cheeta into the chopper."

"They were all armed?"

"Only Banning. Burner and Haiphong Hannah were getting into the chopper ahead of them."

"You are certain it was Banning?"

"He wearing sunglasses and a big hat," Remo said. "The only thing I was sure of was his kilt."

"What color was it?"

"Green plaid in Atlanta. Brown plaid in New York."

"They are called tartans, not plaids," Chiun corrected.

Smith consulted a computer file. "Clan tartans do not change color," he said, frowning. "It is possible the abductor was not Banning."

"So why'd Captain Audion shut down when he heard Banning was dead?" Remo asked.

"Perhaps because he wanted to foster the impression that Banning was the culprit, and that this was a Canadian operation."

"Does that mean Burner and Haiphong Hannah are the real bad guys?"

"It is a reasonable working theory," Smith allowed.

"Okay, let's find them."

"All Federal resources are bent toward that purpose. But so far there was been no sign of them, or Burner's helicopter."

"We're at a dead end then?"

At the word dead, the Master of Sinanju sipped in a shocked breath. "Cheeta is at the mercy of Canadians and there is no helping her," he wailed, throwing back his head and placing a clenched fist to his amber forehead.

Remo was looking at Smith's TV set. "Hey, when did you spring for cable?" he asked, indicating the cable box.

"Today. With broadcast television out of commission, it was absolutely necessary. I must stay on top of events in every way I can."

"Don't sound so miserable. Lots of good stuff is on cable these days—if you like stale thirty-year-old sitcoms. Wait a minute, check this out."

Smith looked up. Turning up the sound, Remo pointed to the Quantel graphic floating to one side of Don Cooder's head.

". . . minutes ago received an extraordinary fax signed 'Captain Audacious'—I mean 'Audion.' " Cooder flashed his anemic smile. "A little slip of the tongue which is not meant to cast aspersions on our colleagues over at KNNN," he added with a nervous laugh. "This fax promises that two days from now, the day May sweeps are set to begin, broadcast television will be shut down for a seven day period. Unless each network and cable service pays fifty—that's fifty—million—million with an M—dollars into a numbered Swiss bank account."

"The fiends!" Chiun shrieked. "Was nothing said about Cheeta? Oh, the heartrending suspense!"

"Here with me now for a reaction to this outrageous demand is BCN news director Loone—"

Smith turned down the sound.

"Don't you want to hear what they're saying?" Remo asked.

"I would rather trace that fax," Smith said flatly.

Smith's fingers worked like pale gray spiders along the keyboard. The intensity of his expression brought the Master of Sinanju to his side.

Smith brought up the BCN AT&T records. He froze the last hour's worth of incoming calls and put them in a window up in the upper right-hand corner of the screen. Then he accessed the MBC list. This went into the upper left-hand corner. The ANC file completed the screen.

Smith initiated a sort and analyze program.

Only two numbers came up in common. Smith frowned. He accessed the Vox phone records and this added a third common number. Then he went to KNNN. The same incoming number showed up. It was a New York area code. Smith isolated it and interrogated the file, murmuring, "This is odd. . . ."

"What is?" asked Remo.

"Of the major news organizations, only MBC does not show a recent incoming call in common with the other networks."

Then Smith saw why.

"My God. The Captain Audion fax *came* from MBC."

Remo started for the door. "We're right on it, Smitty."

"No, you are not," Smith said tightly.

"Huh?"

"Thanks to Master Chiun, you are both wanted by the New York City Police. We cannot put you back in the field so soon."

"So what do we—?"

"*I* am going to MBC," Smith said.

"What about us?"

"You will remain here, by the telephone, ready to move on my signal."

"Emperor Smith," Chiun said suddenly. "I have a brilliant suggestion."

"Yes?"

"Pay the ransom. It is only money and Cheeta is—"

"No."

Chiun turned pale and said no more.

Without another word, Harold Smith went over to a filing cabinet and took from it his briefcase. From the top drawer he extracted an old Army issue .45 automatic and a clip of bullets. He placed these in his suitcase and walked from the office.

After the sound of the elevator came to his ears, the Master of Sinanju turned to Remo and said, "This is all your fault."

"My fault! If you hadn't run ahead to ANC, our faces wouldn't be on every light pole and post office in Manhattan."

"If you had not been late, I would not have had to seek out Cheeta in dangerous places."

"And if you had come with me to Atlanta, we wouldn't have lost Cheeta in the first place!"

The Master of Sinanju froze, his face stung. Slowly, the tight pattern of his wrinkles disintegrated.

"Cheeta! Poor Cheeta! Who will soothe her troubled brow while I am forced to abide in a madhouse among white madmen?"

There was panic at Multinational Broadcast Company when Harold Smith presented himself, Secret Service photo ID in one hand, at the MBC security desk. Staff was pouring from the building as if from a fire.

"What is wrong!" Smith demanded.

"They're running haywire again!" the guard cried, pulling his sidearm free of its holster and pushing against the human tide.

Smith followed him into the building, through a rabbit warren of corridors and cubicles in which secretaries cowered under desks and technical staff hid behind heavy editing equipment.

The guard came to a heavy steel door marked SET. There was a bulbous red light over a sign that said ON AIR. He put his back to the door, holding his pistol high in a two-handed grip. He closed his eyes and took a steadying breath.

"What is wrong?" Smith repeated.

The guard didn't reply. He slammed into the door, whirled, and legs spread apart, began firing into the news set.

Eight closely spaced shots came out. Gun smoke wafted back in Smith's horrified face.

Then, the guard stumbled back and said in a shaken voice, "I can't stop them! Bullets don't even faze them."

Smith grabbed the man by his jacket front.

"Get hold of yourself," he said tightly. "And tell me what is wrong."

"It's those damned Nishitsu robot cameras!" the guard said.

Smith scowled. "Robot cameras?"

Smith released the man and eased the door open. He saw the familiar MBC news set. There was the anchor desk that Tim Macaw usually sat behind.

Only now Macaw was up on the desktop cowering on his knees as a trio of wheeled unmanned cameras were blindly bumping into sets, backdrops, and live monitors and into the desk itself, their bullet-pocked teleprompters frozen on the words, THIS IS THE MBC NIGHTIME NEWS.

Macaw saw Smith and wailed, "Get security before these things kill—I mean terminally inconvenience—me!"

As if responding to his voice, the number two camera shifted away from breaking the world map that made up one wing of the background and joined the number one camera in banging into and retreating from the news desk. Big chunks began appearing in the thick formica top, threatening Macaw's shrinking perch.

Smith's gaze raked the set. Through a long glass panel, he could seen control-room staff frantically throwing switches. One turned and threw his hands up in a helpless gesture of defeat.

Harold Smith strode in, stepped gingerly around the struggle over the news desk, and went up to the number three camera, which had jammed its square glass lens into the monitor array and was furiously spinning its smoking rubber wheels, trying to disengage.

Smith found a panel marked FUSE, popped it open, and unscrewed the fuse. The camera abruptly shut down.

Still clutching his briefcase, Smith went to the remaining cameras and, with more difficulty, pulled their fuses.

Tim Macaw climbed off the chewed-up island that had been his desk.

"Thanks," he said shakily. "I owe you. Wanna do a two-shot? We can take turns asking the questions."

"No," Smith said flatly. He flashed his Secret Service card. "I am investigating the Captain Audion threats. Earlier this evening, ANC and BCN both received a new demand fax from this terrorist."

"Yeah, I know."

"How do you know?"

"We got one, too."

"According to a search of your phone records, you did not. And it is impossible for you to have received one."

"What business of it of yours to look into network phone records?" Macaw demanded in a voice that shook with righteous indignation.

"You reporters do this sort of this all the time," Smith snapped.

"But we're a news organization. We're above the law."

"And I represent the lawful United States government," Smith said, his voice going testy.

"Oh. You'd better talk to legal about that."

"I am talking to *you*," Smith pointed out.

"Uh, I don't know if I can talk on the record."

"Who has access to the fax machines in this building?"

"Actually I have the only one."

"A network this large and there is only one fax?"

"We lost so much money sponsoring the '92 Olympics we had to sell off a lot of stuff," Macaw admitted. "Why do you think our cameras are robot-controlled? We saved three camera operator salaries."

Smith glanced around the destroyed news set, calculating that the run-amok cameras had cost the network the equivalent of thirty cameraman's salaries.

"Who discovered the fax?" he asked Macaw.

"You mean who found it?"

"Yes."

"Guess I can tell you that. It was our technical director, Nealon." Tim Macaw pointed to the control room. "He's the one with the helpless expression."

"Could you be more specific?" Smith asked.

"In the red shirt."

"Thank you."

Harold Smith worked his way through the confusing maze of satellite rooms surrounding the MBC news set. Security guards challenged him at one point and, impressed by his falsified photo ID, allowed him to roam at will.

Smith entered the control room without knocking.

"Nealon?"

The horse-faced man in the red shirt looked up from an exposed control board. "Yes?"

"Smith. Secret Service. I understand you were the first to discover the latest extortionary fax."

Nealon licked a pasty upper lip and said, "Yeah, I was walking past the thing and it was coming off. I knew it was important so I gave it to Macaw."

"Do you recall what time that was?"

"Yeah. 7:31. I know because the 7:00 feed had just wrapped."

"You are lying."

Nealon blinked. "Say that again?"

"AT&T phone records show that the demand faxes received by the other networks originated at an MBC faxphone. And there were no incoming calls received here at the time you state."

Nealon said nothing. His eyes lost their focus. They began to cross slightly.

Harold Smith had in his pre-CURE days been a CIA bureaucrat, a field operative, and before that an operative for the OSS. He understood how dangerous men behaved under stress. The telltale signs of a man reaching for a weapon were red flags to him.

Smith had his automatic out just as Nealon's fingers took hold of the butt of his own concealed weapon.

"Do not make a mistake you cannot survive," Smith warned without evident emotion.

Nealon looked down the barrel of Harold Smith's formidable handgun, looked up to Smith's gray patrician features and, balancing the threat of one against the resolve of the other, made a mistake that many men who had gone up against Harold W. Smith in his past had made.

He completed his draw, producing a flat .22 pistol.

Harold Smith squeezed his trigger once. The bullet smashed the tiny .22 against the man's stomach before he could fire—and continued on into his ribcage.

The bullet richocheted off three ribs and exited Nealon's throat. He took hold of himself with his free hand and the flood of blood told the man all he would ever know. Eyes rolling up in his head, he crumpled to the control room floor.

Harold Smith went to the body, his gray features grim.

"Now long has this man been working here?" he demanded, his voice sharp.

A technician croaked, "Six months. Came over from BCN after their last round of layoffs."

Smith became aware of a frantic pounding on the other side of the Plexiglas panel overlooking the newsroom.

It was Tim Macaw. He was banging with one fist and pointing at the dead technical director with the other. Someone flicked a switch, and Macaw's voice came through a intercom.

"—tures! Somebody get a camera in there. We can do a live cut-in. We'll *own* this story!"

"What is that man saying?" asked Smith.

"He wants this to go out live."

"Absolutely not," said Smith. "This is a Secret Service investigation. I hereby order this control room sealed pending the arrival of a federal coroner, and all camera equipment is excluded until further notice."

"Can you do that?" asked Tim Macaw from the other side of the glass.

"I *am* doing it," Smith said.

The news director was called in. He took one look at the dead man and asked, "Did anyone get the shooting on tape?"

When the answer came back no, he lost interest in the body and told Smith, "You can't suppress the news. This is news. I stand on the first amendment rights of the great peacock-proud MBC network news tradition."

"This is in your interest," Smith said.

"It is *never* in the public's interest to suppress news."

"My investigation shows conclusively that the MBC technical director is responsible for transmitting the latest extortionary faxes from the terrorist who calls himself Captain Audion."

The news director took a sudden step backward as if hit by a blow.

"MBC is as much a victim of this nut as anyone else," he protested.

"The fax Nealon said he had received was falsified. Nealon is an operative of Captain Audion."

"Did I tell you we got him from BCN?"

"Immaterial. He is an MBC employee. Now."

"Look, what'll it take to put this on ice for a while?"

"Your complete cooperation," said Smith.

"I'll have to check with legal."

"Do so."

A representative from the legal department who came down from an upper floor threw up over the body when it was shown to him. Covering his mouth with his handkerchief, he retreated to the relative safety of his office.

"I guess we're cooperating, then," the news director said thickly.

Harold Smith was allowed access to MBC employee records and staff and was shielded from all news and camera crews, although Tim Macaw had to be locked in the film storage library until he stopped crying.

After twenty minutes, Smith had determined that Dennis Nealon had come from BCN less than four months ago.

"What happened to the previous technical director?" Smith asked.

"Cooke? Hit and run victim."

"Was the driver ever caught?"

"No. It was one of those drunk driver things."

"I see."

"See what?"

"That Dennis Nealon was a plant. Tell me, isn't there a redundancy system for putting out your signal?"

"You mean the microwave feed?"

"Yes."

"Sure."

"Why did the microwave feed not go out to the affiliates?"

"We don't know. Nealon was in charge of—" The news director paled.

"Could the feed have been disabled by Nealon?"

"Sure, but why would he—"

"Why would he attempt to assassinate Tim Macaw with robot cameras?" Smith countered.

"That was a short circuit. We get those from time to time. Back when Cheeta Ching was working here, one of them up and goosed her. She turned around and slapped us with sexual harassment suit. We had to settle out of court."

"Dennis Nealon just attempted to kill Tim Macaw."

"Why would he do that?"

Harold Smith said nothing. His mouth was a compressed, bloodless line.

A shout went up from the control room.

"Hey, KNNN is broadcasting again!"

"Hoorray!" came the muffled voice of Tim Macaw. The MBC anchor was liberated as staffers crowded into the cramped control room to watch the KNNN feed.

Two anonymous KNNN anchors were interviewing one another, interspersed with footage of the downed satellite dishes.

"At this hour," one said, "there has been no word of KNNN owner Jediah Burner and wife, Layne Fondue, missing since the outrageous attack on KNNN's broadcast signal by persons unknown."

"They don't know any more that we do," Macaw said unhappily. Smith noticed that he was standing on the stomach of the dead technical director, Dennis Nealon, in an attempt to see above the heads of the others. Everytime Macaw shifted his feet, blood gurgled from the dead man's open throat and mouth.

While the MBC news staff was fixated on the
KNNN broadcast, Harold Smith slipped out a side
door and hailed a Checker cab.

Half an hour later, Smith was seated on the bed in
a corner room in an aging hotel near Madison Square
Garden, his briefcase open on the drumhead-tight
bedspread.

The TV was on and Smith was tuned to KNNN.
The sound was off. Smith was speaking directly to the
President of the United States, straining to be heard
over the rock music playing in the background.

"Mr. President, I have made some progress."

"Good. We can use it."

"I have discovered Captain Audion had placed a
mole in the MBC news organization."

"A mole?"

"An agent, whose job it was to facilitate the imple-
mentation of his blackouts. This man was responsible
for the latest demands."

"Was?"

"He is dead. I was unable to interrogate him. It is
unfortunate, but even in death he may be useful."

"How?"

"I would like the Secret Service to take possession
of the dead man's body and throw a blanket of secrecy
over the death."

"I kind of doubt that MBC will go along."

"They will go along, Mr. President. At least long
enough for me to implement my plan."

"If you can do that Smith, you're a better man than
I am. That MBC White House reporter all but jumped
down my throat during my last press conference."

"Thank you for your cooperation," said Smith,
hanging up before the President could ask questions
that Harold Smith had no time to answer.

Smith logged into his computer and typed up a blind
fax. It stated in bare-bones, journalistic sentences, that
Dennis Nealon, technical director for MBC's news division, had been taken into custody by the Secret Service
in connection with the Captain Audion threat.

Smith transmitted it to all news organizations except MBC.

Then, turning up the sound, he waited for something to happen.

KNNN broke the story first. ANC and Vox followed. Smith flipped between BCN and MBC to see who would jump on the story next. It turned out to be Don Cooder.

His stentorian voice broke in, saying, "This is a BCN Special Report. Good evening. Don Cooder reporting. The latest salvo in the struggle for the soul of broadcast television—if not human civilization—and the faceless monster calling himself Captain Audion has been fired. BCN has just learned that the Secret Service has taken into custody one Dennis Nealon, technical director for the Multinational Broadcasting Corporation, in connection with the Captain Audion terror transmission. Whether this implicates MBC management—and we want to be extra, extra careful about this—no one is saying. Officially. The word from MBC is a tight-lipped 'No Comment.' There are no further details available at this time. As always, we here at BCN stand ready to break in with new developments as they happen in this, our continuing effort to stand vigil over your right to know. Now, back to *Raven*."

For its part, MBC news issued a terse written "no comment" nonrelease unstatement and did not break programming.

Smith smiled thinly. Captain Audion, wherever he was, was certain to panic over the reports. It was reasonable to assume that his agents, whom Smith was now convinced were planted in every broadcast news organization in the country, would hesitate to implement the threatened broadcast blackout set for three days hence.

In the game of high-stakes chess he was playing against an unknown opponent, Harold Smith was confident that he had checked his opposition. Perhaps irrevocably.

28

Don Cooder's frozen smile stayed frozen until the tally light over the number one camera winked off. Then he reached under the desk for the producer phone and asked, "How was I?"

"Fantastic, Don," gushed his producer. "As always."

"So what's the latest?"

"Nothing, Don. Our sources have all dried up."

"Can't we get anything out of the Secret Service?"

"They're worse than the CIA. They refuse to talk off the record, never mind on."

"If we send a camera crew over to MBC, how do you think it would play?"

"That's a precedent I don't want to set, Don."

"What the hell's the matter with you? This is big. Maybe the biggest story of the last decade of the twentieth century. We can't just let to go rolling past like sagebrush ahead of a Texas twister."

"Upper management says hands off. They're hoping the Secret Secret rips the lid off this thing before the deadline."

Cooder lowered his voice. "They're not talking about paying, are they?"

"They're not talking. Period."

"Well, next time you talk to them, tell them they'll pay this blackmailer over Don Cooder's dead body."

"Don, you sure you want me to say that?"

"Why not? I'm a man of principal."

"You're also dead last in the news ratings. They're very sensitive about that."

"And if Don Cooder breaks this story, he'll be first in the ratings."

"Don, listen to me: Dieter Banning is dead. That automatically bumps you up a notch. Cheeta has been kidnapped. KNNN is reporting Jed Burner as missing, too. And MBC is hinting that there was an attempt on Tim Macaw tonight. You know what that means?"

"I'm number one?"

"No. It means Captain Audion is targeting news anchors by ratings and your low numbers are probably all that've saved you so far."

"Don Cooder is not afraid of high ratings. He will gladly lay down his life for a solid three share!"

"Fine, Don. But let's not encourage the brass. Don't forget they took a ten-million-dollar insurance policy out on you."

"Good thought. Let's keep this conversation between ourselves, shall we?"

"You got it, Don."

Don Cooder hung up, straightened his tie, and clumped on ostrich hide boots to his office, where he picked up the telephone and dialed a number.

"Frank, it's me again. I need a reality check on something . . ."

29

Harold W. Smith left his Rye, New York home the next morning and almost broke his neck tripping over an obstruction on his front step.

Smith recovered his balance, and for a moment his mind refused to accept what his gray eyes told him was on the step.

It was his subscription copy of his morning paper. And it was twice the size of the usual Sunday edition.

Except that this was Saturday. Or Smith thought it was. Was his mind going? Smith stooped to pick up the paper, and a telephone book block of color advertising inserts popped out.

He was forced to set his briefcase down and use both hands to lift the paper. Even then, slippery inserts kept sliding out.

Groaning, Smith carried the paper to his waiting station wagon. He had to make two trips. Finally, briefcase holding down the pile of paper, he drove toward Folcroft.

According to the masthead, today *was* Saturday. This simple confirmation lifted a great weight off Harold Smith's mind. If he had one fear as head of CURE, it was that his mental faculties might slip. He and he alone was responsible for the day-to-day running of CURE.

The day would one day come, Smith knew, when he could no longer shoulder those responsibilities. Retirement was out of the question. He knew too much about how America kept its political head above the waters of anarchy and social chaos. Smith expected to die at his desk, serving his country. Or in the field.

Upon his demise, CURE would either be shut down by the presiding President or a new head of CURE would be installed. That would not be Harold Smith's problem.

But if Smith's mind showed any signs of failing, it was his responsibility to take his own life with a poison pill he kept in the watch pocket of his gray vest when awake and in his gray pajama pocket when sleeping.

At a stoplight, Smith scanned the headlines.

The entire front page was devoted to stories about the five-hour TV broadcast blackout.

The lead story was long and told Smith little he hadn't known before.

It was the sidebars and companion stories that held his attention even after the light changed and the honking of horns brought his head up and his foot to the gas.

Buried in the human interest angles of video rentals surges, predictions of a mini-baby-boom nine months in the future, and a 3 percent increase in incidents of domestic violence, were scattered reports of riots in certain inner cities—Los Angeles, Chicago, Baltimore, Detroit, and Miami.

In most cities, the riots had begun as protests over the loss of television signal. Police were theorizing that these incidents were the result of a frustration with useless TV sets. Smith understood there was more to it than that.

Television had become a social sedative, without which certain elements, having too much time on its hands, got into more trouble than usual. But beyond that there was a deeper psychological warning. People had come to depend on TV as their chief source of news and main connection with the world beyond their neighborhoods. Deprived of the electronic window on the world, they quickly became uneasy, restless, disconnected, and worried. In these scattered events there was the shadow of a darker menace—widespread civil unrest, if not panic.

Smith had foreseen this even before the President. What he had not foreseen he saw as he scanned the inner pages, was the international ramifications of the problem. Mexico and Canada had also ceased broadcasting over the air. In those countries, cable stations continued carrying signals. That told Smith that Captain Audion was targeting U.S. networks primarily, and the spillover was due to the enormous scope of the broadcast null zone.

Still, the government of Mexico and Canada did not grasp this. They saw only that their airwaves were being disrupted. There was growing instability in Mexico. But the greater problem lay to the north. The Canadian government was threatening to close its borders with the U.S. if the interference did not cease.

As Smith turned into the gates of Folcroft Sanitarium, he promised himself that he would hunt down Captain Audion before the situation could escalate further.

But how to do that? Until Audion resumed jamming, there was no way to trace his transmitter. And Smith had seen to it that Audion would not dare to carry through on this threat.

Remo Williams greeted him when Harold Smith, bent almost double by the weight of his morning newspaper, stepped off the elevator.

"Here, let me get that," Remo said, taking the bundle of newsprint from Smith's thin arms. Seeing the size of the edition, Remo looked puzzled. "Is it Sunday already?"

"No, the blackout has panicked advertisers into taking out newspaper ads in anticipation of Captain Audion's next attack."

Remo's dark eyes lifted hopefully. "Does that mean they've doubled the size of the comics page, too?"

"I have not looked."

Smith unlocked his office, saying, "Where is Master Chiun?"

"In his room. I don't think he slept. I could hear him pacing all night. He's worried sick about Cheeta, and he's not talking to me."

Smith laid the newspaper and briefcase on his desk, took his seat, and touched the concealed stud that brought his CURE terminal humming out of its hidden desk reservoir. Smith logged on.

Remo turned on the tiny TV and checked every channel. All stations were broadcasting normally, and he settled on KNNN.

"When did KNNN come back on?" he asked Smith.

"Last night," said Smith, not looking up from his scan of the morning news digests. Smith preferred to get his news in digest form. Commentators only diluted the facts with their personal prejudices, he felt. Smith's computers continually scanned wire services feeds, gathering and summarizing events according to a program Smith had long ago set up.

Remo abruptly snapped his finger. "Hey! I just remembered something."

"Yes?"

"When we were at Cooder's office, Chiun impressed Cooder by quoting from the Bible."

"How so?"

"Chiun's name was in it."

"Really? Do you recall the citation?"

"No."

Smith pulled up his Bible concordance, input the name Chiun, then depressed the Search key.

"There is only one reference to a Biblical Chiun," he told Remo. "But in context, I do not understand it."

"Neither do I. Chiun gave me a cock-and-bull story about one of his ancestors. Chiun the First. But he wasn't exactly generous with details."

"According to this footnote," Smith added, "Chiun is a transliteration of the Hebrew Kaiwan, a name that goes back to the Babylonia word, Kayamanu, which has been identified with the planet Saturn, which in turn can be equated with certain obscure Babylonian deities, such as Ninurta and Rentham, whom the Hebrew people worshipped during their desert exile."

"That tells me a lot," Remo said dryly. "Anything else?"

"Kayamanu, or Saturn, was called 'the star of right and justice.' But we could be here days backtracking obscure references," said Smith, abruptly logging off his Bible database. "We must unmask Captain Audion before the deadline."

"I don't see what the big deal is."

"Read the front page," Smith suggested.

Remo did. People had been killed over satellite dishes. Stores reported massive dropoffs in sales—apparently because without commercials to motivate the average citizen, he held onto his money. The economy was taking a further beating. "All this because of no TV for a crummy five hours?" he complained.

"Try to imagine the consequences of the seven-day blackout—sports riots, domestic strife."

"Maybe the networks will pay up."

"They might. But it would not solve the basic problem."

The red telephone rang and Smith said, "Excuse me. That is the President."

"Give him a message for me."

"What?"

"Drown the Vice President."

Smith frowned and put the receiver to his ear.

"Yes, Mr. President?"

"I have some news. I just spoke with the prime minister of Canada. His CRTC was tracing the pirate transmitter until the signal went off the air."

"Did they get a fix?"

"Not exactly. The prime minister tells me he has the longitude line."

"And we have the latitude."

"I offered to exchange data, organize a joint assault operation on the transmitter, but he refused and demanded I surrender the latitude coordinates as a good faith gesture to demonstrate U.S. noninvolvement."

"You, of course, declined?"

"Damn straight. I wasn't about to let them swoop down on this transmitter, grab the bad guys and phoney up a scenario implicating a U.S. citizen or his government."

"You did right," said Smith, "We have to be prepared for the probability that U.S. citizens *are* behind this plot."

"I know," sighed the President. "And here is something else: I've spoken with the heads of the major networks. They say they can't afford a seven-day blackout. It would break them. They're losing millions in advertising money to newspapers and magazines already. You should see my *Washington Post* this morning. The Secret Service thought it was a bomb and detonated it."

"Capitulation to terrorism is always a mistake."

"I know. But I have no control over what the networks do. Civil unrest could explode if TV is blacked out again. And the economy is hurting. I had no idea how much spending was motivated by TV commercials."

"Can you convince the networks to give us twenty-four hours?"

"I can try. But they sound ready to wire the ransom into the numbered Swiss account today."

"Do your best, Mr. President," said Smith, hanging up. He looked to Remo.

"The networks are prepared to pay the ransom."

"Damn. I couldn't care less about the networks, but I can't stand the idea of this nut getting away with this crap. Once he's paid off, he can vanish and we'll never find him."

Smith was staring at the greenish field of commands on his terminal screen.

"There must be some clue," he said, "some lead. We know that the transmitter is in Northern Canada. But where?"

"Let's put our heads together."

Smith's prim mouth tightened. "How do you mean?"

"You work your computer . . ."

"Yes?"

"And I'll pull up a chair and watch KNNN."

"Why KNNN?"

Remo grinned. "Because they always break stuff first."

"It is worth a try," Smith said without enthusiasm.

Hours later, a bleary-eyed Harold Smith looked up from his screen and began polishing his glasses with a handkerchief.

"Anything?" asked Remo, looking away from the TV. He had the newspaper spread out over his end of the desk.

"The only anomaly I can find in scanning Canadian news feeds is a rash of car battery thefts in the area of upper Quebec called the Canadian Shield."

"Car battery thefts?"

"From parked cars and auto supply stores and gas stations."

"What would that have to do with a pirate transmitter?"

Smith frowned. "I do not know. . . ."

The red telephone rang. Smith lifted the receiver.

"The networks have just paid the ransom," the President said in a subdued voice. "I did what I could. They were looking at their economic survival."

"The trail may end here, Mr. President."

"But the crisis *is* over. Isn't it?"

"For this month. Perhaps this year. But Captain Audion has just earned 100 million dollars by extortion. The combined ad revenues of the big three networks exceed five billion dollars annually. What is to stop this madman from asking for one of those billions next time?"

"We can only hope he isn't that greedy."

"I would not count on such a likelihood, Mr. President," said Smith wearily. "Now if you will excuse me, I intend to continue my search for the transmitter."

Remo, having overheard every word, asked glumly, "Does that mean Cheeta's going to be released?"

"We should know before long," said Smith.

"Then our problems will *really* start," Remo muttered.

They went back to work.

Hours passed.

*   *   *

In his sparsely furnished room in the private wing of Folcroft Sanitarium, the Master of Sinanju sat before a television set, his face stone, his eyes fixed unwaveringly on the screen.

He was watching BCN, trusting that news of Cheeta, beloved Cheeta, the flower of Korean womanhood, would be given.

Never had he felt so helpless. Never had been forced to endure such tortures. First, fair Cheeta is kidnapped and then his emperor refused to allow a reasonable ransom to be paid. Were all whites mad? What was mere paper money against the life of a mother and child? No doubt this was a subtle example of the virulent anti-Koreanism that infected the white mind.

Now he was reduced to watching *Bowling for Bucks,* as if every fat white wheezing in victory or sobbing defeat was important. It was unendurable.

But there was nothing he could do. His emperor had forbidden him from taking action.

Then, abruptly, the screen went black and a sonorous voice said, *"There is nothing wrong with your television set . . ."*

Remo was reading *Calvin & Hobbes* when the KNNN anchor said, "On a lighter note, Canadian authorities are unable to explain the discovery on a remote mountaintop in Quebec of a religious statue of a kind normally seen perched on South American hillsides."

At the sound of the word "Quebec," both Remo and Harold Smith looked up from their reading.

A Quantel graphic materialized beside the anchor's serious face—and the screen turned to snow and static.

Remo changed the channel. And got blackness.

"There is nothing wrong with your television set . . ." a voice began saying.

"What's this crap?" Remo exploded.

"I do not understand," Smith muttered. "The ransom has been paid."

"Maybe the checks bounced."

"Wire transfers do not bounce," said Smith as Remo changed channels. Not every channel was blacked out. A number of cable stations was in service. The networks were down. As was Nickelodeon and MTV, and a smattering of others.

"Try KNNN again," Smith directed.

Remo obliged. The KNNN transmission was just snow.

"Think their dishes went down again?" Remo said.

"Coincident with the new blackout? Not likely."

Then KNNN came back on. With a technical difficulties graphic depicting a broken anchor. A voice-over said, "Please stand by while KNNN switches to its backup film library."

"Must mean that robot-controlled room I saw," Remo said.

The graphic went away. And filling the screen was a slab of unreflective basalt decorated by the words: NO SIGNAL.

"Impossible," snapped Smith. "A cable transmission cannot be masked like that."

Captain Audion began speaking. *"There is nothing wrong with your television set . . ."*

Remo switched channels. On the network feeds, Captain Audion was already deep into his recitation.

"It's not the same signal," Remo said.

"You are right," said Smith.

Just then, the office door burst in and the Master of Sinanju, eyes ablaze, leapt in.

"Emperor Smith! The faceless fiend has struck again! You must do something. We must ransom Cheeta before it is too late."

Smith picked up the red telephone and was soon speaking with the President.

"If we move quickly, we may be able to trace the signal," Smith said.

"So will the Canadians."

"My people can move on instant notice."

"The fiend will die with his very own anchor wrapped around his lying throat," Chiun shrieked.

"What was that?" asked the President.

"Later," said Smith. "Time is of the essence." He hung up.

Remo asked, "Anything we can do?"

Smith frowned at the black TV screen.

"There must be some reason Audion went back on his word so quickly. But what?"

"But that's good, isn't it?" said Remo. "He can be traced now, right?"

"Yes. But it will take hours for the tracking planes to . . ." Smith's bloodless lips thinned.

"What? What?" squeaked Chiun.

"Perhaps there is another way."

"Speak the words, O Emperor Smith, and your loyal assassins will wreak your holy vengeance on the Canadian pirates."

Remo stared at the Master of Sinanju. "Holy?"

Chiun glowered back.

Smith winced, "Please, I must think."

The Master of Sinanju came down off his toes and dropped his upflung arms. He squinted one eye thoughtfully at Harold Smith.

"Captain Audion had a reason for restoring the blackout, despite being paid," Smith was saying. "A reason that overrode the danger of his signal being traced."

"Not necessarily," said Chiun.

Smith looked up from his thoughts. "Excuse me?"

"Everyone knows that Canadians are notoriously irrational."

Smith's frowning mouth grew puzzled. "Why do you say that?"

"The fiend swore to eradicate all television for seven hours, but ceased after only five. This is not how one strikes fear into an enemy nation. Therefore, he is irrational."

"Sound like inescapable logic to me," Remo said dryly.

"Thank you," said Chiun.

Remo rolled his eyes.

Smith said, "I find it difficult to believe this is a

Canadian operation, even though all evidence points
to a Canadian transmission site."

"Do not forget the vile-tongued spy, Banning,"
Chiun added.

"I have not. But I wonder if Banning were not a
red herring?"

"He was a Scot. A white Scot. They are a cunning
race—cunning and stingy. Worse than Canadians."

"Did we ever work for the Scots?" asked Remo.

"Who do you mean we, white thing?"

"Jed Burner is not Canadian," said Smith slowly.
"Neither is Layne Fondue. Yet the finger of suspicion
has pointed to them, to Dieter Banning, and via
planted fax transmissions, to KNNN and MBC both."

"You saying that Audion been throwing suspicion
on everyone he could?"

"It is obvious. And his targets might point to the
identity of the terrorist."

"Who does that leave . . ."

Remo's voice trailed off. A light jumped into his
deep-set eyes.

Before his mouth could open, a voice jumped from
the silent TV screen that was still broadcasting black.

"This is a special report. Captain Audion speaking."

Remo and Chiun hurried to the set.

The screen head was still black. Then, the blackness
shrank and retreated, until the picture showed a television set perched on the broad shoulders of a figure
wearing blue pinstripes.

The TV screen was blacked out except for the NO
SIGNAL.

Then a hand reached up into the frame and turned
a knob.

The TV screen within the TV screen winked on,
showing a rugged face that was known to millions of
television watchers across the nation.

"Hear ye! Hear ye! Cheeta Ching, broadcast ancho-
rette, is about to have a cow. That's right, folks, her
water has broken. Stay tuned."

"Aiieee! The unmitigated fiend! He has shown his
face and now must die!"

30

Don Cooder had locked his office door against the constant demands of his staff. They were forever pestering him at all hours, the shameless syncophants. So he had established a locked-office period, usually around three in the afternoon. He called it Sanity Maintenance Time.

His staff had other names: Nap Time, Fetal Position Hour, and Don's Thumb-sucking Break.

The truth was that it was at three in the afternoon that Don Cooder touched up the gray in his hair. If the aphorism that TV news is about hair, not journalism, is true, Don Cooder had a take on it no one else in television ever dreamed of. Where other anchors used Grecian Formula to take the gray out of their hair, he had a special formula to salt his virile black locks with mature gray.

Another anchor might have been proud of his luxurious helmet of jet-black hair. Not Don Cooder. He had inherited the Chair from the most distinguished anchor of the last two decades, Dalt Conklin, the affable and avuncular Uncle Dalt whose shoes Don Cooder had been trying to fill for ten years now.

From day one, the critics had been merciless in their unfair comparisons. The public changed channels in droves. His own staff had a pool betting on the week he would be let go.

After only two years in the Chair, Cooder had come to a ego-deflating realization. He would never, ever,

no matter how low he pitched his voice or faked a
catch in his voice, fill Dalt Conklin's shoes.

So he decided to copy his hair instead. The gray
was painted in slowly over the months until his hemor-
rhaging ratings stabilized. Another year was spent in
perfecting the perfect salt-and-pepper mixture.

Cooder had created a calendar chart for each week
in the year. A photo of his black-to-gray hair ratio in
the Sunday slot and his Nielson and Arbitron ratings
scribbled over Saturday.

When he found the perfect balance, it was just a
matter of holding it stable.

And so now, in his eleventh year anchoring the
BCN Evening News, Don Cooder sat at his desk, an
illuminated makeup mirror propped in front of him,
touching up his artfully placed gray streaks with a slen-
der brush.

A knock brought a scowl to his craggy face.

"Go way, I'm maintaining my sanity!"

"Turn on the TV. Turn on your TV." It was his
news director.

Cooder reached for the instant-on button of his desk
TV set and saw his own face staring back at him—
framed in a TV set framed in his TV screen.

"This is Captain Audion of the Video Rangers," a
voice, very much like his own, was saying. *"Greetings
Earthlings!"*

Don Cooder shot bolt upright in his chair.

"That's not me! That's not me! It's a frame! We've
got to get the word out."

"We can't," the BCN news director shouted
through the locked door. "We're in black; everyone
is in black."

"There's gotta be a way. My whole career, my credibility, my reputation for honesty and sincerity is
about to—"

The clatter of his bottle of hair color dropping to
the floor brought a question from the other side of
the door.

"You all right, Don?"

"Knocked over a Diet Coke in my excitement. Nothing to worry about."

"What are you going to do, Don?"

Don Cooder strode over to his office window, looking down Seventh Avenue toward Times Square.

"I know exactly what I'm going to do," he announced in a deep, manly voice as he yanked his office window open.

Hearing this, the news director screamed, "Don! Don't do it! Don't jump!"

"Too late," said Don Cooder, climbing out on the ledge.

The news director of the Broadcast Corporation of North America was frantic.

"Help me someone. Help me to break down this door."

"We can't. There's trouble at the front door."

"What kind of trouble?"

"Press. They're clamoring for an interview with Don Cooder."

"He's left the building!"

"Then they're going to want an interview with you."

"Somebody help with this door. I'm going out the window, too!"

But there was no budging Don Cooder's reinforced door.

The news director ducked into Cheeta Ching's office and waited for help. No one came. In fact, the shouting from the front of the building died down. After a few minutes, someone came for him.

"It's okay," he was told by his floor manager. "They left."

"They did?"

"Yeah. They found Cooder."

"Is he . . . dead?"

"No, he's broadcasting from One Times Square."

"How can he do that? We're off the air."

"Remember at the last Democratic National Convention when we opened with a talking head shot of

Cooder, then pulled back the camera to show that
it was a simulcast with the screen up on One Times
Square?"

"Yeah, that was a spectacular shot. Cooder was his
own Quantel graphic."

"Well, it must have given him the idea. Because
he's in that building doing a remote bulletin."

"The man is a genius. A fucking genius. And worth
every cent we overpay him." The news director
blinked. "He *is* denying the story, isn't he?"

"I guess."

They ran out into Times Square.

Traffic had stopped. Newspaper reporters were
pushing through the gathering crowd as the giant face
of Don Cooder, the bags under his eyes as fat as prize
Holsteins and an inexplicable splash of gray in his
well-combed hair, stared down at them as if from
some electronic Mount Olympus.

"I categorically deny being Captain Audion. I am
not Captain Audion. This is a frame, a cheap frame.
A conspiracy by my many enemies in the media.
They're trying to kill me. But Don Cooder can't be
killed. As long as there is news to report, Don Cooder
will live on, unbowed, unbloodied, immortal—"

"He's losing it," the floor manager said.

"Yeah, he's no good without a script. Never was."

"Good thing this isn't going out nationwide."

"Yeah. Wait a minute." The news director shouted
back toward the studio. "Hey, somebody get a camera
on this for rebroadcast later."

"Are you crazy? He's falling apart up there!"

"Yeah," said the news director, "but it's great
television."

31

Harold W. Smith stared at the bizarre image on his tiny television screen and said, "That is not Don Cooder."

"Are you blind!" shrieked the Master of Sinanju. "It is the fiend himself."

"A minute ago you were blaming Dieter Banning and the Canadians," Remo pointed out.

Chiun's voice grew frosty. "Who is to say this man is not in league with the wicked Canadians? Or a secret Canadian himself."

"Not you, that's for sure," Remo retorted.

"His mouth looks Canadian—thin and merciless," said Chiun, padding up to Harold Smith and facing him across his pathologically neat desk. "Emperor Smith, the villain has revealed himself for all to see. His motives are clear."

"They are?" Smith said.

"Yes, yes. Are you blind too? He is jealous of Cheeta. You yourself heard how he threatened her on television."

Remo caught Smith's eyes. "He has a point there."

"Perhaps. But that is not Don Cooder," Smith said flatly. "It is an animated graphic."

Remo took a closer look at the TV screen. His eyes were so heightened by the discipline of Sinanju that he had to focus hard, otherwise all he saw were the changing pixels, like colorful amoebae living out some superfast life cycle. "Yeah, you're right," he said. "Does that mean Audion is trying to frame Cooder?"

"It fits Audion's pattern to date. He has thrown suspicion on virtually every network and its news division."

"But why the news divisions every time? I mean, if he's attacking the networks, why go after the news? Aren't they the least profitable?"

"But the most visible for Audion's purposes. Each anchor functions as a kind of living symbol of his network. No, this is sound strategy."

"So we're nowhere?"

"No," said Smith. "We have an abundance of facts. There must be a way—"

Chiun made clutching motions with his long-nailed fingers and said, "Emperor Smith, allow Remo and I to descend upon every television station and I promise you we will wring the truth out of the secret oppressors."

"Like you wrung the truth out of Dieter Banning?" asked Remo.

"Pah! He is but a tool of baser fiends."

Smith raised his hands. "Please, Master Chiun. Reckless violence will not smoke out Captain Audion. We must attack this with logic."

Chiun made a face. "I am a Korean, not a Greek. I do not practice logic."

Harold Smith was staring at the TV screen on which the talking TV set with Don Cooder's face continually gestured and spoke. The sound was off.

"There is a reason for this," Smith mused. "Just as there was a reason Audion prematurely terminated his earlier transmission."

"Sure," said Remo. "Because he wanted everyone to think he was Banning."

"Possible. But he is not Banning. Yet he has to be someone in the television industry, if not currently, then at one point in the past."

"How do you figure that?"

"It takes enormous technical skill to engineer a broadcast and cable interruption of this magnitude," Smith explained. "As well as sophisticated equipment and deep financial reserves."

Chiun spoke up. "Those anchors are paid obscene amounts of money. Remo has said so."

Remo snapped his fingers suddenly. "Hey! Maybe Cheeta's behind this!"

The Master of Sinanju turned a slow crimson and stared at his pupil coldly.

"Then again," Remo amended, "maybe not."

"This person must have the contacts to plant his agents in many networks and TV stations for sabotage purposes," Smith continued as if speaking to himself. "He is powerful. He is wealthy. And he has a compelling reason for attacking television."

"Comes back to Captain Audacious, Jed Burner," said Remo. "Both are captains and Burner's company symbol is an anchor. It all fits."

"Emperor," Chiun said breathfully, "I will go to Atlanta this time, to atone for my previous mistake. I will tear through the evil tower of Jed and topple it into ruins, as the walls of Jericho fell. This will end the darkness that has blighted your kingdom, O Smith."

Frowning, Smith changed the channel to KNNN. The bizarre computer image of Don Cooder was playing there too, but in what seemed to be a three-minute delay.

"This is a cable signal," he said, "microwaved from the KNNN tower to a satellite and downlinked to an earth station. It should not—"

Then, Harold Smith's TV screen gave out a hissy pop and the screen went dead.

"What was that?" he gasped.

"Looks like the tube blew, Smitty."

Reaching for the selector knob, Smith changed channels by hand. The blackout signal returned.

"Guess it's fine," muttered Remo.

Smith switched back to cable. He got snow.

"Then why am I not receiving the cable signal?" he mused.

Lips thinning, Smith put in a call to his local cable company. He spoke for several minutes, then hung up.

"The cable company has been knocked out of commission," he explained.

"How?"

"Captain Audion is very clever. He can mask broadcast signals for as long as he continues broadcasting, but his plants in the cable-only stations can get away with covering up their sabotage of the outgoing signals only so long. Audion has figured out a way to knock out cable companies, one by one."

"Yeah? How?"

"Because of the proliferation of nonauthorized cable boxes, the companies had developed the technology to remotely disable the boxes when they are illegal or illegally tampered with to obtain an unauthorized channel. It is called a magic bullet—a fanciful name for an electronic pulse sent through the cable itself and designed to short out the box. In practice, an illegal box owner would be forced to call the company for a service call, thus exposing himself to the company."

"Yeah, I read about those. But your box isn't illegal—is it?"

Smith looked pained. "Of course not. Someone at the local cable company has sent a magic bullet that has disabled every box, legal or not, in the system. The company tells me their phones are ringing off the hook."

"Great. Audion keeps raising the ante. But why? He's got his money. Is he asking for more?"

Smith turned up the sound.

Captain Audion was saying, *"What's the frequency, Kenneth? People say that to me a lot. They want to know what it means. The truth is it doesn't mean anything. It's just a lot of bull's wool. Like Cheeta Ching's hair."*

Smith lowered the sound. "It does not sound as if he is doing anything more than dominating the airwaves for his own amusement."

"Air hog," sniffed Chiun. "Why does he not let Cheeta speak?"

"Why he is back on the air is what concerns us," Smith said. "It makes no sense. Unless . . ."

"Yeah?"

"Unless there is something he did not wish to go out over the air. Remo, do you recall what you were watching when KNNN went off the air?"

"Nothing. I was reading *Calvin and Hobbes*."

"Er, yes. I remember now. A report had just come on. Quebec was mentioned, was it not?"

"Yeah, I remember now."

"What did the report say?"

"Search me. I wasn't looking at the TV. When I looked up, I saw snow."

Smith smoothed his tie. "Snow . . . KNNN is not a broadcast station, yet it was knocked off the air. When it came back on, it was blacked out just like the others." He picked up the telephone with one hand and queried his computer with the other, stabbing out the phone number that appeared on the screen.

"Let me speak with your program director," he told the person who answered. "This is Smith, with the Secret Service."

Remo and Chiun crowded close to overhear.

"This is Melcher," a harried voice said. "We're a little busy down here, Smith. What can I do for you?"

"You went off the air at approximately 3:30."

"Three twenty-eight. I know because that's when my heart stopped, too. We couldn't get out a signal no matter what we did, so we switched to our backup tape library to run the most recent feed. The master monitor showed a No Signal. We can't figure it out. We got so desperate we tried airing commercials only, and got the same damn thing."

"You might enter your tape library, pull a tape at random and play it on a machine," Smith suggested.

"What good would that do?"

"Try it please."

Smith held the line. A minute later, the program director came back on. "The fucking thing—excuse my Cajun—is coming up No Signal on the tape deck.

It's prerecorded to go out black. And there are other tapes with that glory hound Cooder on it wearing a TV set for a helmet."

"Your tape library has been sabotaged," said Smith.

"I know that now."

"Who is in charge your prerecorded library?"

"Duncan. Why?"

"He may be the saboteur."

"Duncan? He's one of the best. We got him from BCN."

"Excuse me. Did you say BCN?"

"That's right. They laid him off and we snapped him right up. Good timing, too. A hit and run driver had just nailed the guy he replaced."

Smith, Remo and Chiun exchanged silent glances.

"One more question," said Smith. "Before you went off the air, you were about to air a taped segment."

"We call them pieces and yeah, we never got it out."

"What was the content of that piece?"

"It was a sayonara piece, you know, a feel-good thing. We always end broadcasts with something light. This one was about a religious statue that just up and appeared on a mountain up in Canada. No one can explain it."

"I see. Where did you get this information?"

"Where else? It came off the wire and we put our Montreal correspondent on it."

As Harold Smith had been listening, his thin fingers were picking apart the international section of his morning paper. He scanned the first page and turned to the second. When his eyes came to page three, they widened.

"Holy Christ!" Remo exploded. "I know what that is!"

"Who's that?" asked Melcher.

"Thank you for your time," Smith said and hung up.

Smith looked up from the paper. Remo and Chiun

were staring at the photo over the headline: MYSTERY STATUE APPEARS ON MOUNTAINTOP.

"That's St. Clare of Assisi," said Remo.

"Yes," echoed Chiun. "It is definitely St. Clare."

"Yes?" said Smith, face and voice equally blank.

"She is the patron saint of television," intoned Chiun. "Pope Pius XII placed that odious burden her frail shoulders in 1958, poor woman."

"How do you both know this?" Smith asked.

"Simple," said Remo. "Don Cooder had a statuette just like this on his desk."

They looked to the TV screen where the computer-generated image of Don Cooder with a television set for a head continued gesturing animatedly.

"So," Remo said. "Does this mean that Cooder is Captain Audion after all, or he isn't?"

32

Don Cooder refused to vacate the tiny television studio in One Times Square.

"Don Cooder is not leaving this studio," he shouted.

"Please, Don," begged Tim Macaw in a wheedling voice.

"Yeah, Don," added Ned Doppler. "You had your turn. Give us a shot."

"Never. As of right now, Don Cooder owns broadcast news. My audience may be small, but it's the only audience there is. When this is all cleared up, I'll go down in anchor history."

"You're already on the front pages of the newspaper," said Macaw. "Isn't that enough?"

"Liar! I did that interview only two hours ago. The paper won't come out until tomorrow."

"They put out an extra," Doppler explained.

Don Cooder's voice grew suspicious. "An extra what?"

"An extra afternoon edition. Just to cover breaking developments. You know, like a bulletin."

"Can newspapers do bulletins?"

"The *News* did," said Doppler.

"So did the *Times,*" added Macaw.

"Care to slip it under the door?" asked Cooder.

"Can't, Don. It's as thick as a telephone book."

"Now I know you're lying. Nice try. Newspapers are dying."

"Thanks to Captain Audion, they're coming back.

Even *USA Today* put out an extra. With today's news for a change."

"Slip the front page under the door."

"If we do," Macaw asked, "will you come out?"

"No."

"Then we're not slipping you anything," snapped Doppler.

"First man who slips me a readable front page will be interviewed on my next newscast."

Paper started cramming and bunching up under the door so fast it tore. Don Cooder pulled pieces free and began to assemble them on the studio floor like a jigsaw puzzle.

A headline read:

TV BLACKED OUT!
Is Captain Audion Don Cooder?

Another said:

NO NEWS FIT TO BROADCAST
Newsprint Makes a Comeback

"Let us in, Don."

But Don Cooder wasn't hearing the pleading of his colleagues. He was looking at a sidebar story that showed a photograph of St. Clare of Assisi, two hundred feet high, standing atop a mountain in Canada.

"I've changed my mind," he said suddenly. "You can both broadcast."

And he flung open the door.

Tim Macaw and Ned Doppler plowed in and tackled the anchor seat like opposing linebackers.

They were literally pulling it and their clothing apart in their frenzy to be the first to plant his posterior in the rickety bentwood chair, as Don Cooder, a feverish gleam in his eyes, slipped out the building bundled up in a belted trenchcoat, dark glasses, and Borsalino hat.

No one in the growing crowd surrounding the big

TV screen overlooking Times Square noticed him as he ducked into an idle cab.

"Kennedy Airport, driver," he bit out.

"Wanna wait another minute, pal? Don Cooder should be back on any second now."

"Don Cooder does not wait for Don Cooder. Drive on, driver."

33

At the BCN studio lobby, security had been tripled in the wake of the death of rival anchor Dieter Banning.

"We're looking for Don Cooder," Remo told the ring of guards who looked at him with hands on holstered revolver grips.

One shouted, "Look, isn't that Wing Wang Wo, the Korean Dragon!"

The Master of Sinanju saw the finger pointing at him and naturally looked over his shoulder.

There was no one there.

"What is this, Remo?" he demanded.

"A long story," Remo whispered. "Look, we admit it. That's who he is. And if you don't want to end up separated from your head, you'll tell us where to find Don Cooder."

"He's missing."

"I heard he was broadcasting," said Remo.

"Yeah. From Times Square. But he deserted his post."

"Damn."

At a payphone, Remo called Smith. "Cooder took a powder. No one knows where he went."

"One minute, Remo."

The clicking of computer keys came over the line.

"According to his telephone records, he has not used his home telephone today. Nor his office telephone." More keys clicked. Then:

"According to his credit cards records, Don Cooder took a five o'clock flight to Montreal, Canada, connecting with Fort Chimo in Northern Quebec."

"He's our man!"

"Do not jump to conclusions. Remember Dieter Banning."

"Here, you tell it to Chiun," said Remo, handing the phone to the Master of Sinanju.

"Master Chiun, I am ordering you to Canada," said Harold Smith.

"Speak their names and their heads will be yours by nightfall," Chiun cried.

"I do not want heads. I want answers. Kill no one unless provoked. Now put Remo back on."

"What's our next move, Smitty?"

"Remo. Go to MacGuire Air Force Base. An Air Mobility Command transport will be waiting for you. I am sending you to Quebec."

"What do you think we're going to find?"

"I do not know. But that statue is squarely on the parallel of latitude line and it is also in the area where there had been a rash of missing car batteries."

"How would car batteries fit into this?"

"That is only one of the answers I expect you to find. Good luck, Remo."

After Remo hung up, he faced the waiting Master of Sinanju.

"You have been telling fables about me, again," Chiun accused.

"Save it. We're off to Quebec. And there's a good chance we'll find out what happened to Cheeta when we get there."

The Master of Sinanju raised clenched fists and a voice like distilled grief to the open sky. "Cheeta! Do not despair, precious one. We are coming to succor you!"

Cheeta Ching was past despair. She was beyond agony. Being flayed by rusty razor blades would be infinitely preferable to the exquisite tortures that were wracking her sweat-soaked body.

She was in her sixteenth hour of labor. Her swollen, jittering belly felt like it was trying to launch into orbit using her splayed legs as launch rails.

If only the damned brat would come out.

"Come on, you little bastard!" she grunted between contractions. "Get out of here or I'll pull you out by your miserable scrotum!"

The door opened and the figure of Captain Audion pushed in. He was lugging a car battery which he added to a growing pile.

"Can I get y'all any little thang?" he asked, turning the blacked-out screen of his square head in Cheeta's direction.

"Yes," Cheeta said through clenched teeth. "A coat hanger."

"Say what?"

"I going to abort this useless little dink if it's the last thing I do!"

"Settle for a jackknife?"

Don Cooder was arrested by Royal Canadian Mounted Police constables the moment he opened his passport for the Montreal customs inspector.

"You can't do this to me. I'm Don Cooder. Premier anchor of our age."

"The charges will include extortion, interfering with the airwaves of a sovereign nation, espionage, and air piracy," said the RCMP sergeant, whose serge coat was a disappointing brown, not scarlet.

"Air piracy? Captain Audion didn't hijack any planes—did he?"

"Then you admit that you are Captain Audion?"

"That dog won't hunt and you know it," Cooder snapped.

The constables stared at him, eyes unreadable under their big yellow-banded hats.

"Would Don Cooder, if he were Captain Audion, telecast his own face to the world?" Don Cooder challenged.

"Whose own face?" he was asked.

"Don Cooder's."

The constables looked at one another.

"Yes, he would," they said in unison.

"Why would he—I mean I—do that? Were I not me, that is?"

"Ratings," said one.

"Ego," added the other.

"How can there be ratings when all TV is blacked out?" Cooder returned.

The sergeant said, "Perhaps the judge will have a theory."

"Look, I've entered your country to expose Captain Audion for who he is."

"And who is he, if not you?"

"I can't say."

The Mounties took him roughly by the elbows.

"Wait. Wait. I can't say *publicly*. It would be libel."

They continued along, despite Cooder's dragging heels.

"But I could broadcast it," he added.

The constables stopped.

"See," Cooder explained. "it's libel if I accuse him without proof, but if I unmask him on television, it will be news. A different kind of libel altogether. Legal libel."

"How can you do that with all television out of commission?"

"That's the tremendous part. I think I know where the transmitter is. We can go there with a remote uplink, knock out the transmitter, and broadcast the unmasking. It will be the ratings sensation of all time!"

"We will have to let the judge decide this."

The judge listened patiently.

"The man is mad!" he exploded.

"He has that reputation," one of the constables said dryly.

Frowning, the judge addressed Don Cooder.

"Your story is preposterous. I will ask you to divulge your suspicions and leave this matter to Federal troops."

Don Cooder pretended the judge was a camera lens and fixed him with unflinching eyes. "I stand on my first amendment rights."

"Well spoken. Except that you are standing on Canadian soil, and have no such rights. And please do not insult this court by suggesting that you are innocent until proven guilty, We subscribe to the Napoleonic code here. You are guilty until proven innocent."

"Then I stand on my principles as a journalist and a Texan—not necessarily in that order."

"Then I have no choice but to remand you into custody."

"You're a mean man in a knife fight, judge. But if you do like I say you're bound to land in tall cotton."

The judge looked to his constables. Everyone shrugged.

In the end, he relented. His country was at loggerheads with the United States of America, and everyone wanted the crisis to end. If only to restore good programming to the people of Canada.

"You will be shackled during every moment of the quest," he warned in his sternest voice.

Don Cooder grinned happily. "No problem. Just tell the cameraman not to shoot below my clavicle."

34

Captain Roger Nodell understood the mission.

Fly from point A to point B, and drop off two passengers.

He just didn't understand what the hell he was doing in an FB-111 Stealth bomber violating Canadian airspace.

Oh, he could take a wild stab and guess it had something to do with the broadcast blackout that had the northern hemisphere tied in knots. That part was easy. But what the hell did it mean? The Canadians were blaming Washington. Some nut with a TV set for a head was taking all the credit, there was panic in the streets, the military was on the highest state of alert, and here he was flying across the Hudson Strait into Quebec.

As he passed south of Baffin Island, he turned on his radio.

Captain Audion was speaking in a voice that sounded like a synthesized version of Don Cooder's voice. If he wasn't going off the deep end, he was doing a great imitation.

"I know something I can't tell. Nah-Nah Nah . . ."

Nodell turned off his radio. It was like this all over. Every frequency from the CB bands to the military channels was masked by the unauthorized transmission. It was screwing up the already jittery upper echelons.

So he flew on over the most godforsaken desolation

he had ever seen. There was literally no place to land for miles around. It was all hard rock and frozen lake chains and some kind of swampy green stuff they told him was called muskeg.

After a while he asked his copilot to take over, and Captain Nodell went back to speak with his mysterious civilian passengers.

He found them arguing over, of all things, television personalities.

"Jed Burner is behind this," the Caucasian was saying. "I saw him kidnap Cheeta with my own eyes."

"Wrong!" the old Asian in black snapped back. "Don Cooder is the villain. He has revealed himself and so must die."

"Nobody famous is going to die. Those are our orders. One Dieter Banning is enough."

Then they noticed him and lapsed into a sullen silence.

"So far, we're doing okay," Nodell told them. "The Royal Canadian Air Force hasn't scrambled a single bird."

"The barbarians," snapped the old Oriental.

"Excuse me, sir?"

"It is bad enough to scramble the eggs of fowl. But to subject the poor mother birds to such torture is typical of Canadian cruelty."

Nodell chewed his cheek while trying to think of a proper response, but nothing came.

"The radio's still bollixed up," he said. "We're maintaining our assigned heading and keeping our eyes peeled."

"Good," said the Caucasian.

"So, where are we going?" Nodell asked.

"Look for a mountain with a nun in white standing on it."

"A what?"

The civilian passed him a folded newspaper clipping, and asked, "Think you can spot that from the air?"

"If I miss this," Nodell said, looking at the photograph, "I should be shot for dereliction of duty."

"That will never happen," said the Oriental.

"Glad to hear it."

"I will personally fling you from this aircraft if you embarrass us."

Nodell started to crack a grin, but the civilian added, "He means it."

Captain Nodell decided two pairs of eyes were needed in the cockpit. The casual manner in which the tiny little Asian man was using his long fingernails to score the titanium floor made him nervous.

Harold W. Smith monitored the steady stream of data flowing in from across the nation.

He was limited in what he could gather. Without broadcast television or radio, news traveled slowly. He had sent a security guard out for an extra. They were appearing every two hours, like clockwork, fat as the Manhattan Yellow Pages.

Meanwhile, Smith monitored computer bulletin boards. They were all choked with reports, some obviously spurious.

One interesting report came out of A. C. Neilson.

It seemed that in certain localities, people had begun to watch their TVs again. Some of it was the curiosity factor of the bizarre spectacle of Captain Audion. But in localities where reception consisted of snow, they were watching, too. Watching in numbers that were estimated to be greater than regular programming.

BCN, for example, was enjoying its best ratings in five years.

But that minor quirk paled before the magnitude of the growing crisis. The stock market had lost over a hundred points in anticipation of a long television siege and the resulting body blow to the national economy.

The word had gotten out that Alaska lay outside the interference zone, and airlines were so overbooked by citizens eager to relocate to the only state in the union still serviced by regular programming that they had quadrupled ticket prices.

Professional sports was at a standstill. The commissioner of baseball instituted an emergency moratorium on all games, pending the resumption of commercial broadcasting.

Irate fans, egged on by ringleaders later identified as bookies, picketed TV stations in all major cities.

They had to fight for sidewalk space. Angry soap opera addicts—mostly housewives—usually got there first.

In most cities, the soap opera addicts forced the sports fans to retreat behind police lines, where they felt safe.

National Guard units had been activated in eight states to help keep order. The President was considering federalizing guard elsewhere.

It was, Smith knew, just the beginning. Unless Remo and Chiun could come through for America.

35

The Master of Sinanju looked up, tension on his face, as the American captain stomped clod-footed into the rear of the bomber.

"We've spotted it!" he exclaimed.

"Great," said Remo.

"Land," said Chiun.

"We can't land. You two are supposed to be air-dropped. Those were my instructions."

The Master of Sinanju arose from his place in the center of the great bomb bay. He padded up to the captain who, although young, towered over him.

Chiun reached up as if to take a speck of fluff from the callow one's chin. The movement was swift and it brought swift results.

"Ow ow ow!" said the captain, dropping to his knees as the exquisite sharpness of Sinanju-hardened fingernails met—with his earlobe caught between them.

"Better change your mind," Remo said. "I saw him do that for three hours straight once. The guy had to be committed afterward."

"Okay, okay! We'll land."

Chiun released the young captain. "Thank you," he said and returned to his place on the floor.

Soon, soon, he would find Cheeta Ching. If only it was not too late . . .

Harold Smith's hand seized the red telephone before the first ring had stopped.

"Yes, Mr. President?"

"The Secret Service has finished interrogating an ANC employee they caught sabotaging one of their microwave relay towers. He's given up his employer."

"Who is it?"

"A man I've never heard of. Frank Feldmeyer."

"Frank Feldmeyer is the science editor for the Broadcast Corporation of North America," Smith said grimly. "He would have the technical background to engineer this operation."

"This is like a bad mystery story. The villain is someone no one would have suspected."

"We have not yet determined that he is Captain Audion. He may be a lieutenant."

"Maybe there isn't a Captain Audion. This guy on my set looks like a cross between Don Cooder and Max Headroom's second cousin."

"I'm sorry. Mr. President. I do not understand the reference."

The President started to explain, and when Smith realized it was some irrelevant trivia, he cut him off.

"Does the Secret Service have a line on Frank Feldmeyer?" Smith asked.

"No. BCN management tell me he's on vacation."

"Where?"

"Quebec is all they have."

"Thank you, Mr. President. Keep me informed and I will do the same."

Smith returned to his computer, his dry features concerned. It was going to be difficult working with a president who had no foreign experience and watched pointless popular television programs.

He returned to his prowling of BCN employee records. One by one he had been identifying those who had been placed in other networks and alerting the Secret Service to pick them up. A number had already confessed . . .

The RCMP cars had been trundling south of Fort Chimo for three hours. They had flown up from Montreal in an official De Havilland Otter and transferred to RCMP cars.

In the back of the lead car, shackled hand and foot, Don Cooder sat ramrod straight, unflinching, unafraid.

"This," he said, "is going to be the biggest story since Hurricane Andrew. That will go down in broadcast history as one of Don Cooder's finest hours. Makes me feel young again. Like Hurricane Carla, back in '61. I cut my teeth on that blow. But this is bigger than any old hurricane."

The RCMP guards were growing bored. One yawned.

"Are there any trees around these parts?" Don Cooder asked suddenly.

"Why do you ask, Yank?" asked the major in charge of the search. His voice was guttural in its French accent.

"Even an anchor has to take a leak from time to time."

The Mounties broke out into peals of rough-hewn laughter.

Don Cooder smiled sheepishly.

He was still smiling when they escorted him to a gully, their .38 caliber Smith & Wesson revolvers holstered and flapped at their sides.

Stopping to unzip, Cooder said, "Mind turning your backs? Bashful kidney."

"Eh?"

"I can't piss when people are looking."

That brought another laugh and the Mounties turned their brown serge backs.

Because he really did have to urinate, Don Cooder did so at great length. When the sound stopped the Mounties waited politely for the sound of his zipper.

Instead, they caught a long length of chain in the sides of their heads and went down, sidearms still flapped and undrawn.

Cooder made a dash for the lead RMCP car.

His driver was on the other side of the road relieving himself. A number of the others were similarly preoccupied.

They turned around at the sound of the idling car engine racing into life.

"*Sacremont*! The American is escaping!"

Don Cooder flipped them the bird and floored the gas.

Some of them ran, holding on to themselves and peeing all over their limping legs. Others finished their business, cursing fluently.

Either way, he had a head start. And a head start was all Don Cooder ever needed to be the first to break a breaking story.

"This," he chortled, pulling a .38 from the glove compartment, "is going to be bigger than Dallas, 1963!"

Captain Nodell was making a preliminary pass, dragging the landing area for stones and muskeg patches when he saw the black-and-white car scoot out of nowhere.

"Uh-oh," he told his copilot.

"Think he saw us?"

"Dunno. Is it a police car?"

"Well, it's got a roof flasher and there's some kind of letters stenciled on the door panel. Begins with R."

"RCMP?"

"Maybe."

"Mounties," said Captain Nodell.

"They still got those up here?"

"Looks like." He pulled up and sent the Stealth fighter sweeping around.

And got a clear view of the speedy little car, distantly pursued by two others, racing toward the mountain that supported the 200-foot statue of a nun—and disappearing into it.

"Must be a cave or something in the base . . ."

"Do we still land?" asked the nervous copilot.

"No choice," said Nodell, feeling his tender earlobe. It felt hot, like a cooked piece of steak.

*   *   *

Frank Feldmeyer was shivering in his blue Captain Audion bodysuit in the great control room under the mountain when he saw the red warning light go off and swore under his breath.

Bolting from the control room, he grabbed up a pistol from a rack by the door.

From down the corridor cut from rough stone, shrieks and wails of pain were coming. He shut them out.

Moving to the spiral stainless-steel steps, he ran down, weapon at the ready, prepared to defend his post.

A familiar voice called up. "Psst, Frank!"

"Don. Is that you?"

Don Cooder, shackled and holding a .38 revolver, stomped up the stairs on his ostrich-skin cowboy boots.

"Yeah," he said, his breath steaming. "Are we still on the air?"

Frank Feldmeyer wiped the cold sweat off his brow and said, "Yeah. But power's getting low. How long do you expect me to keep this up?"

"It's time to wrap this up."

"Great. Let's get out of here."

"Can't."

"Why not?"

"Mounties are on my trail like a pack of redbone foxhounds in heat."

"Mounties! What the hell do we do?"

"They think I'm trying to break this story. I'm covered."

"What about me?" Feldmeyer demanded anxiously. "Look at me, I'm dressed up like Captain Audion, for God's sake."

"You can hide once we set things up. Where are Burner and that loudmouth bitch?"

"Cheeta?"

"No, the other loudmouth bitch."

"On ice."

"Okay, let's get them out."

Ignoring the shrieks of pain, Don Cooder moved through frost-rimmed stone corridors to a stainless-steel door like a walk-in freezer and yanked on the handle. A blast of cold air wafted out, along with the chill dead smell of frozen meat.

They entered a small cave. Past shelves of frozen steaks and chicken parts, they pushed to the dimly lighted rear of the natural freezer.

Cooder knelt beside two motionless figures.

"They look kinda blue," he muttered.

Feldmeyer said, "They weren't dead when I looked in on them last."

Cooder put his ear to the still chest of Jed Burner.

"This man's heart is beating like a stone, which is to say it's not."

"Oh God, I didn't count on murder."

"Shush. Let me check on old Haiphong Hannah." Cooder listened, his face contorting. "I got a beat."

"Great. Thank God."

"Okay, let's get them into the control room."

Rattling his chains with every step, Don Cooder lugged Haiphong Hannah down the corridor to the control room and dumped her into one of the console seats. Jed Burner was dropped into the other, not quite fitting because his joints had stiffened.

"Where's the damn helmets?" Cooder demanded, looking around.

Feldmeyer pointed unsteadily. "In that cabinet. Why?"

"We're going to set it up so that it looks like they're the black hats. Why do you think I had you abduct them in the first place?"

"Will it work, Don?"

"Burner's dead and Haiphong Hannah's got the credibility of Saddam Hussein. How can it fail?"

Shrugging, Frank Feldmeyer helped Cooder set the Captain Audion helmet over Jed Burner's frost-rimmed head.

"Now let's get old Hannah set up and this thing is in the barn."

When they were done, two television-headed figures sat at the console that controlled the most powerful broadcast TV signal on earth.

"Okay," Cooder said panting, "let me have your gun."

"Why?"

"I'm going to shoot Burner."

"Why?"

"Why? The low-down goat roper had the nerve to ask 'Who the hell is Don Cooder?' when I was holding onto the Chair by my sphincter. Made me a laughing stock. Nearly ruined my career at a crucial time."

"No, I mean what good will it do?"

"Dead men tell no tales."

Then the ringing of steel stair treads came from beyond the open door.

"That's the Mounties," Cooder snapped. "Right on cue. We gotta shoot them right now or it's boot hill for us both."

"I can't shoot anyone," Feldmeyer said shakily.

"Tell you what, you shoot Burner. He's already dead. And I'll shoot Hannah. Deal?"

"O-okay."

Together, the two men lifted their weapons and pointed them at the unmoving backs of their targets.

"Count of three," Cooder said.

Swallowing hard, Feldmeyer nodded.

"One!"

"Two!"

"Three!"

Closing his eyes, Frank Feldmeyer steeled himself to pump a single round into the cold back of Jed Burner, and never opened them again.

The roar of Don Cooder's pistol in his ear reached his eardrum just as the bullet had gouged out one ear canal and exited the other in a spray of grayish curd.

Cooder emptied the cylinder into the back of Hai-phong Hannah's head, shattering her screen with its steady NO SIGNAL message.

Taking the dead hand of Jed Burner in his, he

wrapped the stiffened fingers around a black handle marked DESTRUCT and pulled hard. A red digital timer began counting backward from 00:00:10.

Calmly, he wiped the gun free of fingerprints and placed it in Frank Feldmeyer's still-twitching hand. From the floor, he took the automatic that had killed no one, squeezed the grip so he left crystal clear prints, lifted both manacled hands to the ceiling, and patiently whistled "Cowboy's Lament" as the Mounties pounded up the spiral stairs.

The shrieking of Cheeta Ching in the torment of childbirth filled the corridor.

"Damn," he muttered. "Forgot one. Oh, well. Next time."

The digital timer reached 00:00:00.

From far above, there came an explosive sound muffled by tons of granite.

36

The sleek black shape of the Stealth bomber rolled to a whining, bumpy stop, and a hatch popped open.

"Wait for us," Remo called over his shoulder as he followed the Master of Sinanju out into the coldest, most inhospitable expanse he had seen outside of Outer Mongolia.

"What if you don't come back alive?" returned Captain Nodell.

"Wait anyway."

"You got it."

Remo found himself standing on hard rock dappled by spongy moss and lichen. Muskeg pools, some no bigger than his fist, speckled the terrain.

"Ready, Little Father?"

"I am prepared for anything," said the Master of Sinanju.

It was a good half mile to the flat-topped mountain which loomed up from the rock-and-muskeg waste. The statue of Saint Clare stood watch like a lonely bride atop an ugly wedding cake.

They started off at a dead run, picked up speed and soon were moving as fast as a speeding car. "Remember," Remo warned, "we don't kill anyone unless we're sure."

Then, as they crossed the difficult terrain, the head of Saint Clare came apart in a noisy black puff of smoke.

A shriek went up to the heavens and the Master of

Sinanju pulled ahead of Remo like a spastic-limbed bat.

"Cheeta!" he squeaked. "I am coming, my child!"

And as they pulled closer, the smoke began to thin, revealing the red top of a transmission tower poking up from the statue's broken stump of a neck.

Then the skin of the statue began to crack apart, coming away to expose the spidery alternating white and red supports . . .

Don Cooder's face and smile looked ready to crack. He had flopsweat, severe eye-dart and cottonmouth all at once.

"You're just in time," he shouted to the arriving Mounties.

They stormed in with their revolvers trained on him.

"What happened here?" demanded the major.

"I was too late."

"You just said we were just in time."

"You were. I wasn't." He rattled his chains in the direction of the bodies. "Mark it. The culprit, Captain Audion, dead at his console with his accomplices scattered around him like so many checked pawns. The weed of crime bears bitter fruit." His grin stretched to the tearing point. "That's going to be my lead."

The Mounties were having none of it. Don Cooder was made to sit on the floor amid the blood, but he didn't care.

"I saw most of it," he was saying as the Mounties examined the bodies. "Feldmeyer shot them both."

"Why?"

"Thieves fall out is going to be my tag. It's up to you nice folks to flesh out the details. On TV, we have to reduce a story to its gut. And man, this one has a lot of guts to it. Back in my field days we called this a 'Fuzz and Wuzz' story. You folks are the fuzz. No offense."

The RCMP major was frowning as he looked at the TV screen faces of the two dead people seated at the control console. He noticed the dead hand of one

clutching a handle marked DESTRUCT and tied it with
the faint rattling of rock that was coming from the
mountaintop, far above this warren of stone tunnels.

"Let's get this contraption off them," he said.

Cooder asked, "What about the cameras?"

"Cameras?"

"Look, this is the climax. You gotta get this on
tape. This will make great television. I could win an
Emmy for this."

"Any tape will become state's evidence."

"You boys don't get it, do you?" He pointed ceilingward. "This is the hidden transmitter."

"A statue of a nun?"

"Saint Clare of Assisi. The patron saint of TV.
That's how I figured it out. I've thrown a few thank-
yous her way in my time. This isn't some misplaced
religious shrine. Dollars to doughnuts the antenna
mast is jammed up the sister's skirts." Cooder lifted
sheepish eyes to the rock ceiling. "Excuse my French,
Saint Clare."

A videocam was trained on the two figures and
when the light was blazing, the major removed the
first helmet.

"I'll be danged!" Don Cooder said. "If it isn't Jed
Burner. Captain Audacious himself!"

The second helmet revealed a head like a Pekinese
that had been used to wipe up an abattoir floor.

"Haiphong Hannah Fondue," Cooder said. "She
came to fame broadcasting for the North Vietnamese.
Now she meets her maker trying to undermine capital-
ism's greatest, loudest voice—free TV."

"She has no face," said the major. "How do you
know that is her?"

"I'm a trained network anchor. I know hair. That's
Haiphong Hannah. Probably a wig."

The major pushed at the hair. It slipped loose. A
wig.

"So who is this individual?" he asked, pointing to
the sprawled figure in the anchor-emblazoned blue
bodystocking.

Don Cooder put on a mournful face. "That, I deeply regret to say, is a colleague of mine. Frank Feldmeyer. He is—was—our science editor. And probably the brains of this insidious operation."

The major looked doubtful. "So which of them is this Captain Audion?"

"You call it and I'll broadcast it that way," Cooder said, winking.

A sudden shriek pierced every ear—long, ripping and bloodcurdling.

"What was on earth was that?" said Don Cooder in a suddenly shocked-dead voice.

The Mounties seized him by his chains and pulled him along as they went in search of the horrible sound's source.

Remo Williams followed the Master of Sinanju into the cave mouth, where three RCMP cars sat, engines still radiating heat, amid piles of discarded car batteries.

His head straining forward, turtle-fashion, Chiun zipped up a set of spiral stairs like a careening black pinball.

"Cheeta, I am coming!"

"Wait up! Chiun! You don't know what you're walking into!"

Another shriek came, louder than before.

Remo skipped the too-narrow stairs and went up the circling rail like a monkey. He still reached the top a full second after the Master of Sinanju.

"Halt!" an authoritative voice cried. "Who goes there?"

"I am Chiun, Master of Sinanju and the man who stands between me and Cheeta Ching has seen his last sunrise!"

"I am Major Cartier of the Royal Canadian Mounted Police and I will know your business here."

Remo got between the guns and Chiun and told the Mounties, "We're from the USA. Take it easy. We're looking for Cheeta Ching."

"Who is Cheeta Ching?"

Behind the Mounties, Don Cooder smiled with pleasure.

Then another shriek filled the cold stone corridor.

Remo could see it coming, but there was nothing he could do about it. The Master of Sinanju leaped for the sound. The Mounties brought their big revolvers tracking around. Fingers tightened on triggers.

And Remo, cursing under his breath, swept in and took them out.

He killed no one. But his hands snapped wrists, his feet exploded kneecaps, and pistols flew everywhere to land clattering and unfired.

Don Cooder backed away, his hands lifted in surrender and his shackles rattling nervously.

"What are *you* going here?" Remo demanded.

"Don't be ridiculous. You know what this place is?"

"I have a good idea."

"Where there's news, there's Don Cooder."

Chiun's voice rose to a keen. "Cheeta, my beloved! What have they done to you?"

Grabbing at a hanging loop of chain, Remo raced to the sound, pulling a hopping Don Cooder with him.

There was a open door and the smell of fresh blood was coming out of it in warm metallic-tasting waves.

Remo put in his head—and the sight sickened him.

The Master of Sinanju was kneeling beside a blood-soaked bed where Cheeta Ching, her face contorted in what looked like a permanent grimace of agony, lay in her own pooled blood. A flap of flesh lay open, exposing her internal organs. And lying beside her, red as if dipped in Mercurochrome, was a wriggling baby.

"The butchers!" Chiun shrieked. "They have killed Cheeta."

"Urrr," gurgled Cheeta, only the whites of her eyes showing.

"Yet the child lives. My ancestors smile." The Master of Sinanju lifted the baby in gentle hands. From its stomach trailed a purplish pink umbilical cord. He severed it with a broad sweep of one flashing fingernail.

Then, holding the baby up, he spanked it once on the backside, producing a wail that made Remo want to cover his ears.

"Takes after its mother," Remo said.

"Son of perfection," Chiun intoned gravely, "I welcome you into the bitter world that has taken the life of your mother."

Then the eyes of the Master of Sinanju fell upon the baby's kicking legs.

"*Aiieee!*"

"What's wrong?" Remo asked, "Is it deformed?"

"Worse. It is a female."

"So?"

"I wanted a male," Chiun wailed. "This is a calamity! I have lost Cheeta, and her only offspring is unsuitable for Sinanju training."

"What is he talking about?" Don Cooder asked Remo.

"You stay out of this," Remo snapped.

Chiun, his voice dripping with distaste, said, "Take this whelp, Remo. I do not want it."

Remo backed away. "I don't want it."

"Neither do . . . I . . ." Cheeta Ching groaned.

Whirling, Chiun gasped, "Cheeta! You live!"

"Barely . . ."

"Name the ones who savaged you so cruelly and I will place their heads at your feet, my child."

"Frank . . . Feldmeyer . . . kidnapped me. The bastard."

"Frank's dead," Don Cooder said quickly. "I found him dead with the other two."

"Other two?" Remo asked.

"Jed Burner and Haiphong Hannah. They're in the control room yonder."

Chiun hovered over the bed. "You have been avenged, Cheeta. The evil ones who cut the child from your belly are no more."

"What are . . . you talking . . . about?" Cheeta groaned. "I . . . did that."

"You—?"

"I couldn't stand it—anymore—the endless labor—the contractions. I used a . . . jackknife."

One bloodied arm came up clutching the dripping blade.

Chiun nodded grimly. "Suicide. I understand. The pain must have been unendurable to drive you to this."

"No," Cheeta said weakly. "I gave . . . myself a. . . caesarian."

Chiun gasped.

Cheeta rolled her eyes up in her head and moaned, "I was magnificent. If only there had been a camera crew . . ."

The Master of Sinanju offered the baby to its mother, saying, "Fret not, Cheeta. Your child breathes. Here . . ."

"Get it away from me!" Cheeta shrieked.

Chiun stepped back, his face stunned. "What?"

"I carried that brat for ten long months, and what does he do? He can't wait until I'm rescued before kicking to be born. Two lousy days and I could have done this in prime time." A sob shook Cheeta's pain-wracked body. "The first self-induced caesarian in the history of womankind and no pictures."

Chiun only stared. His wispy beard shook uncontrollably.

"Come on, Little Father," Remo said. "Cheeta's just freaked out. She'll get over it."

Cheeta gasped. "Vino? Is that you?"

"Vino?" Remo and Chiun said together.

Cheeta smiled dreamily. "You're my wine . . ."

The Master of Sinanju laid the squalling infant on its mother's chest and backed from the room, his hazel eyes unreadable.

"Cheeta has gone mad. . . ." he breathed.

"In the business," Don Cooder said, "we call it ratings-induced dementia. Some people just can't take the pressure."

Remo closed the door after them.

The Master of Sinanju turned, his hands slipping

into his sleeves. His gaze came to rest on the stiff face of Don Cooder.

"It was your face the fiend showed to the world," he said.

Cooder showed his white teeth all around. "Frame."

"And it was the statue you worshipped which crowns this mountain of wickness," Chiun added.

Don Cooder shook his head. "Frank Feldmeyer, crooked as a snake. I still can't believe it. Can you imagine him, a traitor to the news organization that made his a household face?"

The Master of Sinanju turned to his pupil. "Remo, do you believe this man's lies?"

"Not really," said Remo, folding his arms.

Don Cooder couldn't believe what he was hearing. He took hold of his fixed smile and said, "The proof is in the control room. The bad guys. They killed themselves rather than be taken alive."

"Show us," said the old Oriental.

As he led the pair to the control room, Don Cooder tried to cover his nervousness with a question. "Was it really one of your ancestors who got written up in the Bible?"

"Yes."

"That's the kind of press a man can be proud to call his own. My ancestors were simple dirt farmers, proud but poor."

Cooder led them past the groaning and unconscious Mounties to the control room and said, "There. A textbook example of 'if it bleeds, it leads' if I ever saw one."

The old Oriental gave the grisly scene only the briefest of glances. "You saw this happen?" he asked.

"The tail end of it. Feldmeyer shot them both dead then turned the gun on himself. Suicide pact, is the way I see it."

"And which one did *you* shoot?"

"Huh?"

"You heard him," Remo added. "Who did you shoot?"

"No one. What are you talking about? The only shooting I ever do is with a video camera." He lifted his chains. "Can't even do that with these fetters."

"The stink of gunpowder is on your hands," Chiun said.

Don Cooder brought his fingers to his hands and sniffed. "I don't smell anything," he said.

"We do," said Remo.

Cooder puffed out his chest. "It's your word against that of the Anchor of Steel."

"That only works in court," said Remo.

"Hey, I'm a prisoner of the RCMP, the finest law enforcement organization since the Texas Rangers. I'll go with their brand of justice."

"Sorry. You go with ours. We've got some old scores to settle with you."

"I don't follow . . ."

"Remember, wicked one, the bomb your lust for ratings caused to be built?" Chiun asked in a grave voice.

"I don't know what you're talking about."

"Because of this device, I lay entombed for many bitter months. This occurred two years ago, but the bitter memory is with me still. Only the wisdom of my emperor enabled me to see the sunlight again."

"What's he talking about?" Cooder asked Remo.

"Long story," Remo said aridly.

"In return," Chiun continued, "I promised my emperor that I would bring no harm to you, for you were not directly responsible for that atrocity."

"I'm not following this."

"But now, your perfidy has changed everything."

"Translate for me, friend," Cooder asked Remo.

"He's saying you're last week's headlines. History."

"History? How can I be history? I'm alive and on the top of my game."

"I might let you live if you truthfully answer a question," Chiun said thinly.

"Gladly."

"Why are your kind called anchors?"

Don Cooder blinked. It was a heck of a good question. Why was he called an anchor? He wracked his brain. "Hold on. It'll come to me in a minute."

But the minute never came because the tiny old man stepped up to Don Cooder and took hold of one arm. Cooder lifted his chains to fend him off as the other one watched with cool unconcern.

Don Cooder experienced a rapid series of sensations in the last minutes of his life. All involving exquisite nerve-searing pain. First in his elbow, then his legs and, as the pain grew to a crescendo that swallowed his screaming brain, the chains that draped his arms and legs were coiling coldly around his throat.

When he was found, hours later, he was strung from the ceiling, his purple-black tongue protruding from his bruise-colored face, hanged by the neck. But that was not what made the headlines next day. It was the twisted pretzel shape of his body, arms curled tight to his shoulders and legs bent at impossible upward angles to his pelvis, broken but somehow curved as if the bones were made soft and flexible and then hardened again.

The Quebec authorities thought the shape was vaguely familiar. It took three of them to decide Don Cooder's mortal remains had been bent and twisted into the shape of a nautical anchor.

No one ever figured out how it was done, however.

37

"It is obvious," Harold Smith was saying, "that Don Cooder was Captain Audion. He had the financial resources, the necessary industry connections, as well as the motivation to point the finger of suspicion at his many rivals, both perceived and otherwise."

It was the afternoon of the next day and Remo and Chiun were in Harold Smith's Folcroft office. Bright spring sunlight flooded in through the big picture window.

"Wait a minute," Remo said. "If he was already rich, why did he try to blackmail the networks?"

"The man had a reputation for instability. From all we've seen, it may be that he simply cracked under the pressure of the relentless race for ratings, and went into a psychotic tailspin."

"That doesn't explain why he had Feldmeyer broadcast that pretaped monologue of himself as Captain Audion."

"He was mad," Chiun spat. "Who can understand a madman?"

"There are several reasons for that," Smith said. "The first is that having pointed the finger of blame at everyone from KNNN to Dieter Banning, adding himself to the list of suspects helped confuse the issue. Also, his ego may have played a role."

"You mean he *wanted* the credit?" Remo said.

Smith nodded. "In a perverse manner. Just as he was willing to sacrifice his confederate, Feldmeyer, to cover his tracks, and incidentally enjoy a final ratings grab exposing Jed Burner as the guilty party before no doubt retiring on the extortion money."

"Did the networks get their money back from the Swiss yet?" Remo asked.

"They are trying very hard. But I am pleased to report that we seem to have rooted out every Captain Audion agent who was planted in the various broadcast and cable stations to facilitate the entire scheme. I must admit Cooder was quite clever in recruiting laid-off BCN employees through Feldmeyer and arranging to place them in his target stations."

"Well, at least we won't have Don Cooder to kick around anymore," said Remo. "I guess it'll be Cheeta five nights a week from now on, now that they've sewn her back up."

"I understand Miss Ching has announced that she will be taking a long leave of absence to care for her baby once she is released from the hospital," said Smith.

"From the way she was acting yesterday, she was all set to drown the kid for blowing her big ratings grab," Remo grunted.

"Miss Ching has received an outpouring of sympathy in the wake of her ordeal," Smith said. "And a great many product endorsement offers. No doubt this has affected her attitude."

At that point, both Remo and Smith looked to the Master of Sinanju.

Chiun had a bleak light in his hazel eyes.

"I do not care," he said thinly. "I will never care again."

"What about the baby?" asked Remo. "Don't you even care about her a little?"

"It is not important, for it is not mine."

Remo's eyebrows shot up. "Wait a minute, what's this?"

Chiun half turned. "I do not wish to speak of it."

"Not so fast," Remo said quickly. "You've been stringing us out for almost a year on this baby thing.

You gotta come clean. Now are you the father or not?"

"Grandfather," Chiun said bitterly. "In spirit."

"How does *that* work?"

"You will remember the time we saved Cheeta from the evil dictator of California?" Chiun asked.

"Will I ever? You went off with her for a long weekend. Next thing we hear, she's pregnant and you're picking out baby clothes."

Chiun winced. "It is well known that Cheeta had been trying to conceive for many years before I entered her life."

"Yeah. She told every live mike in the Western hemisphere."

"It is not, as is commonly believed, her husband's fault."

"Which? That she couldn't have a kid or that she did?"

"The former. In our brief dalliance together, I told Cheeta of my feelings toward her and she of her disappointment in her husband's inability to fulfill her."

Remo looked skeptical. "So you fulfilled her?"

"I sensed in her an imbalance, which prevented her womb from fruiting with a proper child."

"Yeah . . . ?"

"And I assisted in correcting this."

"How, Master Chiun?" asked Smith, leaning forward in his chair.

"Wait a minute!" said Remo. "Maybe we're better off not knowing."

"It was a simple matter of diet," Chiun explained. "I told Cheeta that she needed to eat the whites of duck eggs boiled in rice four times a day."

"Sounds like an old wive's tale to me," Remo said.

"It is a remedy that goes back many generations and never has been known to fail, ignorant one," sniffed Chiun.

"So you didn't make it with Cheeta, after all?"

"Remo! My love for Cheeta is too pure to be sullied by such things. Besides, were I the father of the . . .

female, it would not be female, but male. I know how to direct the correct seed to its proper destiny."

Chiun glared at Remo pointedly. Remo frowned. He had a daughter he had not seen in years, whom the Master of Sinanju believed would—and should—have been a boy if Remo had paid more attention to what he was doing with the mother rather than enjoying it.

"Look, there's nothing wrong with baby girls," Remo said hotly.

"Except that they are always the first to be sent home to the sea and cannot be trained in Sinanju," Chiun returned.

"Because no one ever tried," Remo snapped.

"And no one ever will. Especially you, who are not equal to the demands of Masterhood and may never be."

Remo turned to Smith. "Let's change the subject. Are the networks back on?"

"Yes. The Canadians shut off the pirate transmitter and are in the process of dismantling the—er—nun. Although I am still unclear on how power was supplied to such an enormous device."

"Forgot to tell you. Remember the missing car batteries? We found a cave filled with them, all hooked up together. There must have been thousands of them. Enough to do the job, ridiculous as it sounds."

Smith frowned. "It is not so farfetched. I recall now an Air Force laser device housed in a remote test facility that had to be powered by great numbers of interconnected auto batteries. It should have occurred to me before. Obviously, Feldmeyer was forced to scrounge for replacements as the supply was taxed under continual broadcast demands."

"So we're back on the air and things are squared away with the Canadians?"

"Yes. But it was an object lesson for society. Our reliance on television, for news as well as entertainment, has taken on the proportions of a shared national addiction. I've recommended to the new

President that he lay this problem before the American people as a challenge for the next century."

"Think he'll go along?"

"No," said Harold Smith glumly. "He is a baby boomer."

"Pah," spat Chiun. "Do not speak that word in my presence again. I am done with babies forever. And with Cheeta Ching, the fickle."

And Remo laughed. A huge weight had been lifted off his shoulders. Turning to the Master of Sinanju, he asked, "Care to tell us about the Chiun from the Bible?"

"When someone informs me why the readers of alleged news are called anchors."

Remo and Harold Smith exchanged blank looks.

When the answer was not found in the CURE computer, the Master of Sinanju stalked from the room, a wraith in crimson silks.

Remo shrugged, indicated Smith's TV set and wondered, "Anything good on?"